An Industrious Woman
by Cinda Brea

I0618562

Copyright© 2015 Cinda Brea

Acknowledgements

Thank you to my Higher Power!

This book is dedicated in loving memory to my cousin Evie Wingo, one the best cooks I've ever known and a lover of children and to my cousin Mary Cleveland, a genius in the field of hair design. You are both loved and greatly missed.

I'd like to thank Amber Qualls, Brenda Smith, Cecily Brea, Esther Alix, and Lessie Solomon, my readers for providing such valuable feedback toward the completion of this novel. You ladies have no idea how much I appreciate you taking the time to assist me with this project and I thank each of you so very much for your support.

Also, thank you again, Judy Bullard at customebookcovers.com. This cover is absolutely fabulous.

Table of Contents

Chapter 1: New Neighbors

A solitary thought enters my head as I peer out my front room window and observe the tall platinum haired woman standing on the sidewalk in front of the house next door. *This cannot be good.* For the better part of five minutes I stand and watch in awe as my eyes dart back and forth between a large capacity rental truck, the two men unloading household items from that truck, and the stacked blond woman. Eventually, I force myself to step away from the window and plop down on my sofa. "This cannot be good," I repeat out loud. After a few moments, I pull myself out of my dazed state and peep out the window one last time, hoping I misread the scene I saw earlier. The truck sits all alone now. There are no laborers or platinum supervisor in sight. The truck tells the story. I am getting new neighbors and those neighbors are in some way connected to Shantrell Melancon. I pray there is only a connection but I know I'm fooling myself. I don't know the woman well, but Shantrell has never impressed me as a person who would spend her Sunday afternoon assisting a friend or family member with a move. Most likely Shantrell is my new neighbor.

I curse Mr. Woodson, the owner of the house. He has a new tenant moving into that place just about every twelve to fifteen months. The last family had been his best tenants ever as far as I can recall and I've seen every one of them come and go over the past twelve years or so.

I hear voices outside. I hate being such an old nosy-assed neighbor but I go back to the window anyway. There's a car parked in the driveway now. Yep, that's Mrs. Melancon, Shantrell's mother. Maybe Miss Mel is moving in. God, please let it be Miss Mel.

"Buddy, grab those lamps and those things out of the back seat. I need to go to the house and load up some more stuff." I hear Miss Mel yell at her youngest son, Budrow aka Buddy. Then to Shantrell she adds, "Shantrell, I left the kids at the house so they can help me load the car when I get back."

Fortunately, I've had new windows installed so unless a person is within a few feet of the window, they cannot observe my voyeurism from outside. "Oh!" I gasp and step away from the window when I realize Miss Mel's oldest child, Ezekiel or Zeke as everyone calls him, is the other man helping with the move. I had forgotten Zeke is related to Buddy and Shantrell. He seems so different from those two.

Zeke, like his mother, is a highly regarded professional. During her time as a bank loan officer, many families credited Miss Mel as the person who pushed their loans through. The woman was known as fair, honest, and influential. Miss Mel saw many managers come and go and although she never achieved the position of bank manager, she had the stature of a bank president. Rumor was that she was indeed the final word when it came to bank loans. If an applicant was not credit worthy, Miss Mel would sit the person down and do personal one-on-one credit counseling and explain exactly what actions were needed in order to get funding and/or make recommendations for sources of funding. In addition to her work at the bank, Miss Mel has been providing free credit counseling as a volunteer at the local community center for years. I work out of a realty office and one of my coworkers has sent several prospective home buyers to Miss Mel for assistance.

Shantrell and Buddy seem just the opposite from their mother and older brother and I have the notion that they don't just live for the weekend but consider every day the weekend.

I can't help but peep back out the window. I know this is a bit weird but I am curious about what's really going on. Who is moving in? I observe Zeke and Miss Mel standing at the back end of her car. I watch as Zeke writes what appears to be a check and hands it to his mother. She, in turn, gives him a warm embrace and a kiss on the cheek.

"Okay, that's enough. You've got work to do, Hannah," I tell myself as I move away from the window, ashamed of spying on my new neighbors. I don't think the exchange of funds and the resulting embrace were meant for the world to see even if the interaction did take place out of doors.

I have been working all morning and most of the afternoon on a good sized luncheon I'm catering tomorrow. There's nothing fancy involved, just finger sandwiches, cookies, and fruit and vegetable trays for eighty ladies. Joykeepers is having a working luncheon tomorrow afternoon and this is the third meeting in a row that they have asked me to cater. This one is the simplest thus far. I've got my fillings for the sandwiches made and nearly all my cookies baked off but I've still got a ways to go before I'm finished with all my prep.

I enjoy the whole catering thing because I have the freedom to accept or decline gigs as I choose. Yes, I've actually told potential clients that I'm booked for a particular time period because I have that time set aside for a *Being Mary Jane*, *Scandal*, *Empire,* or *How to Get Away with Murder* marathon weekend. Scandalous, right?

Currently, there is a black television drama feast on American television. Next year we might not be able to find a sister with a role in a television series so I'm taking advantage of all this beautiful color and preparing myself for the eventuality of the famine of black leading ladies. I'm just pleased that there are people who are close to my skin color with nappy hair under those wigs and weaves. Hopefully, I'll soon get over the joy of watching all these black women on the screen and spend less time in front of the television.

There was a time when I prided myself for watching so little television. I was actually a bit of a snob when talking to people hooked on certain shows which shall remain nameless (Atlanta Housewives). I would either turn my nose up or look down my nose at the perpetrator and declare. "I don't watch much television and especially not reality television." I know, snarky, right? Over the past two years, I've had to take all that attitude about television back because I am wearing my sets out.

With all that TV time, I still work hard. I have two jobs, each of which I schedule as I choose. Of course, there's the catering but my main job is Property Management. I have had my California Realtor's license for the past four years. I had no intention of becoming a realtor but after I got stuck managing properties in and around my hometown of Seaside for several of my family members, realty became a natural career choice.

You see, all my immediate family abandoned my grandmother, Ina, and me, moving on to other places. Initially, I was left with only three homes to manage. Eight years ago my mother and stepfather moved to Winston-Salem, North Carolina, leaving me the responsibility of both their homes, one of which I lived in. I also took care of my grandmother's home. Not long after my parents moved away, I moved in with my grandmother and rented out the home I had been living in, thus planting the seeds for a lucrative but sometimes challenging career in property management.

After that huge subprime mortgage debacle, my older sister and brother both bought houses here in the Monterey area and insisted I not only manage their properties but buy investment property of my own. They refused to take "no" for an answer. Not that I told either of them "no" because there's only one person in my family I feel comfortable telling "no" but that's another story. So, I very quickly became responsible for nine homes, including my grandmother's house. Once I was knee deep in houses, my brother was so impressed with my management skills that he declared I had found my niche and suggested I get my realtor's license. Did I mention that I seldom tell my family "no?" Before I knew what hit me, I had completed the realty course and had a spot lined up in the office of a friend of a friend. Now I'm waist deep in properties and I must confess I have indeed found one of my niches.

Two bells sound at once, the oven timer alerting me that my cream cheese bars are done and my cell phone. "Hey, Brie," I answer the phone to my sister Brianna's exclusive ring tone."

"Hey, girl, what have you got going on today?" Brianna asks with no real interest. This is Brianna's almost daily check in call. Sometimes these calls are less than a minute long but she calls nearly every day, if I don't call her first.

"Just working on an order I need to get out for a meeting tomorrow afternoon."

"I'm just checking in. You haven't mentioned Granny lately. Have you been to see her this week?"

I find this question odd because everyone knows I visit my grandmother three to four times a week. She is my first and most important priority. "Granny is good. She said "Hi" when I went in this morning. She seems content as always."

Brianna hesitates before she continues. "I thought I might try and get down there this weekend to see you guys. Maybe we can take Granny out for a picnic or something. Are you free?"

I'm tempted to say "Hell no!" just for the hell of it. Granny has been in a care home for a little more than three years now and I am her only close family still living in the area and her only regular visitor. One might think that when my mother, sister, or brother comes to town they would relieve me from the grind of visiting my grandmother. No, each complains how much they dislike visiting the home without me. Even when they come into town together, they want me to drop whatever I have planned so they can stroke their conscious with an outing, a dinner, or a shopping trip for Granny. On one occasion, my mother and sister declared we were to have a sleepover for my grandmother and two of her old friends and one of the friend's daughter. Of course my mother insisted this grand gesture occur on a weekend that I was completely free. I cannot recall working so hard in my life. Granny's friends were pleased to see her and enjoyed lounging around, gossiping, and giving advice to the younger women. Granny was hardly awake the entire time and was overjoyed to get back to her cozy room at the home the following afternoon. She was worn out. I was the only person more tired than my grandmother but my mother and sister were quite pleased with their efforts. God spare me!

Don't get me wrong. I appreciate my family wanting to do things that make Granny's life more enjoyable. I just wish they would leave me out of their plans once in a while. Let me rephrase that. I want them to include me but I would like the option to decline and for the party to go on without me. Because, you see, if I don't participate the shit don't happen. They cancel, postpone, reschedule, change venue until I say "okay." I can't bring myself to say "I refuse to participate in another damn activity you plan for Granny. No one helps me when you guys aren't in town and I manage just fine."

Well, actually, I have said just those words to Brianna but I can't bring myself to say them to my mother. Mom would give me "the look" and then cut me with that razor she carries that we call a tongue.

I haven't seen my sister for a while and she has visited with Granny once or twice on her own since I told her how I feel, so I'll cooperate and be nice. "I don't have anything planned. When exactly are you coming?" I ask, resigned to my fate as the ever present family member in attendance to my frail yet lovely grandmother.

"I thought I might drive down early Saturday and spend the night. I'd head back here late Sunday morning."

I'm not looking for an argument but I know my sister all too well. "Brie, if you're not going to get here until late afternoon on Saturday, I can take on a job for that day. I don't want to miss out on a gig because I'm expecting you at noon and you don't show up until after two or three o'clock."

"Hannah, please don't be in the kitchen when I get there. I want to take Granny on a nice outing," Brianna whines.

See what I mean! I'm trying to be nice here but Brianna feels my world should stop so she can spend time with her grandmother. Obviously, I don't need the pittance I could possibly make in my kitchen on a Saturday morning.

"If you're hard up for money, I will gladly give you what you could make in that kitchen on Saturday." My sister sounds indignant and I am amazed. Get thee behind me Satan. I will not curse.

"Brie, if you don't want me to take on a job, you need to be here before noon."

"What is the big deal?" Brianna asks with even more indignation.

"The big deal is you always give me these flaky maybes about when you're coming and tie up my entire day. Last time you were supposed to be here mid morning and showed up just before four in the afternoon. We were supposed to take Granny out to lunch that Saturday."

"Well you could have gone and taken her, Hannah. You didn't have to wait for me to get there."

This is what pisses me off. It was Brianna's idea to take Granny to lunch that day. I do lunch with my grandmother and dinner, and short walks, and trips to the park, and shopping trips, and when I'm feeling really energetic and I mean really energetic we do an overnight visit. I don't call up to Sacramento and ask my sister to join me and Granny in these outings. Well, I don't want to argue anymore. "Life is too short," Granny used to say when she still talked. "Please be here early enough for us to take her out. This is your idea, not mine," I remind Brianna but get no response. I know she doesn't like me telling her to respect my time but she's a good sister. She'll get over it. I change the subject. "You'll never guess who is moving in next door."

"Who?" is her only response.

Yeah, she's a little hot with me. This will cool her off. "Shantrell and or her mother," I say.

"Shantrell Melancon?" Brianna is too curious to be angry any longer.

"The moving van is out there right now."

"I hope it's not Shantrell. I haven't seen her in a few years but the last time I saw her she looked ratchet, I mean top shelf ratchet, like someone out of the cast of *Babs*. You remember that pitiful Halle Barry movie. Shantrell had a flaming red weave slicked to her head and hanging down her back, nails so long I'm still trying to figure out how she wiped her behind, and way too much makeup. How many kids does she have now?"

"I don't know. I haven't seen any kids. They're just moving in," I respond.

"There goes the hood." Brianna laughs at her comment. This house that my grandparents purchased brand new over fifty years ago does not sit "on the hill" and the ocean is barely visible from the front window. I was surprised to learn that living up on the hill was considered something exclusive but the houses on the hill are newer, larger, and have better views so I guess it stands to reason that we humans would make a distinction. Brianna has been calling my neighborhood "the hood" for years now. I don't take offense. Before she left for college, all those years ago, she spent just as much time in this part of Seaside as I did.

"Hopefully, they won't be too bad. The people who moved out were nice. They kept the yard up and were very friendly. I'll miss them," I reflect.

"You better hope Budrow doesn't spend much time with whoever moves in. Budrow has always been such a user." Brianna does her best to make me feel worse about my new neighbors.

"I saw him over there. Zeke too, helping move the furniture in."

"Zeke is over there? Oh, I know Deidra is livid. She can't stand Mrs. Melancon. Says she's always begging."

"Is Deidra still seeing Zeke? I forgot they had a thing," I say, feeling somewhat deflated.

"More than a thing I'd say. I haven't talked to Deidra in a while but the last time I heard from her they were still together. It's been a few years now. They've come up to visit us a few times. Zeke and David get along well. I asked Deidra when they were going to set a date. She said between his mother and Shantrell he was too broke for her to even think about marrying. Don't no woman of sound mind want no broke-assed man."

I realize I do not have the almonds I need for my Mexican Wedding Cookies, the Joykeeper's favorites. I find the news that Deidra and Zeke are still together a bit disturbing and I'm relieved to have a good reason to end the conversation. "I gotta go, Sis. Please call me and let me know what time you'll be here Saturday."

"I will and keep me posted on your new neighbors. I'm going to call Deidra and see what she's talking about."

--

I feel a little guilty about my thoughts and all the bad-mouthing of the Melancon family Brianna and I just shared. My grandmother and mother would have already been next door to extend a welcoming hand. In that vein, I decide to pick up a welcoming token for my new neighbors. I consider flowers but I can see the contempt all over Shantrell's face if I step up to her house with a bouquet. "What are we suppose to do with some damn flowers," I imagine her saying to Miss Mel after I've left the house. Fruit – I can't imagine Shantrell eating fruit. A bottle of wine, some Moscato maybe? I don't care for the stuff myself but it seems to be the drink of the day. Somehow wine doesn't seem right.

I stroll around the store trying to think of what to purchase for my neighbors. I've picked up all the items I need and a few I don't as I contemplate. A roasted chicken – I've got two in my cart already. I'll give them one of the birds and a bottle of the Moscato. That should do; hell, that's almost dinner. Add a salad and you're good to go.

--

"Who's there?" I hear Shantrell yell at the door in response to my knock. I tried the doorbell but it must not be working because after pushing it twice and getting no response I started knocking. The rental truck is gone but there are two sedans and an SUV parked out front.

"It's Hannah Jacobs from next door." Before I complete my sentence the door swings open and I see Budrow standing there gazing at me with a face that goes from curious, to surprised, to flirtatious. That's Budrow, always on the prowl for some woman with low standards. I feel any woman who messes with Budrow has to have pretty low standards. Don't get me wrong; Buddy is a good-looking, smooth-talking, well-groomed and dressed brother but, as my Granny used to say, without a pot to piss in or a window to throw it out of. He is mostly unemployed and cannot keep a job but does keep a woman. I do not know his current lady or ladies but I'm sure he's got at least one.

"Hi Buddy, is Shantrell or your mother around?" I ask, feeling uncomfortable under his roaming eyes.

Buddy doesn't bother to answer my question directly or invite me in, but yells, "Mom," near the top of his voice.

Shantrell exits the kitchen and stands there looking at her younger brother with disgust on her face before turning her eyes on me. "Hey Hannah, come on in, girl," she says with a warm smile. Then to Budrow she snaps, "Why did you leave her standing out there like that, Buddy?" Budrow rolls his eyes and closes the door behind me as I enter.

"Do you live around here, Hannah?" Shantrell asks.

Before I can answer I hear and see Miss Mel coming from the depth of the house. Her oldest son, Ezekiel, is dead on her heels. She has a question and a smile on her face. "Hi, you're one of Miriam's girls aren't you? Yeah, you're the baby, Hannah. I knew

I knew someone in that house next door. That's your grandmother's home. How's she doing and how is your mother? What do you hear from her? Where is your sister living now, still up in San Jose?" Miss Mel then asks Shantrell, "Did you offer her a seat, Shantrell?" Without waiting for an answer to any of the questions she's posed, Miss Mel goes on. "Have a seat, baby. Everything is such a mess." Finally, the gregarious woman takes a breath as she looks around for a clear spot for me to sit down.

"Don't worry about it, Miss Mel. I saw you outside earlier and wanted to bring something over as a welcome. I don't need a seat. Mom's good and Brianna's up in Sacramento."

As I hold the bag with the chicken and wine out to Shantrell, I see her two boys coming from the back of the house. Oh goodness, one chicken for six people. What was I thinking? "I didn't realize your babies were here, Shantrell. Let me go get the other chicken."

Zeke finally looks up from his cell phone and speaks for the first time since I entered the house. "You don't need to do that. I was just going out to pick up something."

"I don't know what you talking about, man. I can eat one of those Safeway roasted chickens by myself," Budrow declares.

"Miss Mel ignores Zeke's comment. "That's so good of you, baby. We were just wondering what we were going to do about dinner.

Zeke says nothing more so I go and get my dinner and hand it over to my new neighbors. I hope it's enough and I hope they enjoy it more than I'm going to enjoy my tuna fish sandwich.

Chapter 2: More Surprises!

I awake Monday morning to the sound of loud voices next door and the ringing of my doorbell. I meant to be up by eight but for some reason my alarm didn't go off. It's late and I've got to get my trays put together for pickup by two o'clock. I grab my bathrobe and stumble toward the door, barely awake. Looking out the peephole, I see Zeke Melancon dressed for a day in the classroom and looking not very happy.

When I open my door, Zeke looks shocked at my appearance but I don't really care if my scarf is on sideways, there's crud in my eyes, drool dried on my mouth, or my face is smashed in from sleeping so hard. His expression seems to actually soften once he gets over the shock. He smiles and gives me a slight nod. "Hey, ah, Hannah, right? I was wondering if I could borrow a hammer and a couple of screw drivers. I usually carry some tools in the car but my mother took out the tool kit to make more room to haul items from the other place. I need to get a couple of shelves hung for her."

"Yeah, sure, come on in," I tell him, now totally conscious and feeling a little embarrassed.

"I can wait out here," he responds.

"Suit yourself. Give me a minute." I close the door in Zeke's face, rush to the garage, and find the tools as quickly as possible. I consider washing my face before I return to the door with the tools but decide that since the man has already seen me, the damage is done.

Zeke seems to have mellowed even more when I hand him the tools without really looking at him.

"Hey, thanks a lot. I'll get these right back to you."

"Take your time. Don't worry about it."

The man hesitates for a moment and then adds, "Thanks for the chicken last night. You saved me time and money. I was exhausted."

"You're welcome."

Still he stands there. I want to ask, "What now?" but finally he gives me a slight wave and steps off. I wish I could have been a little friendlier or a bit more talkative. He seemed to want to talk.

I'm just not the talker. People used to say I was slow and probably still do. No, I'm not quick witted and yes, I see no point in doing a whole lot of talking when I've got nothing to say, but I am intelligent and have a decent portion of common sense.

There was a time when I thought I was not capable of performing at a high level but I know better now and have known for years. My family is a little protective of me. Well, actually, a better description is involved, because they think I need them to monitor my affairs but I don't.

No, I don't claim to be a genius like Brianna or a quick witted intellect like my brother, Bill, but thank you Jesus, I know how to handle my business. I admit it would have been nice to have something witty to say to Zeke just now but he's a man who could tie up any woman's tongue. I've noticed Brianna's tongue get thick in her mouth when trying to talk to Zeke. Hopefully, I'll get to practice on him when he brings my tools back.

In recent months, I have occasionally seen Zeke running along the beach trail when I'm out walking. He always waves. I'm pretty sure he didn't remember me as Brianna's sister. He seems more down to earth than I thought. Not that he was ever unfriendly, just kind of full of himself. At least that was my impression the times I had seen him about town. Maybe I got that sense of the man because he got into Stanford and everyone made such a big deal about his acceptance. Brianna applied to Stanford and was not accepted. She settled for the University of California at Santa Cruz where my brother was attending. I think once Brianna, the whiz kid, was turned down by Stanford, many of our friends and acquaintances realized what an accomplishment Zeke's acceptance was. Then when he graduated with honors, everyone was talking about the town's favorite son who had done little Seaside proud. Now he's an associate professor at California State University at Monterey Bay, divorced, and dating or shacking up with Brianna's best friend from high school, Deidre. That Deidre is one lucky woman.

--

I finally get to work on my trays and have them just about finished when I receive a call from Lois, the founder and president of Joykeepers. She wants me to deliver the trays and asks if I can get them there by two o'clock.

"Hell no! That's the time you were supposed to pick the food up," is what I want to say but don't. I agree to deliver free of charge. Joykeepers does good work providing cancer patients with daily assistance around their homes, child care during appointments, transportation, and companions for appointments. They provide these services on a shoestring budget and I am willing to do what I can to help so I agree to deliver the order but not before two thirty. Lois is grateful and I speed up my action.

After dropping the trays off to Lois, I stop by Carmel Homes. My mother's mother, Ina Lorraine Williams, has lived in the care facility for nearly four years. Granny has Alzheimer's. Seven years ago, when she first started displaying signs of the disease, I moved in with her. Within a two-year span, the disease had progressed to the point that I could no longer work and take care of Granny. I hired a caregiver for a short while but the illness was progressing so quickly that before long, I needed someone with Granny every hour of the day. It got to the point that my mother's calls focused more on my health and well-being than Granny's. I got little to no sleep most nights because Granny was up and about. Every small object and piece of paper had to be secured away from her. It took her getting out of the house and roaming the neighborhood twice before I had special locks installed on the three doors leading to the outside.

Placing my grandmother in a home was a difficult thing for my family, my mother and me in particular. I tried so hard to keep Granny in her home but my life had become miserable and I was ashamed to admit that to anyone. I put on a good face and attempted to keep up with my realty classes but I was a mess. I cried like a baby when my mother called and told me she had found a place for my grandmother. I felt like a failure and thought I had let my grandmother down. Mostly, I felt guilt about the relief I felt. That seems like decades ago. Granny is settled in at the home now and seems quite comfortable with her routine. Thankfully, my guilt has diminished and she and I still have a special relationship, although she doesn't seem to know who I am most of the time.

--

The traffic is heavy on the short drive from Pacific Grove to Seaside and it's late afternoon before I make it home. No sooner than I pull into my driveway I see a woman with a stroller and two shopping bags camped out on my front porch. I decide not to pull into my garage because I don't recognize this person. She is most likely at the wrong house and I need to let her know.

As I exit my car and approach the unkempt looking woman, I get a closer look at her face and recognize my cousin Dana approaching me with a huge smile. I have not seen or spoken with Dana, who is my father's niece, in over two years. The last time she stopped in she stayed four days before she got angry because I wouldn't give her money to get her hair and nails done and expected her to do dishes and pick up behind herself. I guess she has finally forgiven me.

I am alarmed by my cousin's appearance. My twenty-eight-year-old cousin has always been a flawless beauty from her thick brown hair to her shapely calves. Her looks have definitely taken a hit over the past two years. She has at least three colors of matted hair weaved in, one of which is a very dirty blond, and her hair looks as if it has not been washed in weeks. On her upper left back, her newest tattoo is a humongous fuchsia colored rose that would be alluring if there weren't so many black and purple tentacle-like vines winding up her neck, onto her shoulder, and down her arm. Her skin which has always been clear and smooth is sallow and scarred with pimples old and new. Dana's nails are chipped and dirty and when she shows me that show-stopping smile of hers, my heart pounds hard in my chest as my eyes begin to fill with water. She now has two broken teeth right up front and it is clear from the overall appearance of her teeth that she has not seen a dentist in a great while. The main reason I didn't recognize my cousin immediately is because she has lost a lot of weight, maybe two or three sizes, but she has quite a belly hanging over her low-rise skinny jeans. I figure the weight loss is because of the drugs.

I no longer feel anger or disgust for Dana because she has once again shown up unannounced and clearly in need of assistance. This is her pattern but she always appeared healthy and looked strong enough to withstand my perturb in the past, but not now, not this time. I hug my cousin long and hard and she holds onto me tightly. After a moment she begins to cry softly and I let her. Eventually, Dana loosens her grip and steps back. "I needed a break and thought I'd come see you for a few days. I hope it's okay."

This is a first. Dana usually acts as if I should be happy to spend time in her magnificent presence. The little person in the horribly grungy stroller makes a noise that sounds very close to a "Hey!" and demands our attention. Dana and I both look down at the child. There is no question she is Dana's baby even though she is dark brown like me, whereas, Dana is very fair skinned.

"Where did you get her?" I smile and reach for the child.

"Where do you think? Not being careful. She's my life now." Dana glows at the fairy.

I keep my eyes fastened on the child as I lift her from the contraption but I hear something in Dana's voice I've never heard before. Dana's in love and I cannot blame her. Her daughter looks straight in my eyes and studies me with deep-set large bright eyes of her own. She then looks at her mother as if to question her about my status. I can't help but hug the child close to me and close my eyes. Wow!

"What's her name, Dana?"

"Dora, Dora Grace Mechum. She's a good baby."

We work our way into the house without me ever taking my eyes from the child. Once we are inside and seated, I turn my attention to Dana. I cannot let her sorry condition or the mesmerizing chocolate fairy in my lap draw me in too much. In the past, Dana has been trouble, nothing major but trouble none the less. I'm certain the baby makes her situation more challenging and likely means she will be more trouble. "So what's going on, baby girl? We've all been worried about you. Aunt Alise kept saying you'd show up eventually but I could tell she was worried. Does she know about the baby?"

Dana is seated in an armchair across from me, looking antsy. She throws herself back into the chair with a deep breath before answering my questions. "I finally had to break down and tell her last month. I'm surprised she hasn't told you or somebody in the family. She called me just about every day for a week after that but

I ran out of minutes on my phone. I was almost relieved because she was getting on my nerves."

"She's been worried about you, Dana, we all have. You need to stay in touch with someone in the family."

"I don't need a lecture, Hannah. I'm here now, ain't I. Mama wants me to bring my baby to her in Greensboro. She's crazy if she thinks I'll let her have Dora." Dana looks at the child and smiles as she walks over and reaches for her. "Mommy will never let her baby go, will she? Not her baby girl – no she won't," Dana coos and snuggles her face into the baby's neck, moving it back and forth to tickle the child. Dora gurgles with laughter and pulls back to escape the caress.

"Where's her father?" I ask without thinking.

"We broke up a month after she was born. He wanted to play house but I'm not ready for that."

"Not really into him, huh?" I ask.

"I liked him okay, but I'm still young. I've got a lot of living to do and I can't do it tied down with some serious man. I just need to find a job and get a place of my own so I can take care of me and Dora. I'm off men for awhile," Dana states with absolutely no conviction.

The lack of conviction might be a good thing. This is not the first time I've heard Dana swear off men and each time before great conviction accompanied her statement. She never says why she's decided to swear off the opposite sex and I'm guessing her obsession with men is about the same as an addiction; it takes a number of attempts before one is able to bring it under control.

"So do you mind if me and Dora stay for a while, just until I get something set up in the city?"

I fight the urge to ask Dana not to return to the Bay Area, but I know her well enough to understand that she will do what her heart, not her mind, tells her. "When did you last talk to Aunt Alise?" I ask instead."

"I told you – a few weeks ago," she answers with the old Dana shining through.

"You need to call her." I rise from my seat and head to the kitchen.

"I will after I've rested a day or two."

I do an about face, pick up my purse, dig out my cell phone and hand it to Dana. "Please call her now. I talked to Dad last night and he says Aunt Alise is worried sick about you. She's been having medical tests ran to figure out why she is so exhausted and losing weight. Call your mother?"

Dana takes the phone. "When did you become so bossy? If I wanted someone telling me what to do, I would have gone to Brie's house instead of coming here."

I have to smile at this. There is no way in hell Dana would show up at Brianna's unannounced unless she felt death knocking at her door or she had a death wish. The simple truth is Brianna doesn't take her shit like me. I'm the chump when it comes to Dana. I'm Brianna's baby and Dana is mine.

Not that Brianna doesn't care for Dana; she does but she knows I've got Dana's back. Brianna encourages me to be careful with Dana because we all know she will rip you off, bring drugs or bad people into your home, or God only knows what. The most she's done to me thus far is steal a few things and lie. I think most people lie or at least exaggerate. I've been working on that and have been amazed at how often I have to retract or back track on a statement I have embellished for a bit more drama and I don't talk much. I figure people who talk all the time must lie a lot.

Anyway, my only close cousin is an addict and now she has screwed up on a child. Once I let this realization sink inside my head, I accept that this Dana sighting will be much more involved than any previous visit from my wayward cousin.

I no longer hear the murmuring of Dana's voice and know her conversation with my aunt has ended. A few minutes pass before Dana comes into my kitchen with little Dora riding her hip. I can tell Dana has once again been brought to tears. I guess it's no wonder she stays away from us; we make her cry.

"Mama doesn't sound very good." Dana tells me with sad eyes. "She says she's okay. What's going on with her?" For the first time, Dana seems concerned about her mother.

"What'd she say?" I ask, a bit put off by Dana's concern. I know my aunt is having some health issues but I assumed there was nothing serious going on with her.

"She says she's fine but she sure doesn't sound fine." Dana looks at me with challenge in her eyes now. I can tell she thinks I know something that I'm not telling.

"I'll call Dad tomorrow and Mom too. Maybe they have some information." I'm just trying to placate Dana at this point. If either of my parents have privy to Aunt Alise's medical condition they will only share that information if she wants it told.

"You mind if I take a bath? I really need one," Dana asks, sniffing and grimacing at her armpits.

I look at the baby and ask, "What about her. She's a little smelly. I think her hair needs to be washed."

Dana gives me a look that used to work and says. "Hannah, will you bath her for me. I'm so tired."

"No, please bath her and feed her before you climb in the tub. I know how you like to hibernate. Once you take care of her, you can stay in there all night if you choose. I've got to get us something to eat for dinner. I was having cold cuts but I need to fix something the baby can eat. What does she like?"

"Pretty much what I eat, table food. I can't afford baby food."

I try not to shake my head in disgust. Dana is an only child and comes from a middle class family full of people willing to help her. She could have had whatever she needed for her baby but her desire for drugs and fast fine men control her.

While she bathes Dora, I pull some tilapia filets from the freezer and slice up a sweet potato for oven fries. After about twenty minutes, Dana brings my newest family member out to me all fresh and clean. Since dinner is not quite ready, I agree to feed and watch Dora so Dana can get the bath she's jonesing for. I sit Dora in the stroller and continue my dinner prep as Dana joyfully heads to the guest bath. The baby watches her mother exit and then turns her eyes on me. Her mouth immediately turns downward and I can see the storm building.

"Don't cry, Dora. Cousin Hannah is with you," I tell her as I pull her from her stroller. She's tired. I can tell. I go to the cabinet and pull out a Belvita breakfast biscuit, which I've concluded is actually a cookie, to hand to her. Dora takes the cookie and then looks at me as if she's asking what she's supposed to do with it. I lean forward and take a tiny bite of the cookie and smack hard.

"Eat it, baby. It's good." The baby's eyes widen as she looks at the cookie and then back at me. "Take a bite." I tell her. I break off a tiny piece and present it to her mouth. She opens up her mouth and smacks on the dry morsel. She likes it and needs no further encouragement.

The doorbell rings just as I start to put Dora back in her stroller. I find Professor Ezekiel Melancon standing outside my door. He smiles as if he is happy to see me. "Hey, you've got company or is she yours?" he asks and then continues before I answer. "I brought your tools back." He raises the tools up for me to see as if he needs proof.

"Thank you," I tell him as I reach out and take the tools with my free hand but don't mention my cousin riding on my hip.

Zeke hesitates once again. "How are Brianna and her family? I used to date a good friend of hers, Deidra Bonner."

I wonder why he's telling me this. "Brianna's good, her and the family. I haven't seen Deidra in over a year or more."

This information seems to have little effect on the man and he continues standing on my porch. I'm being rude so I ask him in and to my surprise, he accepts. "Can I get you some coffee or something?" I ask, trying to hide my discomfort.

"No thanks," Zeke responds as he stands and looks around my living room. I put Dora in her filthy stroller and feel embarrassed. I swear I'm buying her a new one tomorrow.

"Whose baby?" Zeke asks once again.

"She's my cousin. I'm in the kitchen working on dinner." I beckon for him to join me and push the stroller close so Dora can see me. She's working on that biscuit and it ain't pretty. I hope Dana's got another clean set of sleepers for her. I wipe her face with a paper towel and try to clean some of the mushy crumbles off her fingers but she resists.

Zeke half settles in on a bar stool. "She's cute. I can see the family resemblance," he says with a smile as he watches Dora. I can tell he is not flirting when he says this. He's just stating a fact. Dora has now captured his attention. This is the gentle side of the man I've heard people say is either quiet and gentle or loud and abrasive.

"Listen, I really want to thank you again for dinner last night,"

"That wasn't dinner. It was just two chickens. I'm almost embarrassed by it now."

"No, it was thoughtful, really. I didn't know people still did things like that." Still looking at Dora, he says "She reminds me of my goddaughter when she was a baby."

I look up from my busy work in the kitchen. I don't think he has taken his eyes off of Dora since he entered the house.

"How old is she?" Zeke asks.

"Nine months, I think."

"I didn't realize how long it's been since I've spent time around a baby." The man laughs at his own delight in watching the child.

The sound of that unguarded chuckle signals a response in me. I look up again and take note of the man sitting at my kitchen counter. I want him to leave because I've become even more uncomfortable and I don't know why he's here. "Are you and Deidra still in touch?" I ask, at a loss for conversation.

Zeke looks a little surprised by the question. "Yeah, we talk every so often. I think she's pretty involved now so we don't talk as much."

He doesn't sound too heartbroken. I wonder if he's still pursuing my sister's friend. "I thought maybe you wanted to see if I knew something about her." This is my way of asking him why he is sitting in my home.

"No, Deidra and I are cool. We agreed to go our separate ways and it's been a while now. You get straight to the point, don't you?" He stands up from the bar stool. "I like that." Zeke points at me and gives me a focused gaze, then makes a point of his own. "Listen, don't let my people next door bug you too much. My mother, my sister, and her children all live there and I hope they get along okay. Do you mind taking my number in case anything comes up? I worry about my mother. She has diabetes and should probably be on insulin but insists she'll control her sugar levels through diet and pills." Zeke shakes his head as he pulls a business card from his wallet. He then hands me the card.

Now I know why he's here. "Sure," is all I say with a stupid smile plastered on as I reach for the card. He wants me to babysit his family. Okay, that's the neighborly thing and I don't mind watching out for his mother a little. Boy do I feel like I've been dropped.

"Well, I've over stayed my welcome. Be sure and give Brianna my regards. I'll let myself out and thanks again for the tools." The handsome man reaches down and gently shakes one of Dora's tiny little gooey hands and leaves without another look in my direction.

Chapter 3: Equal Consideration

I manage twenty four rental properties from Monterey to Marina and three in Salinas. This responsibility keeps me pretty busy but I usually spend no more than thirty hours a week at my desk or in front of a computer screen working my property management duties. I love being my own boss. It's nice to have the freedom to step away from my job whenever I choose. I'm taking advantage of that freedom today to check on my houseguests. I'm surprised to find my house empty when I arrive. I know Dana has some old school friends still living in Seaside, so she may be visiting with a friend or taking the baby for a walk. I quickly dismiss the walk theory when I look in the guest room and see Dora's stroller.

I start straightening up the house but no sooner than I get started, my house phone rings. It's my mother, Miriam. She tells me she had a call from my Aunt Alise earlier and wants to know about Dana.

"I didn't get to talk to her very much last night, Mom. She was so tired that she went off to bed just as soon as we finished dinner. I thought she was avoiding a conversation but I heard her snoring hard almost right away," I say.

"And Alise tells me Dana has a baby. What is she planning to do? Where's the baby's father? How is she looking?" My mother asks all these questions out of frustration because she is powerless to fix this situation. Miriam is a fixer. Whatever the problem, she tries to find a solution and put it in place. She's been fixing me since I got knocked unconscious out on the elementary school playground in the second grade. I let her work her magic on me and she continually tweaks my brother, Bill, and Brianna but she has had no luck with Dana and has pretty much stopped trying.

"I don't think Dana has any solid plans. She asked me if she could stay a few days. Her baby is a jewel but Dana is not with the child's father. She didn't mention who or where he is." I answer the questions I remember.

"Well, I hope she's getting some support for the child. I'm certain she can get assistance from the state also. There's WIC and food stamps, Medi-Cal. You make sure she's taking advantage of these programs. She's got a whole lot of family paying out a lot of money in taxes for these services. She might as well take advantage of them just like the next person."

I hear Dana at the door and get my mother off the phone. Dana enters carrying a sleeping Dora on her shoulder. Shantrell comes in right behind Dana with a lit cigarette in her hand. Both ladies stop abruptly when they see me. "I didn't know you were home, Hannah. I called myself looking out for you but I never saw the car pull into the garage," Dana says.

"I just got here a few minutes ago," I reply.

Shantrell makes no effort to put out her cigarette. Who does this shit? I mean, you'd have to have your head buried in the sand to not know the dangers of secondhand smoke. "Hi, Shantrell. Are you and the family getting settled in okay over there?" I ask in an attempt at being friendly.

"We're coming along alright. How are you doing? Did you work today?" Shantrell asks.

"I'm fine and yes, I did work for a while. Shantrell, please don't smoke in here or around the baby at all. I don't mean to be rude but secondhand smoke is not good."

I notice Dana roll her eyes and I want to slap her. I shouldn't need to tell Shantrell not to smoke around Dana's child. That's Dana's damn job. Shantrell looks ashamed, reaches for the door knob, opens the door, and flicks the cigarette out into my yard.

Dana takes Dora to the bedroom and I offer Shantrell a seat. When Dana returns, she and Shantrell sit next to each other on the sofa looking like the rainbow of fruit flavors in a bag of Skittles with platinum, purple, yellow, and brown hair; red and blue nails; and an array of colorful tattoos. I won't even mention their clothing except to say they both have on brightly colored skinny jeans with spiked heels. If I didn't know better I'd say they coordinated their outfits.

I head into my kitchen because I cannot wipe the smile off my face and I'm fighting the urge to burst out laughing. This is the very first time I have had the urge to take a picture and post it on Facebook or Instagram. I would give almost anything to be as content with my appearance as these ladies appear to be with theirs. I might need to make some changes. "I didn't know you two knew each other." I say before offering Shantrell something to drink.

"We just met today. I'll take a glass of water, Hannah," Shantrell replies.

"Me and Buddy have known each other since I was in middle school," Dana tells me.

"Is Buddy living with you?" I ask Shantrell.

"When he's not shacking up with some woman. I wish he'd get with one and stay. I'm tired of him running back in the house with me and Mama. One of us always lets him stay. Zeke won't. He doesn't even try to stay with old mean-assed Zeke. Now that Mama and I are in the house together, we can't take turns dealing with Buddy." Shantrell smiles at me with this comment and accepts her water.

"I'm surprised Buddy can't keep a woman. I remember the girls really liking him when I was in school," Dana says.

"Buddy likes women who have something going for themselves. His women have to have good jobs, nice homes, nice cars and plenty of money. He's usually working when he gets with them but once he gets his foot in the door, he quits his job for one reason or another. No woman with any self esteem is going to put up with his sorry ass." Shantrell's phone begins to ring but I don't see it. Girl reaches in her abundant bosom and pulls out the phone. The call is obviously more important than her visit with Dana and me. Shantrell heads to the door and gives us a casual wave on her way out.

This might be a good time to have a talk with Dana. I'd like to know what her plans are for taking care of her family but the somewhat contrite Dana who I found on my front porch two days ago has vanished and the Dana I know well has replaced her. I should have known things were back to normal when I saw the dirty dishes in the kitchen sink.

I decide to let Brianna tackle Dana when she comes on Saturday. Brianna has even more questions about Dana than my mother had.

--

By week's end I've fielded a barrage of questions from my father, my stepfather, my brother, my aunt, and my two best friends, Erika and Marshon. All questions concern Dana and Dora who should feel quite important. I'm sure neither has any idea of the stir they are causing.

Brianna arrives in town before noon on Saturday. She and I go shopping and pick up the items we need for our little picnic at Lover's Point. We swing back by my house and pick up our cousins before going to the care home for Granny.

It's a warm day on the peninsula and we manage to have an enjoyably relaxing time eating, watching the small watercraft out in the bay, gawking at other picnickers and people out for the day, and reminiscing about old times. Granny doesn't understand what we are saying but she laughs when we kid with her and glows the entire time we are out. We remain on the Point for nearly two hours and have Granny back at home by four thirty. She will have a peaceful night's rest for certain.

"You mind if I ask a few people over for dinner tonight?" Brianna asks with a doubtful glance in my direction as we ride back into Seaside after dropping off Granny.

I can sense Dana sit up straight in the back seat. She has been bored with me almost since the moment she arrived, so much so that she was even happy to see Brianna's face. "Who are you having over, Brie?" Dana asks.

"Just a couple of old friends, if Hannah gives the go ahead."

"It'll be good to have some company. That house is too quiet. I don't know how Hannah can stand it," Dana complains.

Brianna looks over at me and I see anger in her eyes. She's getting ready to attack Dana and I want to get her also but I won't. She's my guest but more importantly, she's in a bad place. I won't baby her but I will not dog her either. I put a finger up to my lips to silence Brianna and to my surprise she respects my request.

"I don't mind. Invite whoever you want," I tell Brianna.

"So can I invite some friends over for dinner too?" Dana asks, excitedly.

Damn it! From what Dana has told me, she had three dollars in her bag when she arrived at my home. I am presently taking care of her and Dora financially. I have spent a nice chunk of change on her and the baby since they arrived and given her some cash to have in her purse. No woman should walk around broke, especially not with a child. She does not have money to have a dinner party and I am amazed that she feels that Brianna or I should foot the bill to feed her friends.

Okay, that sounds callous. It's not just that I'm callous but when it comes to Dana's friends I might be considered downright Bougie. Dana's friends are the neighborhood dope dealers and crack heads. I'm sorry, but could you at least pretend that selling drugs is not your primary occupation and doing drugs your primary recreation.

Brianna gives me a look I interpret to mean, "Do you believe this cow?"

"Not this time," I answer reluctantly. Dana always wants more than I'm willing to give.

"That ain't right. Why is it okay for Brianna to invite people to your house but not me?"

I don't how to respond to this question because I can't think of a nice way to say, "Because your broke ass is broke and you hang with people I don't want in my house."

This is Dana – so damn inconsiderate but wants equal consideration. Everything is a test with her. She resents the fact that Brianna and I are sisters and so close; whereas, she is a mere cousin. She always wants us to prove we love her as much as we love each other. How crazy is that. It's not enough that we love her. Insecurity is a difficult companion.

Chapter 4: Disappearing Act

When we get home, Brianna takes off and heads back to the market. I wanted to ask Dana to help me straighten up my patio and pick up the house a little but she closes up in the room with Dora. I have everything from the picnic put away and the house and patio looking pretty good in a little more than half an hour, so I jump in the shower. No sooner than I get dressed, I hear Dora crying so I knock on Dana's room door. When I get no answer, I go inside and gather up Dora. She is wet and probably wants a snack. The guest bathroom door is closed and I decide not to disturb Dana from her marathon bath. I find one diaper and a container of wipes on the dresser and change Dora before taking her out front with me. "I got the baby, Dana," I yell toward the bathroom door. The spoiled brat doesn't bother to answer.

Brianna shows up with bags of groceries and a number of items for Dora. Dana doesn't come out to help us so we can only assume she's still sulking. I want to talk to her honestly but I know from past experience, the more honest I am the more upset she will become.

I tell myself to stop worrying about Dana and her feelings. I just want to do the right thing when it comes to her. My Granny always told us to "treat people the way you want to be treated," but what do you do when you feel you have to protect yourself from a person like Dana. If I treated her like I wanted her to treat me, she would have used me up by this time and I would probably be living up in Sacramento with Brianna or out in North Carolina with my mother. I have to maintain boundaries with Dana. She is the one person in my family I frequently tell "no."

I'm so preoccupied with thoughts of Dana that I still do not know who Brianna has invited to dinner. "What time are your guests coming and who did you invite?" I finally ask.

"Oh, just Deidra and Zeke but Deidra is bringing some guy she's dating. They should be here at about eight."

I look at my sister and wonder if she has lost her mind. "What are you thinking, Brie?"

Brianna rolls her eyes and throws a hand up dismissively; you know how we do. "I know, I know, when I talked to Deidra on

Monday she did not say a word about having a new love in her life and sounded devastated that she and Zeke were no longer together, so I thought I'd try and get them back on track. I had already invited Zeke when I called Deidra back with an invite. I called Zeke back and told him Deidra is bringing a date but he said he'd still like to come. I can't very well tell him not to, especially with his people right next door."

"Oh God!" is all I can say to this mess up by my sister.

Just then a strong whiff hits my nose and I know Dora has a dirty diaper. I tell Brianna in a lowered voice. "I have spent more time with this baby than Dana has since they've been here. Open that front room window and let some fresh air in before your friends arrive. There's some incense in that coffee table drawer."

I gather Dora up from the second hand portable crib I purchased on Craig's list a few days ago, along with a nearly new top of the line stroller. The child seems quite happy to have relieved herself. It is time for her mother to stop sulking and take care of her. If Brianna and I are such horrible people, why isn't she trying to keep her child away from us? I knock at the bedroom door but get no answer. I can't believe she is still in the tub. I can't help but think "what a sorry excuse for a mother." I feel guilty right away for this unkind thought. For all I know, this may be the first time Dana has had the freedom to leave Dora in someone's care.

I decide to change the diaper but there are no diapers in the bedroom. "Dana, I'm coming in to get a diaper," I yell at the bathroom door but get no response. I knock but still get nothing. What the hell is going on? I hope she's okay in there. I knock harder and then open the door to an empty bathroom. I look around with Dora still on my hip needing to be changed. I probably smell like her shit at this point. I get a diaper, spread a towel on the bathroom floor, and get her cleaned up as my eyes fill with water and my nose starts to burn. At this moment, I feel sad for this little girl child. Dana is so irresponsible to take off like this. Once again, I've been too easy on her. I'm going to get her ass when she gets back here. She could have told me she was going out.

I enter the kitchen and watch my sister prepare for her guests, who are due to arrive in less than an hour. "Is she still in there acting stupid?" Brianna asks as she moves around the kitchen putting the finishing touches on her impromptu dinner party.

"She's gone out," I say as casually as possible.

Brianna stops and looks at me for a moment. "Gone out where? When did she leave?"

"I don't know. She's not in the room."

My sister's eyes turn to saucers and this scares me. "She didn't tell you she was leaving?"

I don't want to answer this question for fear of the follow up questions. "I thought she was in the bathroom. She must have left while I was in the shower. She's just being a baby." I start to say Dana will be back but I tell myself there's no need to affirm her return. She has to return for Dora, her most precious treasure. "I need to get Dora fed before your friends arrive." I end the discussion and Brianna shakes her head as she heads off to shower and change.

Dora is perfectly content once she has her dinner. I take her to the bathroom and brush her few little front teeth and wash her face and hands. When I go back out front, I hand the child over to Brianna who changes her harsh expression to one of joy just for Dora's sake and plays with the child while I move the portable crib into the bedroom. After about ten minutes, I take the child and sit her in the crib where she quietly entertains herself with two new toys her cousin Brianna bought her.

I help my sister set the patio table and light Tiki lamps in the back yard. We sit down to relax over a glass of wine for Brianna and a cup of tea for me until the doorbell rings, announcing Zeke Melancon. Zeke enters the house with a bottle of red wine which he hands Brianna and a lovely bouquet of yellow roses for me. "For my thoughtful new friend," he tells me with a warm smile. I'm embarrassed by my unbridled pleasure.

Brianna gives me a "you go girl" look and I blush all over my body.

"Can I get a hug?" the charmer asks Brianna as he grabs her up in his arms and she returns the embrace before heading off to the kitchen.

"What would you like to drink, Zeke? "We've got Scotch and Tequila and red or white wine. I can make you a Margarita on the rocks, if you like," Brianna offers.

"I think I'll start off with a glass of the red. I don't want to get too zooted before Deidra and her date arrive. I need all my wits about me when I crush his skull."

Zeke keeps a straight face when he makes the statement, causing my mouth to drop open and eyes to grow wide. I see Brianna lean around the corner and look back into the front room with the same expression.

Zeke laughs. "I'm just kidding ladies. I work with Mykol. We were all at an alumni function together a couple of nights ago, even shared a table. I introduced Deidra and Mykol and yes it was after she and I split. Of course I didn't know they would get together but it's cool."

"That was mean, Zeke. You scared me for a minute there," Brianna tells him with a smile.

"How's your old man?" Zeke asks Brianna as he and I migrate into the kitchen. "Tell him I think I'm about ready for him on the links now. I won't need him to handicap me the next time we meet. Have him call me when he's planning on coming down this way and has time to get in a round or two."

Brianna hands Zeke his glass of wine and picks up her glass. "You're not joining us, Hannah?" Zeke asks.

Okay, I know this sounds silly but I can't help feeling happy that the man is now sure of my name. Now keep in mind that he looks me directly in my eyes when he says "Hannah" and then waits for my answer to his question. I find myself waiting for Brianna to answer on my behalf. Hell, maybe I am slow. "No, not yet, I never drink on an empty stomach." Slow and dull.

"Well we need to eat. Where are Deidra and Mykol? Are they the only ones we're waiting for?" Zeke asks.

"Yes, just the five of us, I guess." I answer, wondering about Dana. I suppose we can throw her steak on the grill if she shows up while we are eating.

We only wait a short time longer before Deidra and Mykol arrive. This is both Brianna and my first time meeting Mykol. He is a large, bald man, well over six feet. He has an open clear expression accompanied by a friendly smile. He dwarfs everyone in the room, including Zeke who has to be right at six feet.

Deidra looks better than ever and I can't help but notice that her breasts are now an overflowing D cup. I do a better job at not staring than Brianna who seems to want to burst out laughing and reach out and squeeze the cantaloupe-sized orbs springing from Deidra's chest. Brianna settles for giving her friend a big wide-eyed grin and a hug.

Once everyone has drinks in their hands, the group moves out to the patio. I go and check on Dora who is sleeping quietly and sucking on her bottom lip. On my way out to join the others, I gather up the steaks.

"Can I help you take something out, Hannah?" Zeke, who I thought was out on the patio, asks from behind me, causing me to jump at the sound of his voice.

I smile at him, embarrassed by my reaction and he smiles back, I mean a serious smile. I don't think a man has ever smiled at me like this before. "You can take these steaks. I don't know why Brie left them in here but I'm ready to eat; how about you?"

"I sure am. These are some good looking cuts. I wonder where she bought them." Zeke drools over the steaks as we exit to the patio.

The two men declare that the grill is a man's domain, so they grill the steaks. We ladies put in our orders, place the sides in the middle of the table, and enjoy a few minutes of gossipy conversation. One subject is Deidra's new girls. "I wanna touch. Do they feel like the old ones?" Brianna asks.

"Just a bit firmer. They feel real to me. Girl, I feel like a freak because I enjoy touching them so much, "Deidra giggles.

"Can I touch?" Brianna cannot take her eyes off Deidra's breasts and starts to reach for one.

"Not now, Brie. I don't know if Mykol knows they're enhanced or not, but if he sees you feeling on my boobs, he'll know something ain't right."

"I hope you're not thinking about breast enhancement, Brie?" I ask, but I'm pretty sure she is. The look on my sister's face says it all.

"Why not? Look at those things. Look at the way they fill out that dress. We're sitting up here looking like somebody burst our balloons next to Deidra and after two children mine could use some help. Yours are still nice and full, Hannah," Brianna whines, then to Deidra she says, "So Mykol likes 'em?"

"So Mykol likes what?" Mykol asks as he and Zeke approach the table.

"Nothing, baby. I was just saying how you love a good steak." Deidra smiles sweetly but instead of looking at Mykol, she looks at Zeke who smiles as if he's in on our discussion.

"I agree with you there, brother. I can't wait to chomp down into mine. Hope they're grilled to everyone's satisfaction. Check and make sure you're happy because mine is bloody so I can switch if anyone's is overcooked. I can eat a good steak however it's cooked," Zeke offers.

We are all satisfied with our steaks and dive in. I'm a little surprised how friendly our three guests are with each other but I begin to sense a little jealousy on Deidra's part as the evening wears on. It starts when I get up to clear the table and Zeke insists on helping. Once we get the dishes inside, I go and check on Dora. When I return to the kitchen, Zeke is scraping and rinsing plates and loading them in the dishwasher. I tell him Brianna and I will take care of the dishes later.

"I don't mind. I was waiting for you before going back out anyway," he tells me.

We finish loading the dishwasher with a little casual strained conversation. Zeke asks me about my parents and my grandmother and how long I've lived in my grandmother's home. He even asks about the care home where she lives. I'm beginning to wonder if he's always this curious. I'm flattered at his interest in me but wonder if he is trying to make Deidra jealous. He hasn't been rude toward her but has been somewhat aloof.

I hear the music come up a little louder out on the patio. By the time Zeke and I return, Brianna and Deidra have moved from wine to Tequila and from mellow to rowdy. "What'd we miss?" Zeke asks.

"Two shots each," Mykol informs us as he points to my sister and her friend who are cracking up in laughter.

When they stop laughing, Deidra looks at Zeke and asks, kitchen all clean?"

Zeke turns his gaze on me before answering. "Nearly, our host refused to let me help her finish."

"Did you check on the baby, Hannah?" Brianna asks.

"She's sleeping hard," I answer.

Zeke and Deidra look at me with a question. "Whose baby?" Deidra asks.

"Oh, I didn't tell you. Our sweet little cousin Dana is visiting from out of town and has Hannah babysitting."

"So where is Dana? I haven't seen that girl in years. Did she think we were too old and crotchety for her to eat dinner with us?" Deidra asks.

I hold my breath, not wanting Brianna to tell our guests that Dana slipped out and left Dora with me. I know that revelation will only lead to more questions and I do not want to discuss Dana with these people. Dana's problems and our problem with Dana are none of their concern.

"I guess we are too old." Brianna answers. "You know Dana is a fly girl.

"Can I see the, baby? Have you seen her, Zeke?"

"I met her the other day. She's a cutie," Zeke responds with a smile.

Deidra sits up straight and gives Zeke a somewhat accusatory glance. "The other day! So you're getting to be a regular, huh?"

I want to explain but what's the point. Deidra looks pissed. Brianna has a little uh oh smirk on her face. Mykol is not paying attention. I wonder if he has noticed his date's jealousy toward her previous love. If he has noticed, he either does not care or is adept at hiding his interest.

"Come on, girl. We'll peep in and see if the baby is okay," Brianna tells Deidra and they both get up to leave the table.

"Please don't wake her," I tell them.

"How long is your cousin staying with you," Zeke asks.

"Just a few days."

"Where is she living?" is his follow on question.

Somewhere in the Bay Area would sound flaky so I say "Oakland" with no conviction in my voice. I look away as I grab a bottle of white wine and pour me a glass in hopes of putting an end to the questions about Dana.

Zeke watches me with a curious little smile for a moment before engaging Mykol in small talk about the Warriors. I have the impression that he knows I am uncomfortable discussing Dana and thankfully, he does not ask more questions about her.

Just as Brianna and Deidra return to the table, Zeke's phone beeps with a text.

"She sure is a beauty. Are Dana and the father still together?" Deidra asks.

"Girl, I don't know who Dana is seeing. You'll have to ask her that question?" Brianna answers without really answering.

Zeke rises from the table as he reads a message on his phone. "Ladies, I thank you both so much for having me over, but I've got a little emergency I need to handle."

"Is it your mother or your sister?' Deidra asks.

"You sure are concerned about Zeke's business. I'm sure if he wanted to share the details, he would have." Mykol surprises us all with that remark. Apparently, he has been paying attention the entire time. I think I might like him. Deidra looks shocked and is left speechless for the first time tonight.

Brianna makes no attempt to rise from the table to escort her guest out so I reluctantly take on the responsibility of a courteous host. "Thanks for coming, Zeke, and thank you for the beautiful roses and the wine," I tell him when we reach the door.

"No, thank you and Brie for inviting me. I don't do much socializing these days. The dinner was delicious and the company even better." Zeke stops just inside the doorway and takes my hand in his. He doesn't let my hand go as he stands there looking at me.

"I hope everything is okay." I nod toward his cell phone.

"Oh yeah, I'm sure it'll be fine. My mother is blowing up my phone. She knows I'm just next door and wants me to stop in before I head home. And I hope everything works out okay with your cousin," he says as he turns to leave. I sensed that he was aware of a problem with Dana and his words are confirmation.

Deidra and her new man friend stay a while longer and seem to be quite content with each other when they leave. No sooner than the couple exits the house, Brianna passes on a message.

"Deidra told me to tell you to be careful with Zeke. She thinks he likes you."

"Really?"

"Yes, really, and she's not the only one. I picked up on that as soon as he walked in and handed you those roses. I wasn't going to say anything but Deidra feels you need to be put on alert. She says Zeke has way too much family drama."

"I'm not surprised with Buddy and Shantrell as siblings," I respond as casually as possible while trying to hide my excitement because I'm not the only person who thinks Zeke likes me.

"Deidra says it's all of them. She must have told me three times to tell you to be careful with Zeke. You want to know what I think?" Brianna asks with a sneaky little grin as we finish clearing the patio table."

"What do you think, Brie?" I ask, afraid of her answer.

"I think you like Zeke." My sister looks at me with a knowing smile.

I give this some thought and shake my head. "I don't know. I don't even know that man. Sunday was the first time I ever talked to him and we didn't really talk then. I've seen him running out on the beach trail when I go for my walks. He always waves and nods but that's been the extent of it. I'm sure he didn't know my name or remember me as your sister until Sunday but of course I knew who he was."

"Well, Zeke is very likable and Deidra is scared shitless that he likes you."

"Why should she care? I think he was paying me so much attention just to get under her skin. They must both still be into each other."

"Don't be naive, Hannah. No woman wants her old boyfriend to start up with someone new, especially not with someone they know well like Deidra knows you. I'm still curious about my old flames and their women. And as far as Zeke putting on a show with you for Deidra's benefit, not hardly; Zeke is not into kid's games. I didn't see any flirting. All I saw was a man very interested in a beautiful woman."

I'm flattered that my sister called me beautiful, a word which hardly describes me. Brianna is beautiful. Deidra and Shantrell are beautiful. I admit I do look good tonight because I've got my best face on. I can't help but glow at my girl. "You really love me don't you?"

"Yes, I do." Brianna comes around the table and hugs me as she whispers in my ear. "Deidra says he's wild in bed. I think that's why she's so upset."

"Brie!" I act shocked.

"Just telling you. You might want to do some reading up, watch some videos are something. If you don't have any, I can lend you some of David's. He keeps a stash." My sister laughs on her way to the kitchen.

Chapter 5: Don't Let the Glitz Fool You

I'm exhausted by the time I climb into my bed but I don't sleep. I turn on the bedside lamp and pick over some magazines and a couple of novels I've been reading. I settle in with Terry McMillan's *Who Asked You?* As I get back off into the novel I remember the one storyline where the mother abandons her children. I love Terry McMillan but her characters and stories are sometimes too real for me, especially when I'm trying to do the escapism thang. I finally doze off at nearly three in the morning but I do not sleep soundly. I keep listening for Dora and the doorbell.

I awake at about seven thirty the following morning to the sound of Dora's babbling. I pray her mother is in the room with her but I find the baby all alone entertaining herself. She greets me with a wide-eyed expression, waiting to see what type of mood I'm in. I know this because as soon as I say, "Good morning, beautiful" and give her a smile, she returns the favor and reaches for me. I swallow hard and try not to think about what may happen to this innocent child if Dana does not change.

After I get Dora cleaned up and fed I break down and call Dana's cell phone but the call goes straight to voice mail.

I put on coffee and Brianna joins me in the kitchen to start making breakfast. We have little to say to each other so we eat and drink our coffee quietly as long as the situation will allow. Breaking the silence, I complain, "I tried Dana's phone but just got her voice mail. I know she has minutes because I paid for them."

Brianna looks over at Dora and shakes her head. "You know you can't let her stay too long or she'll declare this as her home and you'll never get her out without an eviction. That's happening a lot now. Family or friends visit and refuse to leave unless evicted," Brianna tells me with a serious look.

The need to evict Dana is the furthest thing from my mind at this moment. I just want the woman to show up and take care of her child. "I can't imagine Dana doing something like that, Brie."

"No one expects that from a guest, Hannah. If they did, they wouldn't let the person in the front door."

"I guess you're right. I wonder where she is." I verbalize my thoughts.

My sister sighs and rolls her eyes. "Your cousin is such a spoiled bitch. I don't know where Alise found her. If Dana didn't look so much like us, I'd think our aunt bought her off the street; I swear. Are you worried she may not come back?"

"I know she'll come back. The question is when."

"Does she have any money?"

"I gave her a little because she was flat broke."

"How much is a little, Hannah?" Brianna asks with a frown.

"A hundred, that's all."

"That's enough to get her back up to the city. What will you do with Dora if she doesn't return by tomorrow?"

"Tomorrow's not a problem. I pretty much manage my own schedule and I can always work from home which is what I do most Mondays. Of course, I don't want to haul Dora with me out to look at properties if I have a problem and there's always a problem. Also I've got a good sized catering job for Friday at noon. I guess I'll have to find a daycare."

Brianna grimaces and says, "See if you can find a reliable sitter. I hate daycares. No matter how well run they are, parents take their sick children to daycares and spread illnesses like wildfire. I'll help with the costs whatever you decide."

"I hope it doesn't come to that. What do I tell Aunt Alise when she calls? She's called every day since Dana arrived. I hate to tell her I don't know where Dana is but the baby is here with me. That will worry her and she's not well."

"You're right. Maybe you should tell Dad what's going on and he can advise you what you should tell Alise."

"Dad's always so hard on Dana. I'd like to wait and see if she shows up later before I put anyone on alert."

Anger is turning Brianna's cool gray eyes smoky in color. It's clear she has been shielding her anger toward our ne'er-do-well cousin. "Dana needs someone to be hard on her ass. Aunt Alise just spoiled her too much. Thank God Mom and Dad were hard on her, not that it helped much."

I have no rebuttal for Brianna's opinion; I agree. We walk out to Brianna's car, both deep in thought. "I wish I could stay but I've got to get home. Tomorrow is a work day and my babies keep texting me. That's their way of rushing me. You let me know as soon as you hear from Dana, okay."

"I will. Thanks for coming down. It was a fun visit, all things considered." I bob my head toward the bundle settled in on my hip.

Brianna gives our little cousin a smooch and me a hug. "Thanks for taking such good care of Granny. I know now why you were always her favorite. Come up and visit soon. We miss your visits."

"That's nice to hear." I get Brianna on the road with a promise to visit on my first opportunity. There was a time when I visited with Brianna, David and the kids once or twice a month. It seemed if I wasn't visiting them, they were down visiting with me. Now my niece, Alise, who is named after my Aunt Alise and my nephew, David Jr., who we call "LD" which is short for, you guessed it, Little David, have these very demanding weekend lives. Brianna's home no longer holds the allure of a place to party or rest. As the children have gotten older, Brianna's weekends have gotten busier and I am not willing to drive all those hours to spend my entire Saturday out shopping or at one of the children's activities, sometimes two or more in one day. Then there is church on Sunday and dinner out or at home. By Sunday afternoon everyone in that household is resting or getting ready for Monday. If I chose to skip out on the Saturday events and just lounge by the pool, I would either be at the house all day by myself or with my brother-in-law, David. David often has a good reason for skipping out on Alise's and Little David's Saturday events. Although David and I are like brother and sister, I quickly realized that it was not a good idea for me to spend too many Saturdays lounging by my sister's pool with her husband while she was out running around with the kids. Nowadays, I visit four or five times a year at most, but I still love the family as much as ever if not more and I'm sure they feel the same about me.

--

I have plans to shop for items I need for a realtor's luncheon I'm catering on Friday. I make up my mind to stop worrying about Dana. Now that Brianna's gone, I have no reason to defend my cousin. This usually means I will begin to vilify her in my own mind. I know I need to remain busy today in order to keep my own anger in check. It is such a beautiful spring day that I decide to take Dora for a walk later. I give Dora her lunch and let her take a nap in hopes that she won't snooze during our outing.

We start out on the trail near the Target in Sand City and head toward Marina. The Pacific is calm and beautiful out in the bay, reflecting the clear peaceful sky. On this stretch of the Monterey Bay Coastal Trail there are not nearly as many people as on the stretches south from Seaside through Monterey and ending at Pacific Grove. I love the peace and serenity. I push Dora along for about two miles and she is content with little to no interaction with me. She seems to be enjoying the ride and the view. I find myself getting tired sooner than usual and I realize it's because of the extra weight I'm pushing. I head back to our starting point without any thought of Dana as I walk along the trail and observe the active people and lovely scenery along my way.

Just about a half mile from our start point, I hear someone calling my name from behind so I turn and spot Zeke jogging up to us. This is an unexpected and pleasant surprise.

He is slightly winded and takes a moment to catch his breath before speaking. "You ladies are out getting some fresh air and exercise, I see."

"We are; just like you." I smile at him and know my cheeks are full but I can't relax my face.

"Looks like the little one is really enjoying it out here. Where is this elusive cousin of yours, anyway?" Zeke stands up straight and looks me in the face with a crooked smile. "Are you sure she's not your baby? There's no need to be ashamed in this day and age."

I feign insult. "Why would I lie about something like that?"

Zeke looks at Dora and then back at me and then at Dora again. "She looks like you," he says with conviction.

I roll my eyes and shake my head. "You think so?"

"Yeah, I do," Zeke says and then asks, "You mind if I walk back with you guys?"

We walk at a leisurely pace with neither of us talking much for the first few minutes. A young couple zips past us at a fast jogging clip and yells out, "Hey Professor Z."

"Hey, guys." Zeke waves and yells at their backs.

Do you enjoy teaching?" I ask as a way of getting conversation started.

"Yeah, I'm pretty much into it now. When I first started I didn't expect to care for teaching as much as I do. I was just looking for a job so I applied everywhere. I was in the financial services industry before the bottom fell out. I got out in time. I made good money but that is not a job for the faint of heart, neither is teaching actually. " Zeke chuckles.

"You don't impress me as being faint of heart,"

"I didn't think I was but when I realized I was encouraging clients to invest in products I didn't understand at all, I knew it was time to go. At first I was just doing what everyone else was doing, but honestly, the deeper I looked into the products we were offering our clients the more confused I became and no one could answer my questions. I decided to take the money and run as the saying goes. I feel bad about the possibility I might have steered my clients into some worthless crappy stock but I was gone two years before anyone really knew what was going on. I like to think that if I had known just how toxic those investments were, I would have gotten my clients out but I don't know." Zeke sounds as if this still bothers him.

"Are you still in touch with any of your old clients?" I ask.

"One or two, not many; they seem to be okay. At least no one has come looking for me." He laughs now. "Some of the guys I worked with caught it pretty bad. Some lost all there equity in some crap stock that they thought would make them rich. Others lost their jobs."

Zeke moves on from a subject he dislikes to one I'd like to avoid. "So where is her mother?"

I start to answer evasively but he gives me a look I'm not prepared for. "I know something is going on. I'm just curious. I think I've been curious about the baby since I first saw her but last night, between you and Brianna, something strange was going on. I know strange when I see it and there was definitely something out of whack last night," Zeke says.

"Well, I mean, it's no big secret or anything. Deidra has known Dana, that's my cousin, for years and Dana has always been trouble. Deidra has never cared that much for her so we did not want to discuss Dana's antics in front of Deidra. To be honest, I don't know where my cousin is. She took off yesterday when I was in the shower and Brie was out shopping for dinner."

Now Zeke stops walking and squats all the way down to take Dora's hand. The child watches him closely and seems to find him every bit as interesting as the scenery. "Has she ever done anything like this before?" he asks with no more humor in his voice.

"Well, yes, often. She comes and goes. I never know when to expect her and she seldom says goodbye. She usually gets offended and leaves. She's our perpetual teenager, you could say."

"So you're not concerned about her?" Zeke stands but Dora continues watching him until we resume our walk.

"I'm concerned about her baby," I tell him.

"Is this the first time she left the baby with you?"

"I hadn't seen Dana for two years before she showed up at my house on Monday. I nor anyone in my family, including her mother, knew she had a child until six days ago. Well, actually, my aunt did learn about Dora a month ago."

"Who goes off and abandons their child like that? You need to notify the authorities." Zeke sounds angry

"I'm hoping she'll show up later today," I tell him.

"Not likely. She doesn't deserve to have this baby. She doesn't care enough. Who does shit like this?"

"Dana knows Dora is safe with me." Here I go defending Dana again.

"No she doesn't. She hasn't seen you in two years. She doesn't know you at all. She remembers you but you might have changed. There's no telling who she's been leaving this baby with. She's too irresponsible to take care of something as precious as a child." He stands there and watches my discomfort for a moment. "What are you going to do if she doesn't show?"

"I don't know. I really don't know."

"Have you got someone to babysit? Don't you work?"

"Yeah, I may need to find someone to care for her several hours a day, at least three or four days a week. I'm my own boss and I work a lot from home.

"You do some type of real estate work, right?"

"I manage rental properties and I also cater. I've got a large event on Friday. I have a friend who helps me sometimes because she's off on Fridays but I'm bringing one more person in for that event.

"An industrious woman, huh, I like that." Zeke smiles.

I smile back and say, "Thank you."

We've reached my car and Zeke helps me get Dora buckled in and the stroller in the back before asking, "So what are you going to do about this situation with the baby?"

It seems he is attempting to take ownership of my family problem and I don't need his help. "I'm just going to play it by ear for the time being. If Dana doesn't show, I'll just have to find a babysitter."

"You know, Shantrell can help you."

"Can she cook?" I ask.

"She's a damn good cook and loves it but I was talking about taking care of the baby."

He's got to be kidding. "Shantrell smokes," I say skeptically.

"Hardly at all. She doesn't need cigarettes. Once in a while she'll smoke if someone else is smoking in her presence. I don't remember the last time I saw her with a smoke and she's good with kids. As a matter of fact I'm helping her with a business plan for a daycare."

"Really?" I say, not wanting to insult him but I can't see Shantrell watching my cat if I had one.

"Don't let the glitz fool you. My sister is eccentric in her dress." Zeke smiles. "Okay, ghetto as hell but she's very intelligent. Keep an open mind. She can help you and you'd be helping her. She needs the extra income."

"I'll think about it. Are you her only reference?"

"If you decide to seriously consider her, let me know. I'll get you references."

"What about her nails?"

Zeke laughs. "I'm sure she can take those things off."

"Well, I hope we're getting ahead of ourselves here. Hopefully Dana just needed some time away and will come back for the baby." I don't even look in Dora's direction because I can feel the emotion rising in my chest and I don't want to stand here and start crying. I was happy to see Zeke on the trail but now he's making me face possibilities I'm not ready to deal with.

"What's she into, this cousin of yours?"

I consider telling him it's none of his business but I need someone to talk this through with. Brianna would get on the phone with me and hash it out but her life is so busy and I know she is exhausted after her weekend here in Seaside. She crammed a lot into the visit and truthfully, I don't want her to know how worried I am that Dana may not return for her child anytime soon. "I'm not too sure." I've had my eyes averted but now I have to look at Zeke. "Nothing would surprise me."

He shakes his head and I get the impression he really wants to help.

"So how long have you been managing properties now?" Zeke asks.

"Well, informally for about eight years, since my mother and stepfather moved to North Carolina. I just got my realtor's license about four years ago. I work out of a friend's office but basically I'm on my own. The contracts are between me and the clients. Right now, I don't plan on taking on any new properties for a while. I just picked up two more last month."

"Do you like being your own boss?"

"I do. It gives me the freedom to do my catering and visit with my grandmother whenever I like."

Dora yells before Zeke can ask me any more questions. This is the first time I've heard her belt out a yell since the day she arrived at my house and I'd swear she's telling me to "hurry the hell up!"

Chapter 6: The Angel Baby's Keeper

I find several messages on my machine when I arrive home. I'm more than a little disappointed that one of these messages is not from my Aunt Alise which means she may call later in the day to speak with Dana. I dread that call.

I return calls to my mother and then my father who I haven't spoken to in a month or more. He and I don't talk so often, mostly on holidays and occasional check in calls. My father is closer to my brother than my sister and me. I don't mind and I've never gotten the impression Brianna minds either. William is a good dad and I love him. He and I do a quick catch up and I tell him about the situation with Dana. My father is of the opinion that I may have Dora with me for a while. He also feels I should tell my Aunt Alise that I have Dora with me. "Alise is going through a rough time right now, but I don't believe it would be wise to lie to her about having the baby with you. Honestly, I think she'll be relieved."

With my dad's advice at hand, I am prepared for my aunt's call but it does not come.

--

I start looking for a sitter immediately. I call everyone I think of who might know of someone who knows someone who could watch Dora for me. My friend Marshon believes she knows an older woman who keeps children in her home. She promises to call me back with the information.

After numerous calls in search of dependable child care, I call Brianna on her job late Monday morning and give her the rundown on the situation. Brianna is a project engineering specialist at Aerojet Rocketdyne Corporation where she has worked since receiving her undergraduate degree in chemical and biomedical engineering. Since I never call her at work, she knows I'm concerned. "Are you considering Shantrell?" she asks.

"I don't know. I'm not having any luck so far. The daycare centers are asking for Dora's shot records and all kinds of stuff. I thought I might be able to just drop the kid off but no way. Do you have any suggestions?"

"I always liked Shantrell. She's a little loud but she's not mean. I think you should at least find out if she's available. I really don't think Zeke would recommend her if she weren't capable."

"Brianna, you should see her nails!"

"I don't think those are her nails, Hannah."

"Zeke says they're fake," I admit.

"Well, if she wants the job, she'll take them off. Just feel her out. It doesn't mean you have to use her."

"Then I'll have a neighbor who's mad at me and Zeke will probably be pissed."

"I doubt it, but what do you care if Zeke gets angry?" Brianna says supportively.

"You're right; I wish he had stayed out of it. I'll talk to you later. Call me if you get some time tonight."

I locate Zeke's business card on my refrigerator and leave him a message to text me Shantrell's phone number. I know she's just next door but I don't want to leave Dora alone while I run next door. Less than twenty minutes later, I receive the number from Zeke but nothing else, not even a "Hey, Hannah." I'm a bit disappointed. I don't know what I expected him to include in the text because anything short of him asking me out would have been a letdown. No sooner than I get Zeke's message, I call Shantrell and ask her to come over for a minute.

"What's wrong?" she asks, sounding panicky.

"Nothing, nothing at all. I wanted to ask you about something but I've got Dana's baby here with me and don't want to wake her. Is it a good time?"

Shantrell comes right over. I'm surprised to see she has gone from platinum to a super short flaming red quick weave with spiked golden blond tips. Girl's hair looks damn good. "What's going on, missy?" She asks with an arresting smile as she enters the house.

"Did your brother tell you I wanted to talk to you about something?"

"Which one, Buddy or Zeke? I guess that's not important because neither of them told me anything," Shantrell laughs.

I thought Zeke might have paved the way for me, although it was wise of him not to mention his suggestion to Shantrell. It wouldn't be fair to have her waiting for me to talk to her if I chose not to. "I'm talking to a few people in an attempt to find a sitter for my little cousin. Dana is gone back to the Bay Area and I'm keeping the baby with me until she gets situated."

"Dana left that angel baby here with you? When is she coming back?"

"Well, she's got to take care of some things and hopefully find a new place for them to live, so." I hesitate. I'm lying and bad at it.

"I'll watch the baby for you. When do you need someone?"

"Probably three or four days a week but I don't have a regular schedule, so it would be up in the air each day. Like I said, I have other people to talk to but do you have that kind of flexibility."

"Girl, you don't need to talk to anyone else. All I do is read and watch TV in my free time. I've been looking for a job but not hard enough according to my mother and Zeke. They fired me off my last job because several of the parents complained my clothes were too tight and the owner said I was too familiar with some of the parents. I tried to tone it down but I just had to be me. I've got three months of unemployment left, so I guess I'll have to find something. That child support won't be enough to take care of me and my boys."

When I can get a word in, I tell Shantrell, "Well, I've already made plans to talk to these other ladies. I hope you won't be mad at me if I choose one of them."

"Hell no, baby! You choose who is best to look after that little angel. She looks like you. And listen, since I'm just next door, I'll be your stand-in when you want to run a quick errand or just need a night out." The woman smiles and appears genuinely willing to help me out.

It dawns on me that this is the longest conversation I've had with Shantrell Melancon and I did not expect such a kind spirit.

My cell phone beeps and I know I've got an important message from a tenant. There is a crisis, at least in the tenant's mind. I ask Shantrell to excuse me while I make a call to Mrs. Horton, one of my nicer but more demanding tenants. No sooner than I get her on the phone, Dora starts to wail as if she just woke up from a bad dream. Mrs. Horton is yelling about a cracked toilet but I cannot hear her very well over Dora's crying.

Shantrell, God bless her, points toward the vicinity of the house where Dora is and asks me if I want her to get the child.

"Please," is all I can say with my hand over the speaker of the phone.

"Okay, Mrs. Horton. Did you get someone to shut off the water?" I ask the lady.

"No! Who would I get to do that? I got towels around the base of the toilet but it's leaking something fierce. You need to get over here."

Mrs. Horton expects me to show up for every occurrence. It didn't take me long to figure out she likes my company. "Let me get Jay over there right away to stop that water from running. I'll be over as soon as I can get there. It may be an hour or so before I can make it by."

"Well, you need to come see for yourself, Hannah."

"I will. Let me get Jay on the phone."

Mrs. Horton is pacified for the moment and the crying has stopped. I make a quick call to Jay, one of the men who service's my properties, and then head to Dora's room.

"What a big girl you are. Look at that pretty smile. I bet you're hungry, aren't you? We're going to get you something to eat. Come on." I hear Shantrell talking to Dora.

I watch as she lifts the child from her crib and recall Zeke's words "Don't let the glitz fool you".

"She was soaking wet," Shantrell tells me once she sees me standing in the doorway. "You'll need to change the bedding." Then to Dora she says, "She's so sweet, yes she is." Dora smiles for her and then to my amazement, the child leans forward with outstretched arms for me to take her.

Shantrell laughs and tells the child, "Okay, missy, go on to your cousin; she's family."

Lord I'm almost convinced. "Thanks, Shantrell. You helped me with my first crisis."

"You're welcome, baby."

I'm just about sold, but I'm looking for a person to care for an innocent, so I need to be diligent. "Shantrell, do you have any one I could talk to from your previous job or jobs."

Shantrell looks at me and I see hope in her eyes. I hate that. I don't want to disappoint this kind-spirited woman.

"I can get references from both of my previous jobs. I quit Kiddie Dreams for more hours at Children's Best. I probably should have gone back to Kiddie but I was feeling pretty down when Children's Best fired me. But the owner at Kiddie will tell you about me. Also the assistant director at Children's Best is still there. Believe me, that's a record because that director runs her assistants off like crazy. Once she thinks the staff or parents are too comfortable with her assistant director, she sends that assistant packing."

The woman pulls her phone from her ample bosom and scrolls through her contacts to provide me with the names and numbers. "Did Budrow tell you to ask me about babysitting?" she asks.

"No, Ezekiel."

A grin spreads across Shantrell's face as she looks up from her phone. "My big brother always has my back. You wouldn't think so as much as he fusses at me. I love him even if he can raise more hell than the devil."

"I've heard that about him. Is he grouchy?"

"Just with me and Buddy. He has little patience for Buddy at all and he constantly harps on me about letting my talents go to waste. Zeke is completely different with my babies. He's stern with them but he never raises hell with them like he does Buddy and he's a complete softie when it comes to Mama."

After sending me the names and numbers of her references, Shantrell makes her way to the door. "You let me know when and if you need me. I've never had anyone call me out of the blue to work and I'm feeling quite special," she laughs.

I see why Brianna likes her. Shantrell is like fine wine, the more time you spend in her presence the more you like her. Damn, I forgot to mention her nails. I didn't even notice if she had them on.

--

I make calls to the two references Shantrell gave me. I get Miss Nancy Martin at Children's Best Daycare on the phone immediately. She tells me what I expect to hear. Shantrell, she says, is good with children and the children liked her. She also surprises me when she tells me Shantrell was the most dependable and self-motivated worker she ever worked with. "I hated to see her leave," Miss Martin says.

My call to Kiddie Dreams Daycare is not as fruitful but I leave a message for the owner/director, a Mrs. Lena Kramer.

After I make the calls to verify Shantrell's references, I gather up Dora and we head out to Miss Horton's home. I'm relieved to see Jay's truck on the scene when I pull up. Jay meets me outside before I have Dora out of the car. He explains that he will need to replace the toilet and makes several cost saving recommendations. I tell him that the new toilet cannot be one Miss Horton will consider high tech, so we rule out the new dual flush toilets. I go inside and ask Miss Horton if she'd like a higher level toilet seat to make it easier to rise after she's done her business. You'd think I had given her a boatload of cash, she's so pleased. Dora and I visit for a good hour and I have coffee with the lady. She considers having Dora in her home a special treat and makes it harder than usual for me to leave.

By the time I get home, I'm beat. I get my second confirmation of Shantrell's worthiness which is more glowing than the first and ends with, "Tell Shantrell I got a part time opening waiting for her if she wants it."

I conclude that Shantrell has not been looking for a job at all. With these references she should be able to get on at just about any daycare on the peninsula as long as the dress code is not too stringent.

--

"Shantrell, I spoke with both of your references. Mrs. Lena from Kiddie Dreams says she has a part-time position ready and waiting for you, if you're interested."

Shantrell laughs off her pleasure at being so highly considered.

"Are you willing to wear shorter nails if you work with Dora?" I get straight to the point.

"Oh, I don't wear fangs when I work with children. Those are just to entice and scare off the men." She laughs again but wickedly this time.

"Which is it, entice or scare them away?" I ask.

"Both, baby doll, I want to scare away the timid men and entice those interested in someone a bit more exotic than the norm."

This woman is a trip. Life won't be dull with her around; that's for certain. "When can you start?" I ask.

"Right now."

"Why don't you come over tomorrow about ten in the morning and we'll talk. We need to see if we can work together."

Chapter 7: That Damn Daughter of Mine

Every morning I awake with renewed hopes of Dana's return. Every day I watch her daughter and pray God's protection over the child and her mother. Every night I climb into bed physically and emotionally drained.

I now divide my time between my jobs, Dora, and Granny. Shantrell has made that possible. The woman is my saving grace. I've accepted a couple of catering jobs I might otherwise have turned down if Shantrell weren't with me. She started working the very Tuesday we met to discuss the job and agreed to also help me with my larger catering orders.

What has surprised me most about Shantrell is her quest for knowledge. Once she learned that I have formal culinary training her thirst for food information became ravenous. Much of what she asks is beyond me so I find myself researching foods and recipes nonstop. My own knowledge base is sure growing. I had two copies of my culinary introduction to foods text books so I gave her one. She left it here at the house and will sit down and actually read through the thing when she's not busy.

I finally spoke with my Aunt Alise. Dana had been gone a full week when Alise called. "Hey, honey bun, how you doing?" Alise sounded especially perky and I felt she was making an effort to sound well. She and I talked casually for a few minutes before she asked me if I'd heard from Dana. With my voice near a whisper, I told her I had not spoken with my cousin.

"I haven't either. I have not heard from her since she got that last bit of money from me. I only sent it because of the baby. I told Dana that I wanted to make sure Dora was well cared for. I worry where they might be sleeping. You think Brie might have heard from them. I stopped losing sleep over Dana ages ago but my grandbaby deserves a chance."

It was clear why my Aunt hadn't called my house over that past week. She thought Dana had Dora with her. As much as I hated to tell Alise that Dana had abandoned her child, I wanted to put my aunt's mind at rest about Dora's well being for the present.

"Aunt Alise, I have Dora here with me."

"What do you mean Dora is with you?"

"I'm keeping her here with me for now," I did my best not to enter tattle mode so I gave as little information as possible to start.

"When did you and Dana make this decision and what exactly is Dana supposed to be doing while you take care of her child, Hannah? She didn't mention a word of this to me. I talked to her maybe three or four days ago. She told me she had found a nice room for her and the baby but needed some money to pay the people upfront." My aunt ranted and made no attempt at hiding her wrath.

The conversation was getting messy. I thought about strangling Dana who was trampling over too many hearts and lives. I had to tell my aunt the truth so she could deal with Dana on a level playing field the next time she received a call for assistance because there would definitely be a next time.

"Dana didn't ask me if she could leave Dora, Aunt Alise. We didn't discuss it at all. She took off over a week ago and I haven't heard from her since. I didn't want to tell you because I knew it would only upset you but you should not be sending her money to care for Dora. Dora is with me and she's fine. I'll send you some pictures this evening."

"That damn daughter of mine. She don't care about nothing but drugs and them streets. Now she's got this baby. Lord help me!"

"Aunt Alise, please try to focus on you. I got the baby. She's happy and doing fine. I have Mrs. Melancon's daughter, Shantrell, helping me take care of her. I checked her references and she is so good with Dora."

My aunt didn't respond.

"Aunt Alise?"

I could hear crying over the phone.

"Would it make you feel better if I brought Dora to see you?" I asked.

"Maybe we can work something out in a month or two, when my chemo is over. I'll send you some money to help with the baby."

"Me and Brianna will take care of this, Alise. Dad and Mom say they'll help if things get tight but right now I see no problems.

I just want you to take care of yourself and I'll get this little fat baby girl up there when you say the word. I love you, Auntie."

"I love you too, baby. I'll call you tomorrow."

Once I got the tattling out of the way, my life took on some normalcy. Dana did contact my aunt for more money which Alise refused to send until Dana sent me Dora's shot records and a special power of attorney, allowing me to make medical decision for the child. My aunt is a wise woman.

I received an envelope from Dana three days later and two days after that, the bitch called. I was nearly speechless. I mean, how do you call and chat with the person with whom you've abandoned your child. During that call, Dana talked to me as if I had signed up for child-rearing duties. Not once did she mention coming to get her child or providing any form of support. I would gladly raise Dora but I know Dana won't allow that. I feel as if Dana, not Dora, has taken control of my life. I can't make any type of long term plans without considering Dora but, of course, Dana may show up for the child any day and I have no doubt that she will return for Dora.

--

I have not laid eyes on Ezekiel Melancon since that day on the coastal trail when he got so deep off into my business. I had expected a call or a visit from him after I hired Shantrell but not one word has come my way. I have to admit my heart is breaking a tiny bit. I like spending time in the presence of all that testosterone. I thought he liked me but I must have been wrong. He might even be avoiding me. His family lives right next door but I never see him. I used to catch sight of him on the trail once or twice a week but not lately.

Recently, Budrow Melancon asked me if I ever go out for drinks. He didn't actually ask me out. It was more like he was feeling me out to determine if I was willing. I gave him a flat out "no." Now if Ezekiel were to ask me that same question I would have told him "sure" and prayed for the invite.

I haven't been on a date in what feels like forever. It's been over a year since anyone asked me out. Up until about two years ago, I was involved with a guy but it was not serious. I met him at Brianna's house one weekend when I was visiting. Bradley, yes, his name is Bradley, would visit me in Seaside on a pretty regular basis. Occasionally, I'd visit him at his home in Milpitas and we shared a couple of vacations together. I liked him and thought he liked me more but at some point during our relationship he met another woman, became engaged, and got married.

Bradley was on his honeymoon when I learned of his marriage. Since I hadn't heard from him in a couple of weeks and he wasn't returning my calls to his cell phone, I called his office for the first time. His assistant happily informed me "Mr. Jackson is away on his honeymoon and will not return to the office until Tuesday, May 1st. May I take a message or would you like his voice mail?" I didn't leave a message though I was tempted. Three days later, Bradley called me. He never mentioned his marriage. He explained that he was in Hawaii on business. We made plans to get together after his return.

I didn't hear from Bradley for nearly a month after that conversation and I made no attempt to contact him. When he finally called, he told me he'd be down on the peninsula the following week and wanted to see me. His words were, "I've missed you something terrible, baby, you wouldn't believe how much. We've got to figure out a way to spend more time together." I remember his exact words because I recorded them. I planned to send our recorded conversation to his new bride. He invited me to meet him at the Hyatt Carmel Highlands and told me not to worry about bringing anything to sleep in and I didn't, worry about lingerie that is. I didn't show up at all for my belated birthday dinner.

Our plan was to meet in the hotel's swanky restaurant overlooking the Pacific. I smile when I think of him sitting there, waiting for me with his cock hard. I imagine him getting antsy and looking over his shoulder in expectation of my arrival, then looking at his expensive Tag Heuer watch.

Twenty minutes into our dinner reservation my cell started ringing. Five minutes later he called my home phone. One hour and thirty minutes after our scheduled meet time, Bradley pulled up in front of my house. It was dark out but I sat in my front room with the lights on drinking a glass of Cabernet Sauvignon as I flipped through the pages of a *Black Enterprise* magazine. He could easily see me sitting here inside my home, but I never turned my head or eyes toward him as he rang my doorbell, banged on my storm door, yelled my name, banged at the window, or blew his car horn. Finally, he drove away after a squad car cruised down the street. I guess one of my neighbors got concerned and called the cops.

Bradley called me several times after that night but I refused to take the calls, listen to, or read his messages. Eventually I blocked his number. Just a few months ago, he showed up at the realty office. After the receptionist told me he was in the waiting area, I left through the side door and haven't seen or heard from him since. I never sent the recording to his wife. I didn't want to hurt her. I'm sure Bradley will take care of that without my help.

All my involvement with men had been pretty dull up until I met Bradley. I admit he made me feel special. Like so many others, that bad experience took away my taste for romance. Since spending time in the presence of Zeke Melancon, I feel my appetite returning.

--

"Hey, Sissy, I was wondering if you want to drive up with Dora next weekend to celebrate your birthday," my sister, Brianna, asks me.

Brianna's thought processes can be somewhat complicated and I often need her to break them down for a simpleton like myself. Seriously, think about it. It's my goddamn birthday not hers. Why would I want to pile me and Dora and all of Dora's crap into my little hatchback and drive three hours to celebrate my birthday with her and her family? Paleeeze!

"No, thank you, Brie, I'm pretty sure Marshon and Erika have planned something here at the house."

"What about Dora?"

"What about her?" I ask.

"I just thought you'd like some time without her to celebrate."

"And how exactly would I get that if I drive to Sacramento?"

"Okay, well, would you and your friends mind if me and mine come down and celebrate with you?"

I do a complete attitude adjustment at this point. This is a first. "I don't mind at all. I would love that, Brie. We could actually have a little get-together. Is David coming too?"

"Yes, if it's okay with you. What about Marshon and Erika? Do you think they'll mind? I know you guys always have your little exclusive party to celebrate your birthday. I just figured since you have Dora with you, it might be okay for us to join in also."

"They won't mind and I want you guys to come. It'll make my birthday really special." I tell Brianna and mean every word I say. She sounds as happy as I feel when we end the call.

Not ten minutes later, Brianna calls again with a more challenging request. "David wants to know if you will talk to Zeke about a round of golf when we come down. You don't mind if we come down Friday night and stay the weekend, do you? That way they can get out early Saturday and hit the course and I'll be able to spend some time with Granny."

"No, that sounds cool. It'll be nice to have you guys here for a few days."

"What do you want me to bring for the party?"

Brianna is making this much more complicated than I'm prepared for. "I'll be honest with you, Brie; Erika and Marshon take care of my birthday celebration. They say what we're going to do, when, and where. That's kind of their gift to me. I don't do anything but show up."

"Do you mind if I call Marshon or Erika and ask them what I should bring?"

"Give them a call. Marshon is probably the one to talk to. She usually does the planning and Erika spends the money. Now what is this about Zeke?"

"When I was down the last time, Zeke told me to tell David he'd like to take in a round of golf the next time David came down. David wants to know if Zeke is available that Saturday morning."

"Oh, okay. Do you want Zeke's number?"

"No, I have his number. I just thought you could ask Zeke the next time you see him but I'm pretty sure David has his number also. I'll just tell David to call Zeke directly. That will eliminate any confusion. You know your brother-in-law; anything he can get me to handle he will."

"I wouldn't mind telling Zeke, but I never see him," I admit.

"You never see him? But his family is just next door and Shantrell is babysitting for you." Brianna sounds baffled and disappointed.

"I know but I haven't seen Zeke in weeks. I see his car parked next door every once in awhile. I can ask Shantrell to give him a message but I never see the man."

"Oh, well excuse me. I thought something might be going on in that quarter. I wasn't asking any questions. I guess I was just waiting for you to volunteer some information. So you're telling me, there's nothing going on?"

"Not a thing!" I say with drawn out disgust.

"You sound a little disappointed."

We both laugh. "Yeah, just a little bit, just a little bit," I say.

"Well, okay. Keep hope alive, sister, keep hope alive," Brianna says jokingly.

Later that evening I get a call from Marshon who says she'd like to bring her husband and children to celebrate my birthday also. I tell her I would like to invite Shantrell, Miss Mel, and Shantrell's boys. Looks like my birthday celebration, which was originally planned for three, is growing closer to twenty three.

--

I am surprised that my sister felt she needed an invitation to come and celebrate my birthday but I understand why she felt that way. For the past five years or so my friends Erika and Marshon have given me a special birthday celebration. They usually ask me how I'd like to celebrate and I always tell them to surprise me. It's always been just the three of us.

Erika, Marshon, and I have been close friends since the second grade. Naturally, we didn't start off as best buddies. They both tell me that I was uppity and that I thought I was cute. I think they just like to tease me with their stories. I honestly don't remember what I was like back then.

You see I had a bad accident in the second grade. From what I'm told, the accident was no one's fault. I simply missed a bar on the monkey bars and fell in such an awkward way that I hit my head on the wood surrounding the play area. I was knocked clean out and carted off to the hospital. I awoke three days later to the sight of my mother, father, aunt, and grandmother standing around my bed in prayer. The doctors were baffled but my family declared a miracle when the CT scan indicated my brain swelling had gone away almost overnight.

I remained out of school for a full two months. My father wanted to keep me out for the remainder of the school year but once the doctor declared I was fine to return to the classroom, my mother insisted I rejoin my classmates. I know now that my thinking was still not clear when I went back into the classroom but I was ready to return and had been begging for weeks to go back to school. Some of the kids ignored me, some would not play with me, and others made fun of me when I first returned. My best friend, Cathy, was one of the children who ignored me after my first day back and her behavior toward me hurt the most.

One day when one of the boys started teasing me, Erika and Marshon walked up to him and demanded that he stop. When he continued, Erika threatened to punch him and Marshon went and found a teacher to report my tormentor. Erika and Marshon have been my ride or die buddies since that day. Erika was the maid of honor and I was a bridesmaid in Marshon's wedding. I am godmother to Marshon's son, Derek, and Erika is godmother to her daughter, Teresa. These are my girls!

Chapter 8: Put Your Foot in This

On the morning of my thirty-third birthday, I awake to a house alive with noise. I hear my brother-in-law on the phone coordinating his meet up time, I assume with Zeke. I hear Dora babbling; my niece, Alise, giggling as she plays with Dora; my nephew, LD, demanding his turn to hold the baby; the television; and Brianna shushing all the noise.

Brianna and her clan arrived late last night and instead of going straight to bed, we stayed up eating junk food and talking. Dora, sensing there were children in the house, woke up and sat up with us like she was a grownup.

I climb out of the bed, get dressed, but don't bother to eat breakfast because my sister has talked me into going to the market with her and to take Granny out for a quick lunch. My niece, Alise, begs to babysit but I explain that I've already made arrangements for Shantrell to come over for a few hours. "You can save your money, Aunt Hannah. I can keep an eye on Dora and LD. Mom leaves me in charge at home all the time," the thirteen-year-old tells me proudly.

"Thanks, baby, but I've already asked Shantrell and I can't cancel on her. She might have scheduled her day around watching Dora. I want you and LD to behave and mind Miss Shantrell."

"We will, Auntie," Alise responds but I get nothing from my nephew.

"You hear me, LD?"

"I'm always good, ain't I, Mom?"

"Don't use 'ain't.' How many times do I have to tell you that, boy?" Brianna chastises.

"Sorry; I forgot," LD responds without taking his eyes away from his video game.

--

We find our grandmother even less lucid than normal. We decide on a little deli near the care home so we can get her right back. Getting her in and out of the wheelchair turns into quite a struggle because she is not helping us at all. Both Brianna and I are breathing hard by the time we get her in the car headed to lunch.

Granny does eat well, probably because cream of mushroom soup is one of her favorites.

We get back to my house four hours later and just ahead of David. "How was the course?" I ask in hopes of hearing something about Zeke.

"Fabulous, you need to take lessons, Sis. I've been thinking on what to get you as a birthday present. Lessons would be just the thing."

I look at Brianna for help. "He's been trying to get me to take lessons for years. I don't know why," Brianna complains.

"So we can play together, baby; why else? You know I like to spend all my free time with you." David pats Brianna on her butt and gives her a look that makes me wish I had someone to ogle me like that.

"Liar," is Brianna's tart response as she ignores his play.

My little cousin starts bouncing for me to pick her up as soon as she sees me and I oblige her request. Shantrell declares that the children were well behaved and heads home to finish up the gumbo she started earlier in the day for the party. The gumbo will also serve as my sample to prove she makes the best gumbo to be had anywhere. Shantrell's gumbo is so good, according to her, that I will make a killing if I add the dish to my catering repertoire. She says she is willing to share her very exclusive recipe with me and I feel quite honored because she has refused both her mother and Ezekiel's requests for the recipe. I have no doubt that the gumbo will be sinfully delicious.

Over the remainder of the afternoon and into the evening, I receive birthday calls from three of my parents. My stepmother, Tracy, doesn't call me personally but she yells a happy birthday wish to me while I'm on the phone with my dad. I also receive a call from my brother, two aunts and two cousins. I always get the birthday calls and online wishes but somehow today feels more like my birthday than any birthday in recent years. I enjoyed my past birthday celebrations with Erika and Marshon but I always felt guilty about taking them away from their families to celebrate with me, the lonely one. I don't have that sense of guilt today but then I haven't felt lonely since Miss Dora arrived; who has the time?

Dora and I go into my room and lie across the bed in order to get some rest before my seven o'clock party. Alise and LD follow us into my bedroom and camp out on my bed also, along with their tablets and cell phones. They turn on the television and entertain Dora. I doze off amidst all the mayhem on my bed. Dora loves the kids, especially Alise, I suppose because she is the only young girl around.

My bed is empty when I awake and I can hear Marshon and Erika talking loudly, all caught up in my real party preparations. I lie in the bed and look up at the ceiling and wonder if I should throw myself into having a good time. It has been a treat having Brianna and the family here. I can't recall the last time they all came on a visit.

I jump in the shower and dress quickly before going out and greeting my friends. I get quick kisses and preliminary birthday hugs and then pushed aside. My three party planners are rushing around like crazy. When I gather up my long-time house guest to get her fed and ready for bed, the planners yell that I'm not to worry about Dora because they will take care of her. They tell me it is my day to chill and that I just need to go put on my makeup and fix my hair. I ignore their protests and spend some time with the baby. She's very excited with all the people around so I figure she'll try and stay awake as long as her little body allows.

Once I've got Dora all ready for bed, David takes her from me. I hand him a book to read to her. Dora looks at him with the same intense curiosity she showed toward Zeke weeks earlier. I think she is noting the distinction between men and women.

--

Shantrell and her two sons, Jameel and Caliel, are the first to arrive. The boys are dressed like twins with khaki pants and short-sleeved blue and white plaid button-down shirts all freshly pressed and heavily starched. They're sporting their "Sunday go to meeting shoes" and fresh haircuts as they stand side by side looking stiff and shy. All that starch in those pants is probably keeping them from loosening up. Once Alise and LD learn that there are other children in the house they grab up Jameel and Caliel and take them out in the back yard to play, thus the kid's party is on.

"Where is Miss Mel, Shantrell? Isn't she coming over?" I ask.

Shantrell smacks her lips together, rolls her large eyes, places one hand on a voluptuous hip, and waves the other in that dismissive fashion we women of color love. "Girl, Budrow is over there. He broke up with his girlfriend, so looks like my boys will be sleeping in the room together until he finds another woman to ride in on."

I can't help but laugh at her because she has so much attitude and looks fabulous in her short canary yellow sleeveless sheath dress. I wonder when she found the time to get her makeup and hair done. I notice my brother-in-law watching her as if she's the most luscious woman he's ever seen. Brianna notices also and snaps her fingers at David. Once she has his attention, she gives him "the look" and points at him. David knows he's been busted and smiles at Brianna with slightly turned down eyes. "You better watch yourself," Brianna tells him.

"Tell Buddy to come over and join us. Should I go and get your mom?" I ask Shantrell.

Shantrell gives me a hard confused look. "You sure you want Buddy to come over here? That boy can eat."

"We've got more food that we know what to do with. We need some eaters. All I'm eating is this gumbo. Girl, you know you put your foot off in this stuff," Marshon declares with Erika nodding in agreement as they both slurp down spoonfuls of the delectable brew. My two friends have made Shantrell's evening complete. She laughs and takes off to gather up Miss Mel and Budrow.

No sooner than Shantrell returns with her mother and brother, Marshon's husband, Mark, and their children, Derek and Teresa, arrive along with Erika's most recent love interest, a petite little redhead named Swan. I'm surprised and pleased to see four of the people who work out of the realty office with me enter the house right behind Swan. I'm not having a birthday party; I'm having a bash and I love it! The food is delicious and plentiful. My friends and family sing both the traditional and Stevie happy birthday songs. I get to blow out lots of candles and take the first piece of my birthday cake, baked just for me by Rosine's Bakery.

The kids are yelling and running around out back in the warm late Spring air and you'd think there was a children's party taking place in the back yard. It's my party but Miss Mel and I seem to be the only two adults who are going light on the alcohol. She and I sit and have a nice conversation for the first time since she became my neighbor. Miss Mel thanks me for being such a good neighbor and giving Shantrell some work. As she thanks me, I realize how happy I am to have them as neighbors and thank her in return.

My brother-in-law, David, is feeling especially good. He grabs Brianna and turns up the music when he hears Missy Elliot's "Work It" over the speakers. Once David gets my sister on the floor, it's clear he can't keep up because Brianna is definitely working it and David has always been stiff as a board. You'd think the brother is really getting down though. He's got his hands up in the air and shuffling from side-to-side with a big old grin on his face as he tells Brianna to "work it, baby!" I'm sorry but I have to laugh.

Budrow grabs my hand and gives me a seductive look. I hesitate. "I'll dance if you mother dances with us," I tell him.

Miss Mel laughs. I can tell she is game. I look over at Shantrell who is standing nearby snapping her fingers, singing along with Missy, and working it in one spot. "Come on Shantrell," I yell as I pull Miss Mel onto the floor.

"I ain't trying to dance with my mother and sister, now!" Budrow protests.

"Shut up, boy! You're getting to dance with three beautiful women instead of one. You're the luckiest man in the world right now," Miss Mel tells Budrow. So he settles in and starts working it and Buddy is not stiff.

I'm having more fun than I've had in years. As I shuffle around my living room floor trying not to get too close to Budrow, I see Deidra walk in my front door with none other than Zeke Melancon fast on her heels. My face drops and I can't keep it up. I know it's obvious to anyone looking at me. This cannot be happening. I have a hard time not staring at the couple until Zeke looks over and notices his family and me dancing and throws a smile and wave our way.

"There's Zeke!" Miss Mel yells, caught up in the joy of the moment, for her at least.

I give a weak-assed smile and turn my head away. I feel eyes on me and look up to see Brianna glaring at me with an angry scowl. She shakes her head, letting me know she likes this no more than I.

Both Deidra and Zeke come over and wish me a happy birthday as soon as the music stops. I smile and try to look as if I still have some of the joy these two have stolen. Deidra hugs me hard and gives me a kiss. These gestures are sincere. Deidra is not a phony and I like her and know she likes me. She's almost family but right now I want to hate her. Brianna makes her way over and gets Deidra away from me so I can stop grinning. Thankfully, Miss Mel has made Zeke dance with her.

I go inside my bedroom, close the door, and sit on the side of my bed. I need a moment to regroup. I cannot let Deidra and Zeke spoil my good time. It's only nine o'clock. I have no reason to be upset and I am determined to enjoy myself tonight. I freshen my makeup and check on Dora who is managing to sleep soundly with all the noise just down the hallway and outside in the yard.

When I get back to the party, I hear a voice from behind me, "Hey, can I get a hug from the birthday girl." I look over my shoulder and see Mykol, who must have come in while I was sulking in my room. I give him a smile and a hug, ignoring the confusion I feel at this moment. Why is he at my party? I hardly know him. Just then I feel someone grab my hand and pull on it. It's Zeke.

"Hey, man, I'm trying to wish her a happy birthday; we're talking," Mykol complains.

"Yeah, well, while you're talking, I'm doing," Zeke responds with a grin as he pulls me away from Mykol. I follow without protest. John Legends "Tonight" is playing and Professor Melancon is one smooth mover on the dance floor. Zeke dances close to me but I refuse to turn my back to him or look in his face. Every time I look up, I find him watching me with a smile. I try to keep some distance between us but the man remains close. My heart is racing so fast that I can't enjoy the moment. I notice Deidra watching us and wonder what's really going on until I see Mykol slide up and wrap his arms around her from behind. At least now I know Deidra and Mykol are still seeing each other and a sense of relief washes over my body.

Over the remainder of the night, Budrow actually tries to compete with Ezekiel for my time. I'm flattered, especially when I notice Zeke watching as Budrow whispers in my ear how good I look and smell. Budrow is full of shit and I know it and normally I wouldn't even entertain such foolishness, but hey, it's my birthday, a time for playing games. At least I know what Budrow is about. I haven't a clue when it comes to his older brother.

By eleven o'clock the party is winding up and nearly half my guests are gone. Brianna, Erika, and Marshon begin wiping and sweeping up in the kitchen. Shantrell has put most of the food in containers and left, taking the boys with her. Before she started in the kitchen she changed Dora, gave her a bottle, and put the child back to sleep for me. I think I'd marry Shantrell, if she'd have me.

Just a short time later, Miss Mel leaves and makes a nearly drunk Budrow go with her. There's no more loud dance music playing, just soft lovemaking stuff. Out of the blue, Zeke pulls me out to the patio to dance, just me and him. He's a bit lit up also, so I don't resist. "I hope you don't plan on driving home." I tell him.

"I don't live far," he answers and then admits, "I'm going to stretch out on the sofa next door."

We dance quietly for a few moments. "Why did you look so sad when I came in? Who pissed you off?"

I thought he had missed that but I guess not. "I wasn't sad or pissed. It's been a great night. I enjoyed my party. It's the first I've had since I was a teenager."

"Okay, I guess I just hoped or imagined you were sad."

"Why would you want me to be sad?" I pull back from him so I can get a better look in his face.

"I don't want you to be sad. I was afraid you might have thought I brought Deidra to your party. I pulled up at the same time she and Mykol parked. He had a call so he told Deidra to go on inside. I ended up walking in right behind her. I know it may have looked as if we came together."

"Why would I care if you came to my party with Deidra? People break up and get back together all the time?"

"That's my point," Zeke says, "but you're telling me it didn't bother you?"

I don't bother to answer his question because I'd be lying through my teeth if I said seeing Zeke come in behind Deidra did not bother me. I could hardly keep from crying but I am surprised that Zeke expects me to care. This means he knows I like him but I have not seen him in weeks. He obviously does not find my interest in him very intriguing.

We take a seat at the patio table and I change the subject. "Where do you live Zeke?"

"I rent a little one bedroom in Marina. I have a home here in Seaside but I've got it leased out for the next seven months. I hate the place I'm living in but I'll be there for another seven months at least."

"What's so bad about it?"

"Noisy students, small windows, tight spaces, old carpet. I was in a rush to settle in somewhere when I leased the place."

"Why did you move out of your home?"

Now he chuckles sarcastically. "I moved in with Deidra. We thought we'd both save money by sharing the living expenses and back then we were spending a good bit of time together."

I don't want to talk about Deidra so I change the direction of the conversation. "Your apartment can't be as bad as you make it sound"

"Wanna bet? I tell you what, why don't you drive me home tonight and you can see it for yourself." Zeke gives me a look that makes my stomach flip.

"And drive back over to pick you up to get your car tomorrow?" I ask. No, I'm not as naive as I sound right now.

Zeke laughs and shakes his head before reaching out and taking my hand. "You're playing with me right?" he asks with that rich, deep, smooth voice of his.

I just smile at him as I gather my composure.

"We'll take my car. I'll bring you back home early in the morning," he promises.

There is no more humor in this situation. Do I look this desperate for a lay? The man knows I like him, has known for weeks now but has made no effort to see me or talk to me. I barely know him. "You know I just met you, right?"

Zeke looks a little baffled but says nothing.

"Do you pick up women like this all the time?"

Now he looks alarmed. "You sound insulted. I wasn't trying to offend you."

"I guess I just thought. I don't know. I expected something different from you. I didn't think you would just come out of the blue and try to get me in the bed. I expect that from Buddy."

Zeke reacts as if I doused him with cold water. "This is not out of the blue, Hannah."

"Oh hell if it isn't. I haven't seen or talked to you in weeks. The first time I ever talked to you was one week before that. So, I've really only known you four weeks, three of which you haven't dialed my number, now you show up and ask me to go to bed with you."

The man leans back in his seat as if he needs to distance himself in order to see me better. "I've thought about calling but I knew you were busy with the baby and all. Forget what I said about going to my place. I was wrong for that. I just had to try. I would have tried the first night I came over for dinner if I thought I had a chance in hell. Another reason I didn't call was because I didn't think you were interested. I asked Shantrell about you several times and after the third or fourth time she got pissed and told me off. 'Damn, I wish you two would call each other. If you aren't asking me about Hannah, she's asking me about you. Just call her and leave me the hell alone.'" Zeke mimics Shantrell and sounds just like her, causing me to laugh.

He smiles and takes my hand again. "When I saw that look come across your face after Deidra and I came in I thought, *Hey, she is interested in me.* Between you, the good time, and the booze, I got carried away. Will you forgive me?"

I think this man is telling me he likes me. As fate does its thing, Erika sticks her head out the door and interrupts what I consider a special moment. "Sorry to interrupt. Little Bit woke up again. I changed her with Alise's help. Alise is putting her back to sleep. The rest of us are leaving."

I rise from my chair. "Oh, I'm sorry. I've abandoned y'all."

"Don't worry about it, baby. This is your party and you should enjoy it however you want. We will have to do this again next year with the same exact people." Erika smiles with satisfaction.

"I agree," Zeke says, amused.

I head into the house to see my friends out and thank them for the wonderful party. Marshon tells me that she and her kids will be back the next day to eat up some of the leftovers and help me clean. Brianna comes from the back to tell everyone goodnight and to wake up David who is passed out on my sofa.

I look around and Zeke and I are the last two standing.

"Well, I guess I'd better go." He reaches in his pants pocket, pulls out a tiny cloth pouch, and places it in my hand. "I bought you a gift."

"Thank you, Zeke. You shouldn't have. We have a no gift policy on our birthdays. This is so thoughtful." I pull the drawstring to open the pouch and pour out a shiny pair of hammered sterling silver teardrop earrings into my hand.

"I hope you like them. I couldn't think what to get you. Perfume seemed too personal but not personal enough. I was at a loss. Well, I hope you wear them for me sometime."

"I will. They're beautiful." I'm both touched and flattered by the gift and the thought Zeke put into choosing them for me.

Zeke stands there looking a little lost so I kiss him, dead on the mouth and he kisses me back. It's a bit awkward at first but then the kiss gets deeper and wetter. I feel his hand under my chin as he pulls my mouth even closer to his. This is the sweetest caress I've ever had from a man. I wish I had taken him up on his offer to go home with him. We pull apart and smile at each other.

"Okay, well, let me go," Zeke says.

I want to ask him to stay but I don't. "Yeah. Thanks again Zeke for helping make this birthday so special."

"Hey, maybe I'll stop by and get some of those leftovers tomorrow," he says.

"Sure. You want to take some with you now?"

"Nah, I want to come by tomorrow." Zeke smiles and gives me a look. I smile back and he's gone.

"Happy birthday to me, happy birthday to me, happy birthday, dear Hannah, happy birthday to me."

"I can hear you," Brianna calls out from the bedroom as she laughs at me.

Chapter 9: HELL NO!

The night of my thirty-third birthday solidifies my friendship with Ezekiel Melancon, at least that's the way I think of it. Zeke describes himself as a rational person who takes time to think through every major decision in his life before acting upon the choices before him. On a recent lunch date he told me impulse control "is the black man's biggest weakness." I asked if that might be the case for all men, even all people. He liked the question and answered in the affirmative.

After agreeing with my theory, my new friend stated that he wasn't particularly worried about other cultures because most in the States had found ways to unite, support each other, and gain wealth. Blacks in America, he said, were in their infancy in learning how to develop community and you need community in order to gain wealth. "The sisters are doing their part as far as I can see. Sisters are getting their educations, starting businesses, volunteering, joining churches, and striving hard to make their lives better. The problem is that there are too many brothers waiting for someone to give them something. I mean look at Buddy. All he wants to do is lie up in some fine woman's house and have her take care of him. He has no idea of the compromises a person needs to make in order to be successful in a relationship. He just wants everything to remain like it was from the very beginning, all lust and partying. The women get tired of him after a while but they let him stay because at least they have a man and one that the other women notice when they're out in public.

"The women Buddy dates usually pay for everything because he's nearly always broke. That dude never pays except maybe the first time or two out with a lady who is hard to catch. Then he calls me, my mother, or Shantrell for some cash. How pathetic is that, an able-bodied man asking a single mother who collects unemployment and is raising one pubescent teen and one prepubescent child for money. Buddy's been with some good women and has drained more than a few bank accounts but these women never drop him until he starts screwing around on them. They make life to easy for the brother."

"Sounds like you're blaming the women for Buddy's behavior," I rebutted.

Zeke had looked at me for a moment and seemed hesitant to share his thoughts. "I've visited you at your house a few times, right?"

"Well, yes, more than a few times I'd say." I was being a bit contrary.

"I mean since your birthday."

"Okay, that qualifies as a few."

"The first time I had to help you clean up from your birthday party because your girls didn't show, right?"

"Yeah, thanks for that. I don't know about that repeat party next year. I ended up working way too hard cleaning after that party. It was fun though." I can't help but grin remembering my birthday night.

"I don't remember if it was the second or the third time I visited but whichever it was, you were so busy that I fed Angel Baby and she did her business in my lap while I rocked her to sleep." With just a tad bit of disgust on his face, Zeke looked at me over the top of reading glasses he had put on to peruse the menu and I had to smirk also as I remembered that load. I wondered what Shantrell had fed Dora for lunch that day. We had to open every window in the house and burn incense. Thankfully, Zeke had been diplomatic about it so I was not completely mortified. Obviously, he had been more traumatized by the baby taking a doo in his lap than he had let on.

I nodded, feeling some of the mortification I had missed when the event occurred.

I didn't know what point Zeke was attempting to make but I was certain he had given me enough instances to support his position, but he wasn't quite finished. "On another occasion, you had me run to Costco to pick up trays, help you make the sandwiches to fill those trays, and deliver the trays to the client. Then you went sound to sleep while we watched the *Equalizer*, a movie you had begged me to bring to your house and promised to watch with me. I have seen the reality of your world, not all I'm sure but a good dose. I realized very quickly that a man who spends time with you on the regular would not be playing video games, watching television, or making Saturday tee times very often.

"Life is hard and you can't succeed by doing what you want when you want. I've known women to change their lives completely for a man. I've seen men act the same but not nearly so often. I'm not saying women make men sorry but I do believe there are too many relationships where women allow men to be sorry. That's cool if she doesn't have to take up his slack but more often than not, she does. When two people get together they need to douse each other with the reality of their lives."

"What if they have a jacked up life?" I asked.

"It doesn't matter what their lives are like, Hannah. The point is that life is hard. It's not easy and we need to teach our children that. And a man or woman bringing a life partner into their world needs to require that partner to participate in the hardship. There cannot always be a party."

"I guess that explains why I see you so seldom."

"Damn straight! You work hard managing all those properties, running a demanding catering business on the side, taking care of your grandmother and Dora. I don't have the energy to spend time with you on regular basis. I mean I work hard too. I stay busy with classes, meetings, counseling students, alumni activities, my mother and nephews. I exercise a lot just to keep the stress level down. So I have to plan out my time and you don't make it easy for me, not at all and that's fine. That's as it should be because if you made it easy for me, it would most likely be harder on you when I'm around."

This was the plain speaking Zeke was known for around town but personally, I didn't like it. He had just told me I was a hard woman to date, that I required too much of a man – too much from him. I sat there and looked at my plate of sea scallops as I tried to think how to respond. Zeke was just being honest. He hadn't been trying to hurt my feelings but he had.

"Did you find it hard to be with your wife or with Deidra? Is that why things ended?" I asked in a pathetic attempt at hiding my anger and my trounced feelings.

Zeke looked up at me and answered my question without hesitation. "Monica, that's my ex, and I were so young and that was so long ago, I sometimes can't even recall why we married or why we split. And no, Deidra wasn't very demanding in that way. She just couldn't abide my family. She felt they were too needy. My brother begs but he wasn't the issue because I stopped shelling out any amount larger than twenty dollars to him years ago. Shantrell doesn't ask for anything but I help her with the boys and they're getting expensive. So between my nephews and my mother always needing extra, Deidra felt I was being played."

The man had gone quiet for a few moments and I wondered if he was thinking about the situation between Deidra and him and if it still bothered him. Without any further prompting on my part, Zeke shared his thoughts. "You probably know that Deidra comes from a pretty well off family and she's an only child. Her father is a retired Army colonel and her mother is a medical doctor. She had an Ivy League education and now has a pretty lucrative job as a speech therapist. Deidra has never hurt for money. Financially, she's set and has been her entire life. She does not understand about people like us. My parents divorced nearly thirty years ago and we've been broke a lot over the years. Shantrell's ex is a lot like my father was, unreliable with the child support. Deidra thinks that since my mother and Shantrell have trouble stretching their limited incomes, they're users. She only complained to me about them twice the entire time we were together but I had to set her straight after the second put down. Afterwards she was cold toward them. She'd speak and show them just enough common courtesy to keep me from complaining. For awhile I liked her so much I ignored her behavior because it was so subtle but when I realized my mother didn't feel welcome in the house I was calling home, I decided to move out. I wasn't calling it quits but Deidra got so pissed about the separation she wanted to end things. I knew that was best and both she and I have attempted to be adult about the breakup."

"Do you still care for her?"

Zeke hesitated thoughtfully before answering. "Deidra's good people. She's just selfish, arrogant, and jealous. That was the real issue. She was jealous of my relationship with my mother and my sister. Yeah, I like her." He looked me directly in my face before continuing. "We had some good times together all over this great state of California and a few other places but that time has passed. She's Mykol's road dog now."

I swallowed hard. Once again my sad-assed feelings were hurt. Zeke had sat at that table with me and told me the truth. Isn't that what we women always want, the truth? HELL NO! Lie to me, nigga. Tell me you can't stand the bitch. Not Zeke, Mr. Plain Speaker himself. He was quiet for the remainder of our luncheon and I asked no more questions.

That lunch with Zeke was two weeks ago and now I want to ask him how he feels about me. I wonder if he was letting me down easy when he said I was hard work. Of course there was no reason for him to let me down at all. I kissed the man one time and he propositioned me once but I'm beginning to think that was because he was half drunk.

Zeke has become a family friend and no more. I thought we were about to get something started and we have, we're friends – a big hoopy doo. We are good friends. We ask each other for favors and all that. I'm even friends with Budrow these days. He sometimes stops by when Shantrell is at the house and I like Budrow more that I thought possible.

Even Shantrell's boys and I have become best buds of late. Our friendship started one beautiful Thursday summer afternoon. I was sitting on my sofa with the remote in my hand feeling a little guilty because I knew there was something I should have been doing but there was nothing that I had do so I just kept sitting on the sofa and relaxing while Dora napped. She hadn't been asleep long and I searched Netflix for a series or a movie I could sleep to. Isn't it funny how you can only sleep well to television you enjoy, at least that's how it works for me?

I was on my way to sleep in front of an episode of "Grace and Frankie" when my home phone began ringing. I answered to find Shantrell sounding slightly winded. "Listen, Hannah, my mother is not feeling well and I need to take her to the doctor's office. I know I said I'd come over this evening and help you prep the filling for those empanadas and the green chili for the enchiladas next week but I may not be able to make it."

I had forgotten Shantrell had offered to come over that evening to help me prep items for an event the following Tuesday.

I should have been out shopping for tomatillos and other ingredients at that very moment instead of sitting on my ass. "That's okay. Don't worry about that. I had forgotten. I hope Miss Mel's not feeling too bad."

"I think it's her blood sugar so I called her doctor and they told me to bring her right in."

"Let me know if there's anything I can do and call me and tell me how Miss Mel is doing when you have the time."

"Okay, I will." Shantrell rushed off the phone.

I checked in on Dora who was still sleeping peacefully before heading next door to see what if anything I could do to help Shantrell. I caught her as she was walking Miss Mel out to the car. Miss Mel, always friendly, gave me a weak smile and waved her hand at me before speaking.

"Where are the boys, Shantrell?" I asked.

"They're in the house. I'm just going to leave them here. Hopefully, I won't be gone too long. I've been trying to get Buddy on the phone but I think he may be out of minutes again and Zeke is out of town at a seminar," Shantrell answered with a furrowed brow as she helped her mother into the passenger side of the car.

"The boys can come and stay with me and Dora until later. That way you won't need to worry about them."

"No, but we'll need to worry about you," Miss Mel joked and again smiled at me weakly. She was clearly not feeling well but was making a good effort at being upbeat as she swatted her daughters hand away from the seat belt, indicating she was capable of fastening it herself.

I followed Shantrell as she rushed around to the driver's side of the car. When she stopped and looked at me I could see the relief on her face. "Are you sure you don't mind?"

"Not at all, we'll be fine. Does Jameel know how to lock up everything?" I asked and then waved off the question, knowing she was anxious to get on her way. "We'll figure it out. I'll get them and get back over to Dora. Just call me when you get some time."

"Oh thank you girl, this takes a load off." Shantrell jumped in her car and was headed down the road before I got inside her home."

The boys both looked surprised when they found me standing at their front door. They didn't hesitate to let me in, explaining that I was one of the people on the list they were allowed to open the door for when no adult was at home. They had already started arguing because Caliel had declared he was fixing himself a sandwich and Jameel was telling him to stay out of the kitchen. Neither seemed the least bit curious as to why I was at their house.

"You guys get your tablets and toothbrushes because you're going home with me until your mother gets back."

"Do we have to?" Caliel had asked.

"Yes, you do," I responded using the same tone I use with my nephew, LD. It's not magic and there's usually no immediate impact but it gets the job done, eventually; whereas, my kind gentle voice is completely ineffective when asking my nephew to do something he is disinclined to do.

"Why do we need our toothbrushes? Are we spending the night?" Jameel had asked.

"I don't know, maybe," I answered, disinclined to commit.

The boys entered my home and looked around as if it was completely new territory and I realized they had never visited me without their mother. Caliel swore up and down that he was starving and Jameel insisted that his younger brother could not possibly be hungry because they had lunch only two hours earlier but was indeed "just greedy." To put an end to the argument, I told them I'd fix them a snack if they would stop arguing and not wake Dora from her nap.

"What you gonna fix us?" Caliel wanted to know before agreeing to anything.

"Not so loud, boy. You'll wake the baby," Jameel had chastised his brother in a whisper.

"What you gonna fix us?" Caliel repeated in a lowered voice, this time looking at me with a glow in his light brown eyes.

After the boys agreed to flat bread pizzas, things flowed along nicely. Once she woke from her nap Dora sat on the floor with her neighbors and was happy to have the company. Jameel and Caliel warmed up to me and started talking and they like to talk. Jameel's favorite subjects are sports, in particular his little league team, and whatever his Uncle Zeke or his Uncle Buddy told him about playing on his little league team. Caliel's favorite subjects are dinosaurs and arguing with Jameel about what his Uncle Zeke or his Uncle Buddy actually said about Jameel's little league team. For some reason I found myself getting particularly tired on that day of relaxation.

Shantrell called after about two hours. She was taking Miss Mel to Community Hospital for some tests. "I still haven't been able to get in touch with Buddy. I hope the boys are not giving you too much trouble."

"Girl, they are no trouble at all. They're fun but lord can they talk."

That observation had made her laugh, a sound I was happy to hear. "Well, I'll keep trying Buddy and maybe I can get him to pick them up."

"Do not ask Buddy to pick up these boys. They're fine. You just take care of your mother. I got the boys and I'm not going to let Buddy take them so leave him alone. If you give me his number, I'll keep trying it and tell him about your mother. Do you want me to try to reach Zeke or did you talk to him?"

"No, I haven't talked to him. I was waiting until I thought he might be in for the day. He's in Atlanta so he may be out of the seminar but if I know Zeke, he's probably at dinner with friends or colleagues. He knows a lot of people in that city. I'll just shoot him a text and have him call me."

Miss Mel had remained in the hospital for two days and the boys stayed with me nearly the entire time. Buddy showed up at my house on Friday evening asking if I had seen his mother and sister. His nephews came running into the house from my backyard before I could answer. I explained that Shantrell had taken Miss Mel to the hospital the day before. He placed a call to Shantrell from my phone and got an update on his mother before leaving and heading straight to the hospital to see her in person

Zeke had called me that Thursday evening because he couldn't get through to Shantrell. He was ready to cut his time at the seminar short in order to fly home and be with Miss Mel. Once he and Shantrell spoke, she convinced him that their mother was not in danger and talked him into waiting until the end of the conference that Friday afternoon and returning home on his originally scheduled flight.

When Miss Mel was finally released she had agreed to go on a regiment of insulin injections to control her blood sugar. Miss Mel seems to feel better and says she has much more energy now that her medicine is so well regimented via the insulin injections she had resisted for several years.

By the time Shantrell showed up at my house to collect her treasures, they had made themselves right at home. These days it is not unusual for me to find Jameel and/or Caliel ringing my doorbell. They just like to come over and visit me and Dora and we enjoy the company.

--

The Melancon family is so enjoyable that Brianna and her family are planning a visit for next week which is Fourth of July weekend and David has already set up a round of golf with Zeke. Brianna wants to barbecue, not just grill steaks but girl wants to do ribs, sausage, and chicken. She also wants me to invite my friends and in particular the Melancons. I think I'll tell Zeke to bring a date if he'd like. I invited Shantrell just as soon as I got off the phone with Brianna. Shantrell said they had no plans other than grilling some hot dogs, so she was happy to accept.

I decide not to call Zeke after all. Maybe David will invite him over. If he shows up good, if not, I will survive.

--

Zeke's a no show for the Fourth of July but Deidra and Mykol join us along with Erika, Marshon, and their people. David did extend an invitation to Zeke but he declined because he had a previous engagement. I survive and everyone else has a blast. The weekend turns into the second best party I've ever had. The day after the Fourth, Shantrell brings over her fixings for hot dogs and s'mores and we sit out back in the cool evening breeze with the children and roast weenies and marshmallows, make s'mores, and play games.

We all laugh as Dora takes her first baby steps around the yard. I swear she's been practicing in private because she doesn't just take one or two steps and fall down. Dora takes ten to fifteen steps or more before plopping on her behind and clapping her hands with laughter. Alise or LD gets her right back up and she takes off again. I make sure I record all this on my cell phone for Dana and Aunt Alise. I send the video to both their numbers. Aunt Alise calls within five minutes of receiving the video. I get nothing from Dana.

Before bed, Brianna, Alise, and I lie across my bed and indulge in some girl talk. Not knowing it was a secret, I ask Alise if she still likes the boy she was telling me about on her previous visit. "Aunt Hannah, you weren't supposed to tell Mom about that!" Alise declares with shocked agitation. I apologize profusely and then Brianna and I pry until Alise gets disgusted and leaves my room.

"What is up with Deidra's old man? Was he mad at her or what?" I ask Brianna. "I mean, he hardly talked to her at all yesterday or today. He was all over her at my birthday party."

"I know," Brianna responds. "I'm beginning to wonder about those two. I think Mykol may be realizing that Deidra is not that particular about him and the feelings may be mutual. Those two may be together just to keep from being alone. Deidra's the type who always needs to be involved with a man.

"I think she thought she had hit the jackpot with Ezekiel; we all did. I remember meeting with her and a couple of other friends for lunch in Oakland one afternoon. She announced she was dating Zeke as if she was announcing her engagement. Girl was glowing and I must admit we were all pretty impressed. Zeke was quite a catch and still is. I don't think a year had gone by before she was pressuring him into moving in with her. She kept saying it was such a waste of money for them to each have a place when they spent all their free time together and he slept at her house every night. Finally, he agreed and leased out his home. I'm surprised she ever let that brother go. I really think Deidra thought Zeke would come back begging. She had him in kind of a bad spot. He moved in with his mother for a few weeks but left all his stuff at Deidra's and still had a key to her place. She expected him back in a week or two. Shoot, girl came home one afternoon and all of Zeke's stuff was gone. From what she tells me, she did not let any grass grow under her feet. I think Mykol is her rebound lover."

"Well, Deidra can sure pick 'em because Mykol is not bad at all. She might not want to let him slip through her fingers but I guess if she's not that particular about him there's no point in trying to make it work," I say.

"He doesn't seem too concerned. Not the way he looks at Shantrell," Brianna responds.

"I know, right. I thought that was my imagination. He does keep an eye on Shantrell and he makes her blush. Deidra doesn't even seem to notice or maybe she doesn't care."

Brianna smirks. "Please, Deidra thinks she's so fine and her stuff is so good that no man would leave her for the likes of a Shantrell. Shantrell may be gaudy as all get out but she is an attractive woman. Deidra doesn't see it because she doesn't talk to Shantrell at all. If she actually talked to the woman she'd know, old girl is a serious threat. I told David he'd better not be hawking Shantrell and I mean that shit."

My sister has gotten serious and is expressing herself with more passion than I've seen in a long time. I laugh hard, causing her to sit up on the bed and look at me indignantly. "You think I'm kidding?" she asks.

"No, I know you're serious. I'm just so surprised. I've never seen you this passionate about David before. I didn't know you were the least bit jealous of David."

"Every woman who likes her man has some degree of jealousy, Hannah. Aren't you a little jealous of Zeke? What's going on with you two, anyway? I thought he might join us this weekend."

"Me and Zeke get along well. I don't see him too often but we meet for lunch every once in awhile. He stops in to say hello sometimes when he's next door but I have no right to be jealous over him. There is nothing really happening between us but friendship."

"Come on, Hannah. I know there's got to be something more than that."

"I wish there was, Brie, but that's it." I throw up both my arms as Brianna gives me a look of sheer disbelief and opens her mouth to say something just as David sticks his head in the doorway and asks, "Are you coming to bed anytime soon?"

Both Brianna and I know exactly what David's question means. "Be right there, baby," Brianna tells her husband before giving me a peck on the cheek and leaving my room.

Chapter 10: Pretty Girls vs. Beautiful Women

"When are you going to use your overnight babysitting gift I gave you for your birthday?" Shantrell asks me one afternoon out of the blue.

"I haven't had a reason to use it. What's the rush? Is there an expiration date on the offer?" I smile and ask as I unpack and put away groceries from the supermarket.

"No, but," Shantrell smirks. "You don't have much of a social life do you? I mean you're always here at the house when you're not working. There's a lot going on around the peninsula and other places but you can't take Dora everywhere with you. If a man was interested in you, you'd run him off with your schedule. You work all the time and don't take out enough time for yourself. That can't be fun." Shantrell purses her lips and seems to expect a response.

With Shantrell's help, I finish putting away the groceries and move into the laundry room to start a load of my laundry. Thankfully, Shantrell does Dora's laundry on the days she's here. She offered to do mine also but I prefer to do my own laundry which has piled up. I glance over at Shantrell as I perform the never ending task of unloading the dryer, pulling a load from the washer and placing it in the dryer along with a dryer sheet, and then loading a load of delicates into the washer. Every time I buy a nice delicate piece of clothing, I wash it by hand the first time or maybe two but who has the time for that? Not me. Eventually every piece ends up in the machine unless it screams, "DRY CLEAN ONLY!"

Shantrell followed me to the laundry room and now stands in the doorway watching me but says nothing. After a few moments, she sucks on her teeth and tells me she's leaving.

"Hey, wait a minute. You haven't forgotten we have a massive job for next Friday. You said that you might be able to find me some extra help. Marshon will not be available so I need to know today if I should hire someone to man the grill. I'm doing the briskets in the oven, but I've got a lot of ribs to grill plus sausage. Also, I'll need you here about five that morning. We have to deliver by eleven."

"I've got you for at least two more people, maybe three," Shantrell says.

"We can manage with two, but three would make life easier. I need someone to deliver with me and for you to stay here with Dora. Can we sit down and go over everything again tomorrow?"

"What time do you want me here?" Shantrell asks, no longer displaying her disgust over my nonexistent social life but excited about the huge function we will cook for on Friday.

"You tell me what time you can be here. Dora and I got nothing planned but rest and some shopping for the job."

"I'll call you in the morning," she says.

Shantrell is still not smiling when she leaves. She tells me I'm all business and no fun. What she doesn't know is that I'm storing up for the winter. I accept only a few catering jobs from repeat clients throughout the fall and winter. I set that time aside for family. Either they visit me or I visit them. I plan to take Dora to see her grandmother, my Aunt Alise, as soon as Alise is strong enough for our visit. Since my father and stepmother, live in the same city, we will visit them also. As always, I will get my grandmother for a few overnights during the holidays. My mother and stepfather, Eugene, are coming for Thanksgiving and will spend several days with me so they can visit with my grandmother. I will meet them at Brianna's for the Thanksgiving holiday before their visit here in Seaside. My brother, Bill, has invited me to spend Christmas at a Colorado lodge with him, his wife and children, and his wife's family. I'm pretty certain I will not be able to make that trip since I would need to take Dora with me. If she were older, I wouldn't worry about taking her into that cold dry Colorado weather, but she's too young. If she got sick, it would ruin everyone's trip and I'd be worried sick for her.

So yes, I work hard through the summer and early fall but I take a nice break in the winter. The bad thing about this business model is that I turn down quite a few catering jobs in the late fall and winter which does hurt my business. Still I find myself pretty much swamped my midsummer. Shantrell has been such an asset with the catering that, if I thought she would continue working with me, I'd consider making the catering a larger permanent operation instead of a side gig.

--

Miss Mel shows up with her daughter on the morning of the Proctor's Texas-style barbecue party. Shantrell tells me she's got Budrow and two others on their way to help. She and her mother go right to work making potato salad, slaw, pasta salad, and breaking up the greens for garden salad. I get two large pots of red beans going.

This is a big job and I can afford to hire all the help I need. My clients, the Proctors, are not only wealthy but generous and I have quoted them a fair price which includes a hefty gratuity. This is my second year catering the event. In past years, the Proctors used a local barbecue joint to cater their event. To my good fortune, the couple happened to be guests at a small barbecue dinner I catered two years ago. They were so impressed with my food that they offered me the gig for their party last year which was half the size of this year's event.

I've rented two large barbecue pits for the job, one from an acquaintance who has his own catering business. He pushed hard for me to give him the job of barbecuing the meat but I was concerned he might prepare the meat to his own standards and I need it cooked to mine. Also his price was too high. I simply told him "If you're not using your grill for those two days, I'll rent it off you. If you are, don't worry about it. It's just a chance for you to make a little extra money, as opposed to having the grill sit idle." My argument was effective and the grill master agreed. I broke down and rented the second grill from a party rental facility and it is expensive. I took time late last night setting up both grills with wood so I could light them early and have them ready to go for my ribs first thing.

The baby backs will only take about seventy five minutes to cook. Then the key is keeping them warm without drying them out. I'm cooking the briskets in the oven using Paula Deen's Texas Oven Roasted Beef Brisket recipe. I got a little disgusted with her about calling her employees "nigger" even though I use the word myself on occasion. But some of Paula's recipes are on point and I simply cannot give them up. My barbeque sauce is a ridiculous mixture of North Carolina vinegary sauce, Kraft Original Barbecue Sauce, and the drippings from the brisket pan minus the fat. I have people begging me for this recipe. It's not too sweet for those who don't care for sweet barbecue sauce but sweet enough for those who do. I don't share the recipe because I don't want to tell people they need to cook and use the drippings from a brisket using Paula Deen's Texas Oven Roasted Beef Brisket recipe as a necessary ingredient to make the sauce be all it can be.

The Proctors like to give the impression that they grilled the meat on site so I do not need to cut up the ribs or slice the brisket. You should see the machinations these people go through to put everything in place. They have on their chef's hats and matching "World's Best BBQ" aprons with a little sauce smeared on them for special effects. They do hire a team of wait staff for the event but I do not stick around after I drop off the food.

I'm placing the first of dozens of slabs of baby backs on the grill when Zeke and Mykol arrive to help. I'm shocked and pleased. I want to question someone about Mykol but I don't have the time to be nosy.

Dora wakes at seven so Shantrell takes a break from the kitchen to get her bathed, dressed, and fed. Then she takes Dora next door to get her boys up and bring them over. After the boys eat, they take responsibility for watching and entertaining Dora in front of the television set.

Budrow shows up at a quarter past seven and bounces back and forth from the kitchen to the grilling area out in the yard. He proves to be indispensable. At nine he starts getting everything wrapped up and in order for delivery. At nine forty five, we start loading up the rented van and Miss Mel, Zeke, and I take off twenty five minutes later. We arrive at our destination with time to spare, unload, and help my clients and their hired staff put all the food in place. I collect my final payment and we are on our way home by quarter past eleven.

"You handled that like a true professional, Hannah," Zeke compliments me.

"Didn't she though," Miss Mel adds with a wink.

"Thanks. I would not have made it if it weren't for you guys."

"You'd have found a way. I'm convinced of that," Miss Mel says.

I smile. Miss Mel is right. Erika has been on standby with Swan and I planned to call them in if I was short of help.

The Proctor job was the largest I've had and paid well but I'm pleased I don't frequently cater such demanding gigs. If I get the job next year and I'm certain I will, I will bring several people in days ahead to help me prep. Shantrell started helping me with the prep early yesterday morning but by the time she left late in the evening, I realized I needed extra help for the remainder of the night and on into the morning. I went to bed at one and was up by three thirty. I will not make this mistake again.

Zeke and Mykol refuse payment for their services and tell me to divide the money between Shantrell, Miss Mel, and Budrow. Zeke asks me to give the boys a stipend also. With nearly twice the amount they had coming in pay plus gratuity, my neighbors are ecstatic when they depart for their homes. "Anytime you need my help, Hannah, just call me. You pay a hell of a lot better than that damn Quik Stop," Budrow tells me.

"No, a good portion of that is because Zeke and Mykol told me to divide their pay between the three of you. I pay good but nowhere near this good," I laugh.

--

Over lunch a few days later, I ask Zeke about his new found friendship with Mykol.

"Mykol and I have known each other for years. I think I mentioned that I introduced him and Deidra. He stopped by to talk a couple of weeks ago. Seems Deidra dropped him. I thought he wanted to lament on what a bitch she is but he has barely mentioned her. Honestly I think he's got a thing for Shantrell." Zeke chuckles as if this is a ridiculous thought.

"Really, how cool is that? Shantrell thinks he's the finest man that ever stepped on the planet."

"Really?" Zeke mimics me and cracks another crab leg. I'm so sick of him and I want to get him in bed so badly. He is well aware of my desire for him but clearly does not want me as much as I want him. He looks up from the two pieces of crustacean dangling from each hand and stares at me for just a moment before he asks, "What do you think?"

"About what?"

"About Mykol? Do you find him attractive too?"

"He's a nice looking man. Why are you asking me my opinion of Mykol? I hope you're not interested in him. That would break Shantrell's heart," I joke. "He watches her like crazy and is so gentle with her. I think they've liked each other for a while now. I hope he asks her out, that is, if he and Deidra are finished for good." I catch myself because I don't want to get all caught up in a nonexistent relationship between Shantrell and Mykol.

"You sound like it'll break your heart if Mykol is not interested in Shantrell. The truth is, I'm sure he finds Shantrell attractive but he's still talking to Deidre and I don't get the impression that he's made up his mind to end things completely between them. I would not encourage my sister in her interest for Mykol. I've seen her hurt too many times before. She doesn't need to get caught up with some guy who can't make up his mind what he wants. Who needs all those complications? Me, myself, I don't do complicated.

"Also, Shantrell likes to play down her best assets and I'm not sure why. She's very intelligent as I'm sure you've learned. She's got her reasons for playing the role and I don't bother her about it as long as she is handling her business. She takes good care of her boys and my mother. Sure, I wish she'd plan for the boy's education but I guess she has me for that. She knows I'll get them through school if they want to go and I will but only if they want to go.

"Anyway, I won't be happy if Mykol messes over my sister and I mean that. I know he's interested in her but that tough exterior is for show. It's to keep the hurt away and it does not always work."

This description of Shantrell and Zeke's feelings toward her exposes another layer of the relationship between the brother and sister he seems to care for so very much. The Melancons are complicated, interesting people and I want to know them on a deeper level.

When Zeke asked me out to lunch I had hoped we'd talk about us but as usual, it was just casual conversation. I continually tell myself to stop wishing for a relationship with the man but long for more with each passing day.

--

Miss Mel had given me hope when it comes to her oldest son. Just a few days ago, she invited me over for coffee along with one of her old friends, Miss Reggie. Years ago, Miss Mel, Miss Reggie, and my mother, Miriam, all belonged to the same social club, church, and NAACP chapter.

Thankfully, Shantrell was at home also and she and I enjoyed listening to the older ladies stories of bygone days in Seaside. Back then there were so many black residents in the small town that many residents swear it was majority black but all records indicate blacks made up only about thirty three percent of the population at most, still a sizable number.

The ladies talked for over an hour about the rich and diverse population of Seaside before Miss Reggie worked her conversation around to Zeke. "When is that boy going to settle down and marry? I thought that pretty girl had caught him. They make such a handsome couple." Miss Reggie smiled at Miss Mel, after rendering the compliment.

"That oldest son of mine has always liked the pretty girls. A big pretty smile, long hair, and a tall slender body; that's always been his weakness," Miss Mel reflected with a long look at me.

I sat there listening to her and wondered if she was trying to tell me I stood no chance with her older son with my short thick thighs, bushy hair, and lack of personality.

"Well, you can't blame him. They say men often marry women who resemble their mothers," Miss Reggie advised.

"I think Zeke is well past looking at those superficial things in a woman. If he's not, he should be," Shantrell added with a huff.

Miss Mel smiled at me. "Yeah, he finally stopped looking for pretty girls. I'm pleased that it's the beautiful women who capture his attention these days. Now Buddy wants his women to look good and have lots of money," Miss Mel laughed but when her laughter died, she once again placed her eyes upon me, causing me some discomfort. I had no idea she was just getting started. "That Brianna was the prettiest little girl I most ever saw when she was young. Wasn't she, Reggie?" Miss Mel asked her friend but kept her eyes on me.

"She was pretty but no prettier than Shantrell," Miss Reggie responded with a look of endearment toward her friend's daughter.

"Thank you, Miss Reggie. I'm glad somebody thought I was pretty." Shantrell smiled and seemed to not mind being disregarded by her mother.

Miss Mel smiled at Miss Reggie and Shantrell and immediately put her eyes back on me. "Miriam dressed you girls so prettily all the time. Brianna's hair hung midway her back back then. She was so beautiful to look at. We all knew she would grow up to be a pretty woman as long as she took good care of herself. You, Miss Hannah, were another story entirely."

"Mama!" Shantrell yelled at Miss Mel trying to put the woman in check.

Miss Mel ignored her child and continued. "You were just as cute as a button before you got hurt. I remember when your mother got up in church and asked us all to pray for you because you had been knocked unconscious up on that playground. You were pretty talkative before that incident but just stopped talking all together after that. I don't think I ever heard you say another word after that injury until you walked off into this house with that roasted chicken and that bottle of wine a few months ago. I didn't even recognize you as the same child. I thought you had dropped off the face of the earth with the rest of your family. Of course, they all moved away but I thought you were gone also. Now here you sit -- a strong, intelligent woman and every bit as beautiful as Brianna. Isn't it wonderful that grownup beauty is an asset we choose?"

"Thank you, Miss Mel," I replied quietly and wished I could disappear as the other women watched me with warm appreciative smiles and nods.

When Dora and I made our escape from the Melancon home, I sat and thought about Miss Mel's words. She had to be telling me that Zeke liked me. She said he no longer liked girls but women and she told me I was a beautiful woman.

I've never been jealous of my sister's beauty, but hearing Miss Mel say that I was as beautiful as Brianna was quite the compliment. My sister is fabulous -- not just physically, but intellectually, spiritually, and emotionally. Brianna, along with my mother, grandmother, and Aunt Alise, is one of my role models.

I'm certain Miss Mel was not speaking of my physical appearance when she said I was beautiful, but about the person I had become. The lady made my day.

As much as I appreciated the confidence booster from Zeke's mother, I have been waiting with baited breath for him to make a serious play every since she gave me that compliment. Now I'm beginning to wonder if old girl was just making conversation. This lunch with Zeke ends as just another friendly meeting. I'm sick of this nigga!

Chapter 11: Nothing Too Specific

One characteristic I figure my role model women possess that I have not utilized is assertion. Yes, I have been assertive in some areas of my life but not when it comes to men. I mean, I'm no doormat, at least not for long. I do, however, go along for the ride and have a pathetic tendency to let the man lead the way. All of that is about to change.

"Shantrell, do you think you can watch Dora for me tonight?" I ask my new best friend and employee.

"Sure, baby. I got nothing going on. What time do you want me over there?"

"Probably not until about nine thirty or ten. Would you be able to spend the night?"

Dead silence on the phone. I wait but get nothing. After a full twenty seconds or so, I say, "Shantrell, are you still there?"

"I'm here."

"Did you hear me?"

"I heard you. I guess I can spend the night if you need me to. Mama will be here with the boys."

"Okay, I'll see you then." I get off the phone as quickly as possible, not wanting to share my plans with Shantrell because I'm not sure of my plans yet.

I pack up my baby cousin and she and I head out to Del Monte Shopping Center. I remember going into Soma with Marshon one time and thought the lingerie in that store suited me better than Victoria's Secret. I push Dora around in Soma trying to look as if I buy sexy undies and lingerie all the time. A nice salesperson starts helping me and I relax and settle on six pairs of panties, two of which are thongs, and the sexiest ever Oscar D black lace chemise with matching thong underwear.

After Soma, I stop off at my favorite nail salon and get a pedicure, my face waxed, and a simple bikini wax for the first time ever, just in case I get lucky. I hope he likes it.

After the shopping, I call Zeke and ask if he's free for the evening. I know, I know, why did I wait so late? I could have saved my money but I needed to spend some money on myself anyway.

"I've got this alumni dinner tonight in Monterey. What's going on?" Zeke asks.

"Nothing," I lie. "I just thought maybe you were free, that's all."

"Don't I wish; I'm free tomorrow."

"Well, call me tomorrow and if I can get a sitter maybe we can do something. Have a good time."

"Yeah, okay," Zeke says. "I'll call you first thing."

I start to end the call but I'm disappointed enough to take some risks. "Hey, Zeke," I yell into the phone but he's gone.

I feel even more of a letdown that I didn't get to ask my question but only for a moment because the phone starts to buzz and it's Zeke. "Were you still talking, Hannah?"

"Yeah, I wanted to ask you about what time you'd be in tonight."

"I'm not sure. I'd guess sometime after midnight. Why?"

"Are you taking a date to this dinner?"

He only hesitates for a moment "Yes, I do have a date. She's a colleague. We sometimes attend these events together."

I want to ask if his "colleague" will be going home with him or if he'll be going home with her but decide not to. I end the call.

I sit down and think about what I can do or where I can go tonight since I have a babysitter. I consider getting a room and just treating myself special. I could wake up in the morning and have a massage and lie around until noon and then come home. I'm sure Shantrell won't mind staying until noon. I could use a break from my ever-demanding roommate. Dora seldom sleeps past seven in the morning and although she is a good baby, she gurgles and giggles and laughs, and babbles until I surrender on sleeping in or napping.

I decide against a hasty plan to spend time away from home doing something I'm truly not inclined to do. So I call Shantrell and tell her I won't need her after all.

"What happened?" she asks, sounding more frustrated than I am disappointed.

"My plans didn't work out but thank you anyway."

"Can I come over and stay the night anyway. I need to get away from these boys and my mother. Everybody got the spirit when I told them I'd be away tonight and they will be so disappointed if I'm not out of the house."

"Sure, if you want."

"You sound upset. Did you have a date back out on you or something?" Shantrell asks.

"I'll tell you when you come over?" I tell Shantrell this, not at all certain I will share my embarrassment with her. I must admit it was silly of me to make plans without ever discussing them with Zeke but sometimes things do get a little scrambled especially when it involves an action I don't want to take. Yes, I want to have sex with Zeke but I sure don't want to proposition him. What if he flat out refused to take me up on the offer? I'd never be able to look him in the face again.

--

Shantrell arrives, bringing good cheer and seems even more up than usual. She has a bottle of Jose Cuervo and some nice Merlot. We sit and watch my old recorded episodes of "Being Mary Jane" and after a few drinks start arguing over which of Mary Jane's men is the hottest. Shantrell likes Andre; she would. He's all tatted up like her. I prefer David; he's smooth and so laid back. In the end we both agree we like the older brother, Patrick. Lord have mercy, he is one broke addict who is trying hard to combat his demons but that brother is fine.

"I thought you were going to tell me why you changed your mind about going out," Shantrell asks.

"I hadn't really made any solid plans. I was just hoping things would fall into place."

"You mean you didn't have a date with anyone?"

I feel like a kook at this moment but I decide to come clean and at least answer honestly. "No, I didn't have a date. I thought he'd be available. I guess I was hoping he'd be available but he had other plans."

Shantrell takes a shot of tequila and looks at me out of the corner of her eye before asking, "Anyone I know?"

I breathe in hard and hesitate. I don't want to hear what she may tell me about my lust for her big brother.

"You don't need to tell me. I already know from the answer you didn't give." Shantrell surprises me with a smile. "He's not going to be out too late. Zeke is a Mama's boy, girl. He'll call me to check on his mother before he climbs into his bed tonight. I tell him not to worry about her but he does. He always checks when he's out of pocket."

It crosses my mind to deny that Zeke is my target but what would be the sense in that. "Can you tell if he's alone when he calls?" I ask.

"That I can't help you with. He always sounds like he's alone but I never give it much thought. Me and Mama have wondered if he has someone under wraps. We never know with Zeke until things get serious. You should go see him, if that's what you want to do."

"What if he has company?"

"Well, don't do no silly-assed Mary Jane shit. If he's got company show some class and bow out gracefully. I would expect nothing less from you and believe me, Zeke will do his best to protect you. He wouldn't want you to be embarrassed."

"I better not," I say to myself more than to Shantrell. "You want to see what I bought myself today?"

"Sure," Shantrell humors me.

I return from my room and show her the lace chemise with matching thong underwear.

"Oohphhh!" Shantrell sighs and breathes in almost at the same time. "That is beautiful! You bought this for Zeke? Where did you get it?"

"I bought it for me. I thought I would let Zeke see me in it though," I giggle.

"That boy is going to pop when he sees you in that. Where did you say you got it? That is so hot!"

"Up in Del Monte at the Soma store."

"Well, I'm going to have to check that place out. That's nicer than anything I've gotten out of Victoria's Secret. I thought Soma only had old lady stuff."

"They've got those also but they've got some spicy pieces."

"You're going to get a hell of a reaction with that shit on, believe me. I wish you could record the expression on that brother's face when he sees you in that." Shantrell starts to laugh as if she can see Zeke's reaction.

Satisfied that Shantrell approves of my choice of seductive lingerie, I pour myself a large goblet of wine and grab up the bottle before heading off to my bathroom, where I immerse myself in a lovely warm tub of water and doze off and on for nearly an hour.

When I come out Shantrell looks like the cat that swallowed the canary. "Zeke called. He's at home already. I told him I thought he was out for the evening. He said he had been out but the event was so boring he made an excuse to get away early."

I know she has something more to tell me but I play it cool. "Good for him," is my lame response.

"I didn't tell him I was over here with you and Dora. No sooner than he hung up with me on that first call, he called your house phone. He was shocked when I answered. He asked what I was doing here. I told him you had plans for the evening and asked me to come and spend the night with Dora. All he could say was, "Tell her I called.""

"Why did you lie to him, Shantrell?"

"I was just messin' with him. I haven't told you the best part yet."

I feel excitement turning my cheeks hot and they begin to puff up with pleasure. I know this is good. "What?" I ask.

"He called your cell phone three times since he called the house phone. He left messages the first two times. Listen to see what he said."

"Shantrell, you are bad."

"I know but I don't have a love life of my own. I figure I might as well enjoy this thing going on between you and Zeke, especially with the two of you acting like you're scared of each other."

In the first message, Zeke simply identifies himself and asks me to call him. The second message came through a full thirty minutes later and he sounds a bit irritated. In the second message, he says it's okay to call no matter how late I receive the message. The third call came only ten minutes ago but he left no message.

"Should I call him?" I ask Shantrell as if she is some sort of a relationship guru.

"Nope, put your face on and put your little hot nightie thingy on and a long coat. Do you have a coat that will cover everything? If you don't, I have one next door you can use."

"You think I should go over to his place. I've been drinking and I don't even know where he lives."

"That's what taxi's are for. Be sure and pack clothes for tomorrow and don't rush home in the morning. Me and Dora will be fine. Ooh this is so exciting! You got to tell me some of what happens tomorrow – nothing too specific. He is my brother after all."

"I don't think I want to do this, Shantrell," I say as I stand in front of her and wait for her to insist.

"Oh, okay, I'm sorry. I don't want to push you into sleeping with a man you don't want to sleep with. You have to do this in your own time, not mine or even Zeke's for that matter. You have to forgive me. I get caught up in love so fast, even if it's someone else's love. I just love to witness love flourishing. I'm a romantic." Shantrell walks into the kitchen and, as if my dilemma is completely resolved, says, "You want some popcorn?"

I'm still standing in the middle of the living room floor waiting for her to push me in the direction I am dying to head toward. "That's all you got to say to me?"

"What else would you like me to say?" Shantrell slams the microwave shut and pushes one button to start her corn to popping.

"I don't want any popcorn." I tell her and head to my room to pack my overnight bag. I place a call to the taxi service and ready myself for what I pray will be a night well worth remembering. I smooth on some Jadore body lotion and my new chemise but don't bother with a coat. I do slip on a favorite overhead dress and a small amount of makeup.

When I return to my living room, Shantrell tells me she sent Zeke's address to me via text. "Don't let the taxi leave until you're sure he's there," is her last bit of advice before I leave my house.

I sit in the taxi nervous and certain I'm making a big mistake, but I go forward anyway. I have been overly cautious most of my life. This one risk won't break me. If things don't turn out the way I hoped, I will survive.

The taxi driver turns the vehicle into a small Marina apartment complex and creeps forward until he spots the correct building number. When he stops, I hand him the fare along with a nice tip before asking him to wait a few minutes so I can make sure my friend is at home. The driver nods with a kind and somewhat sympathetic look in my direction.

The stairs leading up to Zeke's apartment go on forever and I see no sign of life from the windows, though the porch light is on. All the apartment porch lights are on. Maybe they come on automatically at dusk. There is no doorbell, so I knock lightly and wait, looking down at the taxi which now has its lights off. There is no sound coming from the apartment but I knocked so lightly that if Zeke is in the back, he most likely would not have heard me. I suck in a little air, as if I need the oxygen, and knock again, hard and long this time. The blinds from the apartment next door move and a woman peeps out. I nod at her but she ignores me and quickly hides back behind the blinds. With disappointment welling up inside me, I consider knocking again but don't. I look back down at my taxi as I reach in my pocket for my phone. The driver waves his hand out the window and I feel a bit less frustrated. Then the door swings open.

Zeke stands there looking at me with a sleep-ridden frown on his handsome face. His uncovered chest is hairy and I notice the man actually has a well defined six pack. The only thing he is wearing is a pair of loose fitting pajama pants hanging low on his hip bone. "Hannah, what's going on? What are you doing here?"

"I came to see you," I tell him hesitantly as I look down toward my taxi which has not moved. I guess the driver is somewhat versed in these types of midnight one-sided rendezvous.

"Is everything okay?" Zeke asks with his face somewhat relaxed.

"I just wanted to come see you. Are you alone? Can you ask me in?"

Zeke still looks slightly perplexed but steps back for me to enter. I wave at the driver and float inside the apartment door.

"Excuse my place. It's a bit of a mess. I never have visitors here." He starts moving around and picking up items but the place doesn't look horrible. I can tell it is just a temporary stopping place. He's still living out of boxes and there is nothing on the walls except a flat screen television. "I called you earlier. Where have you been?" he asks.

I sense a hint of jealousy. "Do you mind if I sit." I point to the sofa he just removed magazines and clothing from but ignore his question.

"Yeah, sit down. Make yourself comfortable, if you can." He looks around and I can tell he's a bit embarrassed by his home. There are golf clubs, tennis rackets, two bicycles and baseball paraphernalia taking up the majority of his tiny dining area.

"It's not bad, Zeke; just a little crowded." I say in an attempt to make him feel better.

He smiles. "Can I get you something to drink?"

"Sure, what have you got?"

"I've got beer and bourbon or if you want something nonalcoholic, I've got water."

I decide to try a little bourbon even though I didn't care for the harshness of the drink the few times I've tasted it.

"Looks like you've already had a few. Where did you go tonight? I left you a message." Zeke watches me as he pours drinks for us both.

"I had plans but they fell through so I didn't go anywhere until now."

"Shantrell said you were out."

"I was -- out cold in my bathtub. How was your evening at your alumni thingy?"

Zeke sits down next to me on the sofa, too close for comfort. "Dull. After you've been to a few of those events, it's hard to work up an appetite for the people or the food. I think I'll recommend you to cater the next one."

"Don't do me any favors," I tell him.

"No, you'd be doing me the favor," He chuckles and takes a drink from his glass.

I follow suit and take a long gulp and nearly gag.

"You don't drink bourbon like that, Hannah. Not unless you're trying to get sick. It's strong stuff."

"Can I have a beer instead or, better yet, just a glass of water."

"So what happened to your plans?" Zeke asks, ignoring my request.

"You were my plans and you weren't available." I keep my eyes pinned to the glass of unwanted bourbon in my hands.

Zeke sits forward on the sofa, looks at me as if he's trying to figure me out, and shakes his head. "Why didn't you tell me you wanted to get together tonight?"

"I did," I say in protest.

"Hannah you didn't sound the least bit concerned. I didn't know what you had planned. I thought maybe you were having friends over or something. We could have planned to meet later." Zeke seems a little frustrated with me.

I shrug off my embarrassment. I feel awkward and wonder if he's just humoring me because he feels sorry for me. That would be sadder than him not desiring me at all.

Zeke takes the glass from my hands and sets it on the small coffee table. "Come here," he says as he leans back against the sofa and pulls me into a nice embrace.

After a moment, I pull back and look at him as I try to guess if he wants me here. He leans forward and kisses me and it feels like he does. Then he wraps his arms around me again and I hold onto him tightly. He seems upset. "Is something wrong, Zeke?" I ask as we pull apart, feeling selfish because I don't want to hear anything negative. I want the night to play out like it has in my mind so many times.

"I don't know. I guess you'll have to tell me that. This thing between us is so iffy and our lives are pretty much up in the air right now. You've got this mess with the baby and your cousin and I've got to get settled into my house and I need to find a place for my mother. She keeps telling me she does not want to stay with Shantrell forever. She says she'll live with one of us later in life but not now. I'm getting off track." Zeke looks at me again as if he can't find the words for what he wants to say so I decide to take the bull by the horns.

"I bought something I thought you might like today."

He smiles. "For me? It's been awhile since anyone bought me a gift."

This breaks my heart a little and I make note to pick him up a nice present, no matter how the night turns out. "I guess you could say it's something for you. You wanna see?"

The man turns and looks at me as if it just occurred to him that he might actually enjoy seeing the item I purchased earlier. "I sure do," he answers with conviction.

I take another one of those "help me, Jesus" breaths, similar to the one I took when I was knocking on his apartment door. Here goes! I stand up and move around so that I am standing directly in front of Zeke and move in closer between his parted knees. He leans back against the sofa cushion to afford himself a better vantage point of whatever I show him. I smile, cross my arms in front of me, gather the lower portion of my dress and pull it over my head in one quick motion. Thankfully, my dress has no buttons or zippers to snag in my hair.

I sling the dress to the side and notice Zeke's face muscles go slack and his eyes open slightly wider as he looks me up and down. "Wow!" he murmurs just loud enough for me to hear. "You bought this for me?"

"Do you like it?"

He swallows. "I love it" he whispers an answer and clasps his hands behind his head as he leans back even further on the sofa. "Step back so I can see you better."

I move back a little awkwardly.

"You mind turning around?" he asks.

Damn! I didn't think I was going to have to model the damn thing, but I do as I am bid and start to slowly make a 360 degree turn. No surprise, when I get half way around Zeke says, "Stop right there." He wants to glare at my butt. Men are so strange when it comes to butts and boobs. Boobs I don't have much of but I've got ass to spare.

I stand there and look over my shoulder at him. "Can I turn around now?" I ask.

"Yeah and come here."

I turn and walk back to him as he leans forward on the sofa and reaches out with both hands to feel the lace of my gown. "This feels nice." Zeke says and looks up at me. "I've never liked a gift so much. I feel his hands running up my outer thighs to the string of my thong undies on around to my butt which he touches very gently. He closes his eyes and bites down on his bottom lip while gently trailing a finger along the string between my buttocks and I like the touch. The man stands, moves me around until I am lying on the sofa before kneeling and kissing me. Zeke allows his tongue to play with mine almost as if we are having a quiet conversation. I feel like I'm about to explode although he has not touched the most sensitive part of my body.

He pulls back for a moment and tells me, "I just want to look at you for a few minutes. I want to enjoy what I'm seeing."

"I don't mind, not at all." I lie still as I become more comfortable with him.

He places a hand behind my head and kisses me again, softer and even wetter this time. When he pulls away, he rubs his thumb across my lips and I take it in my mouth and suck on it. This causes him to laugh lightly. "You're hot, aren't you?"

"Yes."

"Sit up" he tells me as he moves back, giving me room to maneuver around. Once I'm sitting, he asks "What do you like, Hannah?"

"What do you mean?"

"Sexually, what do you like?"

Is he really asking me this question? "You, right now, I just want you," I answer.

The man kneels down in front of me and positions my feet up on to the sofa so that he has a full on view of all my intimates. The thong is useless with me in this position. His mouth is now slightly open and his eyes droop as he licks a finger and runs it softly along my exposed crotch. He makes this soft touch three or four times before actually inserting his finger inside me and pulling it out slowly. Then he takes his other hand and moves my soaking wet thong to the side and plays with my hardened nub. I can't help but moan loudly when he runs his now saturated fingers to lower more exotic places.

"I want to wait but I think we'd better do this now or I might not make it inside you" he tells me. "I've got to get my condoms."

"Pass me my bag. I have some," I tell him as I move myself into a less vulnerable position.

"You came prepared, didn't you?" he asks as he hands me my overnight bag.

I hand him a condom and smile. "I hope it fits."

Zeke smiles back at me as he unties the drawstring on his pajama bottoms. I reach up and pull the bottoms to the floor for him to step out. Now it's my turn to savor what I see before me. I remain seated and reach out to touch the tip of his hardened body which jumps in response to my touch. I move closer. Zeke is watching me but he no longer has as smile on his face. I take him in my fist near the very head and move my hand up and down the shaft, allowing the head to peep out of my firm grasp. "You'd better stop," he whispers.

"In a minute," I tell him as I pull him into my mouth. I run my tongue around the head of his swollen body and relish his excitement. Zeke begins to move inside my mouth and after a few strokes he grabs me by my shoulders and pushes me away. "Not like this. Not the first time. I want to be inside you."

I lie back on the sofa and watch as he puts on a condom. He then lies over the top of me, kisses my mouth and enters me all at once. "Damn, baby!" he moans and begins to move, with long easy strokes which keep going deeper and getting juicier. He's moving slowly and our bodies start to make noise from all the moisture we are releasing. When I start to moan loudly, Zeke begins to move faster. I know he's trying to wait for me and when he begins to draw nearly completely out of my body and apply more pressure on that nub as he goes back inside, I have to let go. Once Zeke realizes I'm reaching my peak, he continues his climb and reaches the top right behind me.

Chapter 12: Joy and Pain

Both my breakfast and my brunch are incomparable. Zeke's apartment may be a drab little place but he can work magic in the kitchen. For brunch he gives me a fourth course of Hannah and Zeke. This particular course is so decadent that I feel the need to take my second shower of the morning. I sure hope Dora is a restful child today because I don't think I have the energy to entertain her.

I enter my home to find Shantrell holding a crying Dora on one hip and using the other hand to hold the phone to her ear while she talks with my mother. I take Dora who seems happy to see me and calms down immediately.

"Yes, ma'am, I'll tell my mother you said "hi" and hopefully we'll get to see you the next time you come this way. It's been a long time," Shantrell says before handing the phone to me.

I find myself with a clinging Dora on my hip and the phone in my other hand. Shantrell makes a half-hearted attempt at retrieving Dora, who turns her head away and clings to my shoulder tightly. I'm not prepared to speak with my mother but have no choice. "Hi, Mom."

"Hey, baby. I've got bad news. I talked to your father this morning and he says they've found more cancer in Alise's lungs. The doctors don't expect her to make it. He wants you to bring the baby out here."

"Oh, Mama, no, no, not Alise!" I drop down in a chair and maneuver Dora into my lap. Tears begin running down my face and I can't stop them. "When does he think we should come?"

"As soon as you can, Hannah. She may only have a few weeks. Have you heard anything from that cousin of yours?"

"Not one word in months other than what Aunt Alise has told me. Doesn't Alise know how to contact Dana?"

"I don't think so. I believe Dana does all the calling. I pray they'll get to see each other before Alise dies. Dana will never forgive herself if she fails to spend time with her mother. If you can think of anyone who might have information on how to reach Dana, give them a call."

"I don't know her old friends who live here. The few I did know have all moved away but I'll ask around."

"I called Brianna and Bill. Brie will call you later on today, after church. I think she wants to fly out with you. That way she can help you with the baby."

"How's Dad doing, Mom?"

"He's pretty upset. I know he wants me to come up there but Eugene can't get off work right now. I could go alone but I think I'll wait until you kids get there. Your father's wife is not that crazy about me. She resents the fact that Alise and I are like sisters and your father and I are still so close. I told Brie to let me know your plans just as soon as you know, okay, baby? What's wrong with that little girl? I think this is the first time I've heard her so fretful."

Dora is now sitting quietly in my lap with her head against my chest. "She's fine, just being a little clingy with me today. Do you think I should call Aunt Alise?"

"Talk to your father first. He's there with her and will know if she's up to receiving calls."

After the call with my mother, I carry Dora to her room and change her diaper. I don't feel like talking but I must. Shantrell is still here and curious about my night and the call with my mother. "Has Dora been crying all morning, Shantrell?"

"She's been pretty fussy. I think she realized that you were nowhere around and got scared you weren't coming back. She went into your room several times. I've had to hold her just about all morning. This is the first time she's acted like this with me. I checked her for fever but she doesn't have one. I checked to make sure she wasn't hurt anywhere but I could tell it was more anxiety than pain or anything like that. She's going to be heartbroken when her mother comes for her."

Shantrell's words are like a jolt of cold reality. I've tried to maintain a healthy relationship with Dora but I am as attached to her as she is to me. I love her so very much and cannot believe it would be possible to love a child of my own more. She has filled my world with joyful purpose.

"Dora's grandmother, my Aunt Alise, is very sick. They don't think she has long to live." I tell Shantrell as the tears begin to well up in my eyes again.

"I know. I could tell from your conversation. I'm sorry, sugar. What can I do to help?" Shantrell comes over and sits down beside be and Dora.

"She wants to see Dora. Do you think you could keep an eye on the house while we go for a visit? It may be a week or two. I wouldn't ask but I worry about Dana showing up and forcing her way in."

"That won't be a problem for me." Shantrell looks even sadder than me for a moment and clearly has something to say but doesn't know how to say whatever it is.

"What's the matter?" I ask.

"I know you had a nice night with Zeke last night. I'm sorry you had to come home to such bad news. Keep the two things separate, okay. It's okay to feel good about your night."

I cannot help but smile. "How do you always know what to say and do, Shantrell?" I tear up just thinking about the joy of last night and today's pain."

--

I would not recognize my Aunt Alise if I saw her on the street. She has lost a great deal of weight and the stress of the medical treatment she has been under is apparent all over her frail body. She does, however, light up like a Christmas tree when she sees Dora. The child is a bit leery of her grandmother at first but warms up quickly and behaves well as long as either Brianna or I are nearby.

My mother stays at my aunt's home and though we visit for hours each day, Brianna, Dora, and I stay at a nearby Residence Inn. My father, William, and his wife, Tracy, also live in Greensboro. In the past, Tracy has complained to my father whenever my brother, Bill, Brianna, or I come into town and do not stay with them. My father makes sure my siblings and I are aware of Tracy's complaints because he does not want to hear them. So, in order to keep the peace in the family and make sure Dad has some peace, Bill stays in the house with William and Tracy.

Alise seems to want to do nothing but have Dora in the room with her and watches the child and I together for long stretches of time. She tells my mother and father and anyone else present to leave the room. She talks to me and engages Dora a little but mostly watches us and naps off and on. Dora loves this situation because it means I am doing nothing but playing with her and reading to her for hours on end.

On our fourth morning in Greensboro, my aunt sends me a message to leave Dora at our hotel with Brianna during my visit to her home that day. I arrive at Aunt Alise's home which she shares with her long-time boyfriend, Christopher, to find my father and another lady present.

Aunt Alise gets straight to business. "Hannah, this is Caroline Gray, my attorney. Caroline, my niece, Hannah Jacobs. Hannah, Caroline has completed my will for which your father will serve as executor. I want you to know what I've put in place for Dora. Six months ago when your father suggested I get you to manage my properties in Seaside, I had no idea God had a plan. I was thankful you took those houses over for me. I've got you here so I can tell you what I've already discussed with Christopher and your father. I want to try and prevent as much confusion as possible. My daughter will receive cash and that is all. Hannah, before you leave, you need to withdraw the funds from my accounts. Christopher and William will assist you with that and help you get an account set up so you can pass money to Dana as you see fit. I suggest you give her a decent portion immediately and hold on to the rest and distribute that on an as needed basis. If you give her a large enough portion right away she'll believe that's all I meant her to have and leave you alone for awhile. That's just my suggestion.

"That is all I am leaving Dana. Everything else is to be divided up between my family members and of course that includes Christopher. Dana does not know I still own my home in Seaside. I did not want her to know because she would have tried to live in the house rent free and would have destroyed the place. She also does not know I purchased the other home. The home on Granada is for Dora. That house on Mendocino is yours, Hannah. I am leaving money for Dora but it will be set up in a way that Dana can never get her hands on it unless Dora gets grown and turns it over to Dana. I am leaving money for you, Brianna, and Bill but your portion will be substantially larger because Dana has been such a financial weight on you over the years and now she has left Dora with you for God only knows how long. Caroline has all the details. My will is finalized but much of this will take place before I leave here so it won't be tied up in probate.

"Hannah, I want to thank you for opening your home to Dana. I know she has been a pain in the rear."

"You don't need to thank me, Aunt Alise."

"Yes, yes I do. I have to admit I wanted to be free of Dana when I took off from Seaside. I couldn't take it any longer. I had no idea she would become such a burden on you. We left you there with so much responsibility but thankfully, you were up to the challenge. Now you've got Dora and I can see how much you love her and she loves you. You fight for her, Hannah. As far as I'm concerned, she's yours now. I know that's not my call to make. You have to do as God leads you but please do all you can to protect my granddaughter."

"I will Aunt Alise. I love you so much and I'll take care of Dora, I promise."

My lovely aunt dies ten days later and I'm so stunned by the sudden loss that I lack the emotion to mourn her properly. I pray to God that he will help me keep my promise to her.

--

No one has heard a word from Dana and it is as if we are all afraid to mention her name. Christopher and my father plan a small intimate gathering for Alise's home-going. Brianna had gone back home to Sacramento and Bill was back home in Denver when Alise passed. They both return to Greensboro with their families to attend Aunt Alise's service.

Zeke flies out, along with Miss Mel and Shantrell. I am deeply touched by their consideration toward me and my family. My mother, father, stepfather, sister, and brother are equally pleased. The Melancon family's presence for Aunt Alise's home-going is an extraordinary show of support and I hardly know how to act toward Zeke I'm so appreciative.

During this heart wrenching occasion, which we try and convince ourselves to celebrate, my family, especially my mother, finds cause for great joy. "He's in love with you, Hannah!" my mother declares. She then looks at Brianna and asks, "Why didn't I know anything about this before now?"

--

Since Brianna and her family leave the afternoon of the home-going service, Zeke changes his flight in order to fly with Dora and me two days later. Shantrell and Miss Mel leave the day following the service on their originally scheduled flight. Once Zeke drops his ladies at the terminal, he moves into the suite with Dora and me. This is our first opportunity to speak intimately since the night we spent together nearly three weeks earlier. I don't have much to say. I'm feeling a bit overwhelmed with the massive changes in my life over the past five months. Sitting in the quiet of the hotel room with only Dora's prattling, I think about my Aunt Alise and how strong she was to the very end. She tried so hard to put things in order, especially for Dora. Every time I think about Dora and her grandmother who loved her so and would have given anything to live and nurture the child, I want to scream. I feel helpless when it comes to protecting her. I simply don't know how.

As I sit contemplating this child I've grown to adore, I realize Zeke is watching me. When I look up, he asks, "You want to talk about it. Talking might make you feel better."

"I wish I believed that. I'm sitting here praying for a way to protect Dora," I say quietly with my eyes on my little cousin.

Protect her from what?" Zeke asks.

I think he knows the answer but wants me to say it. "I know I won't be able to protect her from everything in life but my concern is that she may need protection from the very person who is supposed to be her most ardent protector."

"Hannah, you've got to get Child." Before Zeke can finish his sentence his phone starts ringing like crazy with quick repeat blasts, almost like a siren. "Excuse me. This is Budrow."

Zeke remains in the room, allowing me to eavesdrop on the conversation. "Where is she right now?" I hear him ask with his eyes turned on me. "Tell her to call Hannah right away." There is a moment's pause before he continues. "No. Don't let her in that house. We'll call you back."

My heart is in my throat. I know who "she" is. Dana has finally returned. When Zeke puts his phone down and looks at me all I can do is throw myself in his arms and sob. He says nothing. He simply holds my head to his chest and lets me cry.

After a few minutes my cell begins to ring. I don't want to answer but I must. "Hannah, where are you guys? I can't get in the house. Did you leave a key somewhere? Buddy says you're out of town." The bitch doesn't even say Dora's name.

"We're in North Carolina, Dana."

"Oh, how's Mama and Uncle William. Give them my love. I need to get in the house, Hannah. I need a shower and I'm tired. How's my baby?"

"Dora's fine. We'll be home late tomorrow. You'll need to stay someplace else tonight," I tell her, trying not to sound upset.

"I don't have anywhere else to go," Dana whines as if I'm letting her down.

"Get a room, Dana."

"A room! Do you think if I had money for a room I'd be here now?"

I put the phone down to my side and breathe in deep. I hear Dana yelling my name over the phone.

"Let me talk to her," Zeke demands and reaches for the phone.

"No," is my only response to Zeke. I then ask Dana, "Is Buddy right there with you?" She doesn't answer right away. "Where's Buddy?" I yell.

"He's right here," Dana yells back.

"Well, give him the phone," I demand. I know Dana thinks I'm going to allow her in my home but no way in hell will she get inside until I return, not unless she breaks in and sets off the security alarm.

When Budrow gets on the phone I ask him, "Is she loaded, Buddy?"

"I don't think so," Budrow responds quietly.

"I hate to put you in the middle of this but can you take her to a hotel that will allow me to pay for the room over the phone?"

"Well, hell, just about every place I know will do that."

"What about the Embassy?"

"I don't see why not. You call 'em and call me on my cell. If they won't do it, I know a few places that will with no questions asked."

"Thanks, Buddy, I owe you. Put Dana back on the phone please."

I tell Dana that Buddy will take her to a hotel to spend the night. She whines in protest until I tell her Buddy will take her to the Embassy or another hotel as nice. After hearing this, my cousin gets off the phone with barely a peep of protest.

I call the Embassy Suites and book the room for two nights and place an extra one hundred and fifty dollar spending limit on the room charges. I don't want to deal with Dana when I get in tomorrow night. Two days will give me time to think. I know I have failed to tell her that Dora's grandmother, my father's sister, my sibling's and my aunt, and her mother is dead. What difference does two days make at this point. My aunt's ashes are already blowing in the wind.

Zeke stares at me when I end the call. "I'm not going to tell her about my aunt until I get home. I need to be there when I tell her," I say defensively.

"I can understand that but why do the accommodations need to be so nice?"

"Dana is a rich woman for the next few months. She can afford two nights at the Embassy Suites," I tell him.

"How much did your aunt leave her?" Zeke asks, awed that Alise left her absent daughter and Dora's neglectful mother a dime.

I look over at Dora who is sleeping soundly in the hotel crib before answering. "Fifty thousand dollars but she's only getting a portion to start. It's up to me and I don't plan to tell her how much she has; otherwise, Dana will go through that money before she finishes counting it."

--

Thankfully, I have a half way decent looking set of pajamas with me but they are so damn drab in color I consider sleeping in my birthday suit. I wonder if that would seem too forward. I feel guilty for wanting to make love when we just memorialized Alise the day before. I should be too sad to enjoy such a wanton pleasure. The truth is I have been hoping to get Zeke alone since he arrived. I'm certain a good intense romp with him will relieve some of the pent up emotions swirling around in my head and chest. I know I'll relax once he makes love to me and I'll be able to think clearly once the edge is off. I sound like a junkie because I feel like one and I can hardly wait to spread my legs and feel Zeke deep inside me.

When I finish my shower, I find Zeke on the phone. "Buddy says all is good," he tells me as he ends the call and heads off to the bathroom.

I call Christopher, my father, and my mother to tell them Dana has arrived back on the scene and that I'm waiting to get back to Seaside before I tell her about her mother's death. My family understands and offers their support. Next I call Brianna, who offers to drive down to Seaside but I decline the offer. We all expect a great deal of drama on Dana's part and of course she has a right to be upset but my cousin will find a way to blame someone else for all the tragedy in her life. I believe I'm in for an ear full for not telling her about Alise right away, but I know in my core that I have made the right decision. Dana has no one in Seaside at present to cry to or to blame. I need to be there for her with this. It would be too much for Buddy and so unfair to expect him to handle this situation and Dana will need to be handled.

I'm so deep in thought that I don't notice Zeke exit the bathroom. "Stop thinking so hard about this situation with Dana. Try to rest. You'll need to deal with her soon enough," he says as he climbs on the bed and lies beside me.

I turn to face him and he does the same. We lie still and watch each other for a few minutes before Zeke reaches out and gently runs the back of his fingers across my face. I capture his hand and kiss the palm. "Thank you so much for flying out here, Zeke, and bringing your mother and Shantrell. I never expected you to come but your being here means a lot to me."

"I wanted to be here. I enjoyed meeting your parents and seeing your brother again; it's been years."

"They like you," I tell him and hope this information doesn't scare him off. It should because my mother is definitely looking for another son-in-law, my father also, I believe.

Zeke smiles and kisses me before saying, "Goodnight, Hannah."

"Goodnight!" I nearly shout and sit straight up in the bed as I twist my torso to look him in the face. He has got to be kidding. I don't want to have a discussion or think about this. I just want him to make love to me. I lie back down and smile at him.

Zeke reaches for my hand and places it on his hard body. "So this is okay then?"

He feels much better than okay. We each reach and turn our bedside lamps off, strip out of our pajamas and fall back into a tight embrace. After a few minutes of wet kisses, Zeke flips me onto my stomach and climbs over my back and enters my wet craving body. We quietly make love twice and I awake with a whole new outlook on life, one which should last at least until I get back to Seaside.

I feel well rested when I awake after a solid night's sleep but there is no Zeke in sight. I find him and Dora out front watching television and eating breakfast. At least Dora is getting her breakfast. Neither notices me enter the room. Zeke speaks quietly to Dora as he feeds her. The child is multitasking with her eyes glued to the television as she listens to Zeke and opens her mouth for the approaching spoon.

"You know I probably shouldn't be letting you watch this show. Your aunt doesn't use the television to entertain you so don't you tell her I have cartoons on, okay?"

When Dora hears the word "okay" she responds with her own language as if she knows exactly what Zeke said.

"What's that you say? I didn't quite get all of that," he tells her with a chuckle.

"Morning," I interrupt their little Powwow.

They both turn their heads and look at me. Zeke smiles but Dora immediately turns her attention back to the television. "Hey, Hannah, you slept hard. I didn't want to wake you. You must've been exhausted."

"I was; how about you? How'd you sleep?"

"Fine," is all he says about his sleep. "This one's been awake for a while. She woke me up talking."

I give Zeke a kiss on the cheek before picking up Dora and hugging her close. "You call that babbling she does talking?" I smile at the baby and pinch her stomach. She ignores me and lets me know she's enjoying her morning without me by reaching for Zeke. "What kept you awoke?" I ask Zeke, sensing from his one word answer that he did not sleep well.

"I guess the strange bed. I'll make up for it tonight when I get back in my own bed," he says with a slight smile on his lips but does not look at me and I know something is wrong. I start to dig deeper but I've got too much on my plate right now to concern myself with Zeke's problem, whatever it may be.

Chapter 13: Biologically and Legally

Zeke, Dora, and I arrive home to a steamy Monterey Bay, tempered by the hottest day of the year. Thankfully, the heat will only last a couple of days before our normally mild weather returns.

It feels good to be home. Dora, who has been crankier than usual the past few days, seems to be happier also. I find my home exactly as I left it nearly three weeks earlier. Shantrell has obviously been over and dusted for me. Dora and I go straight to bed when we get in. I let her sleep with me and we both sleep as if we haven't slept in days.

My home phone awakens me at nearly nine the next morning. It's Zeke and he wants to stop by before he goes in to work. I hang up the phone and look over at Dora who is still sleeping soundly. Poor little thing is exhausted.

No sooner than I get my face washed and teeth brushed, Zeke knocks at my door. He enters my home looking solemn and I begin to worry what this visit is about.

"I need to tell you something and I hope you won't be upset with me for keeping it from you." Zeke starts out before I can offer him a seat or a cup of coffee and his solemn expression scares me.

"What is it, Zeke?" I ask anxiously.

"Dana is pregnant. Buddy says she's trying to hide it but it's pretty obvious." Zeke looks at me and breathes in hard, without another word.

I am numb but my mouth is working. "When did Buddy tell you this?" I ask.

"The night he took her to the hotel. I didn't tell you because it was clear you were exhausted and I wanted you to get some rest."

I take a seat. "I don't need you to protect me like this, Zeke. I'm a big girl. I have to deal with things my way."

Zeke paces the room for a moment before he speaks again. "I'm sorry you feel that way, Hannah. I wanted you to rest, that's all and you did. I'll try to stay out of your business from here on out."

He looks hurt but not angry and I want to take my words back. It feels good to have him looking out for me, real good. "Thank you, Zeke. It just seems as if there's one thing after another piling up when it comes to Dana. There's Dora, Alise's death, another baby, the money Alise left Dana. This is becoming my life," I shake my head in futility.

"Can I give you some advice?" Zeke asks.

"I'll listen," I answer.

"You need to get with a good family lawyer and discuss this entire situation. I still think you need to get CPS involved."

"I'm not going to CPS. What if they take Dora?"

"What if Dana takes her away? You know she might take her now that she has money? At least let them have a record that she's abandoned Dora once. We don't know where she'll leave her the next time."

I leap up from my seat on the sofa. "Stop! I can't deal with this right now," I say firmly.

Zeke shakes his head in frustration. "I wasn't planning on getting into all this but there hasn't been a good time." He approaches me and tries to grasp my hand but I step away from him and he doesn't persist. After standing there and looking at me for a moment, he tells me, "I've got to go. I've got a class in less than thirty minutes. I'll call you later."

--

Dana calls at noon, demanding I pick her up. I tell her to take a cab but she swears she doesn't have the fare. "I'll pay the taxi when you get here," I say.

Nearly an hour later, Dana arrives looking worse than the last time she showed up on my doorstep. I already feel sorry for the baby growing in her belly. Dana and I barely speak and she marches right to Dora and picks her up with some effort before kissing her repeatedly. "Look at mommy's little girl. You're so beautiful and chunky. What has Cousin Hannah been feeding you? I missed you so much. Mommy missed you, Dora."

Dora looks from her mother to me and back at Dana with a long stare. From her behavior, I think she may have some memory of Dana even though she hasn't seen her in months. I leave them alone for a short while. After about thirty minutes, I call Shantrell and ask her if she can come over. After she arrives, I explain that I may need her to watch Dora while I talk with Dana. Shantrell understands and takes a seat to wait until she is needed.

I find Dana in the bedroom with the baby, actively engaging her with toys she brought. Not cushioning the news in any way, I pick Dora up as I tell her mother, "I've got bad news, Dana. Aunt Alise died last week."

Dana looks at me for a moment as if my words don't sink in. "What are you talking about?"

"None of us knew how to contact you or where you were living. The cancer spread quickly and Aunt Alise is gone." I feel unexpected tears rising at the harshness and finality of my words.

"Stop lying. She was in remission. I talked to her a little over a month ago and she was better." Dana yells at me loud enough to startle Dora. Shantrell enters the room, takes the child out of my arms, and leaves the house.

"She thought she was better but when they looked further they found more of the disease," I tell my cousin bluntly.

Dana gets up from the floor and sits down on the side of the bed before starting to cry. I want to console her, so I do. We sit on the side of that bed with my arm draped over her shoulder as she sobs.

Finally, Dana asks why I waited so long to tell her about her mother's death.

"I wanted to be here with you when I told you. I didn't want you to be alone."

"Someone should have told me how bad things were. I called her just about every month. That goddamn Christopher could have warned me. I should have seen her before she died. Mr. Big Stuff answers the phone every time I call. He didn't really care about my mother. He just wanted her all to himself. I wanted to go to their home when I was pregnant with Dora but I knew he didn't want me there and would have made things hard for me. That's why I didn't tell Mama about Dora, because she would have wanted me with her and Christopher would have got in the way."

I can't recall Dana mentioning Christopher before today. Now, according to her, the poor heartbroken man is the reason she never visited her mother in Greensboro. This is Dana's way. Someone other than her is always to blame. She is powerless in the missteps of her life.

"Did my mother leave a message or anything for me?"

"I mailed a box of items she wanted you to have. They will arrive in a day or two." I reach in my back pocket and hand over a small envelope I have stashed. "She left you this note."

I have no idea what Alise wrote in her letter to Dana. I pray there are words to comfort my cousin but I am certain Dana will read condemnation in the words no matter what my aunt's intent. I stand awkwardly and watch her for a few moments before realizing that she may want to be alone. I lean over and hug Dana but her body only stiffens in response to my gesture. "I'll be out front," I say as I leave the room.

--

My good friend Ezekiel is once again keeping to himself. I thought I had broken some type of barrier when I showed up at his home unannounced and he and I had such a good time together. At that point I was all in, and when he brought his mother and sister all the way to North Carolina for my Aunt's funeral, I was certain he was in as deep as I. Now we're back to hit and miss lunches and occasional phone conversations. I'm beginning to conclude that I have no true knowledge of how to have a relationship with a man. I've had so few serious relationships. The mix up with Bradley was the most serious and I can't honestly call that a relationship. It was a farce.

I want to talk to Brianna or Marshon and ask them if Zeke's behavior toward me is normal. Is this what guys do? Does this behavior mean he's just not that in to me like in the book that was so popular a few years ago? I won't bother asking Erika because she's a player and I honestly think she sees things more from a male point of view. She changes up girlfriends worse than Budrow Melancon and some of the women she's dated seem like good catches to me. Both Brianna and Marshon have had man-troubles with the whole boyfriend or husband misbehavin' thing but I'm too embarrassed to broach the subject. I don't want anyone to know how much I like this man. After Bradley the buzzard, I pledged to never get in a position to be hurt again and I meant that thang and I still do but my insides are feeling squishy and I don't like being vulnerable.

--

We buried my Aunt Alise nearly a month ago and Dana has been here with me and Dora every since. Her behavior has been okay. She's pregnant and eating up just about everything. She complains of morning sickness but I have seen no signs of those symptoms. What I have seen is all day laziness. She lies around a lot and does little in the way of helping around the house other than holding Dora, occasionally changing her diaper, and once in a blue moon feeding the child. Thankfully, Shantrell is still helping me and working more hours than she was before Princess Dana returned to the realm. Although Shantrell and I never had an agreement for her to do housework other than keep Dora's room clean, Dora's laundry, and pickup after her and Dora, she has taken on the responsibility of picking up after Dana also.

Shantrell and Dana don't get along as well as I had hoped. They are not rude or mean to each other but they don't care for each other and both choose to keep their interaction to a minimum and neither seems to wish for more.

I was pleased and surprised when Dana had me take her to the bank to open a bank account. She seems to believe she is very well off with the five thousand dollars I handed over to her. Dana has no idea of the amount of money I am holding in her behalf and I will not tell her because I have a strong feeling that she will need more money soon. Hopefully, one day in the not too distant future, she will settle down and make a home for her children and she will need money to make that happen. If she never makes a decent life for her children and she remains on the streets chasing drugs and fast men, she will always be in need of money for one thing or another. If I give it all to her now, she will be at my doorstep in a year, maybe less, flat broke and begging for more money. I've got to stretch the funds my aunt left for Dana as far as possible.

Dana did throw a thorough fit for the first few days after learning of my aunt's death. She was mad at everyone. She refused to speak to my father when he called to talk to her. She said my father never cared about her before so why was he pretending to care about her since Alise's death. That hurt my father deeply. He always cared about Dana but he never babied her like he did me but he never babied Brianna or Bill either. I was his only baby because I had been injured and he feared life for me. He's long past that now. I get no more babying from him. Dana's behavior toward my family is so ugly that I haven't told anyone she's expecting another child, not even Brianna.

Dana yelled and screamed at me on several occasions during those first few days. She was mad at my aunt and it was as if I was a stand-in for Alise. Dana cursed Christopher for getting my aunt's share of their North Carolina home, even though he and Alise purchased the home together. Dana feels she is entitled to part ownership of that house and that Christopher exercised undue influence to get my aunt to leave him what should have been hers. She says Alise was not thinking about Dora and her when she left "that stranger," who her mother had been living with for over ten years, her share of her house. Dana also challenged my assertion that none of the family knew how to find her or get in touch with her. She wanted to know exactly what lengths we went through to locate her. On several occasions she has told me that Alise would have left things differently if they had spent time together, an assertion I don't doubt.

Mostly, I ignored her screaming and whining. I did pay attention when she cried over the loss of her mother. Dana had a good and loving mother. Was Alise a perfect parent? I doubt it, but what parent is? I love my aunt and I want her back with us because she was the sweetest person I have ever known. I feel so sad that I relished her love so much more than her daughter did and I feel sorry for Dana for that very reason.

After a few days Dana calmed down and went into her usual behavior of being easy to live with for a day or two and then becoming difficult. I thought she would sleep in the room with Dora when she returned but she complained that the noise from the television would keep the child awake and I had to agree. One weekend when Brianna planned to visit for a couple of days, Dana complained that it would be too much trouble for her to move into the room with her child and insisted Brianna sleep in the room with Dora. I was actually relieved when Brianna cancelled her visit. I'm beginning to wonder if Dana has any motherly instincts toward her daughter and I can't help but think it sad that she's about to bring another child into the world. I am relieved that I have seen no signs of drug use of any type other than her prenatal vitamins.

Yesterday Shantrell asked me if it would be okay for her to keep Dora next door at her home because she does not like the way Dana yells at Dora. "Angel Baby is just that, a baby. All babies cry sometime but Dana can't stand to hear her cry. I think it would work out better all the way around if I kept Dora at my house. I'll bring her back just as soon as you get home. I haven't noticed Dana yelling at her as much when you're around," Shantrell tells me.

Also, Shantrell does not like picking up after Dana and neither do I but I just don't know what to do. I have lectured her repeatedly but it does no good. "No one wants to pick up behind you, Dana. You've got to do your fair share. At least take out the garbage, sweep a floor, clean out the bathtub when you finish. We can't put Dora in the tub behind you unless we wash it out. That's not fair. It's clean when you get in, so clean it when you get out."

At first Dana would say, "Okay, I'll do better," or "Oh, I forgot," or "I'll get it in a minute." Now my cousin is responding with "Would you get off my back," and "What's the big damn deal?" as if she is fourteen or fifteen years old.

Nothing about this situation is easy for me because I have no idea what to expect. I have tried to talk to Dana about her plans but she has no desire to discuss the future and I don't have the will or the fortitude to pursue the mountain range that is Dana's life. I do my best to be upbeat and happy with the one ray of sunshine in my life. Dora has become even more attached to me since her mother's return. I am uncomfortable with this dynamic but Dana does not seem to mind at all. By every standard except biology and legality, I am Dora's mother at this point and have been for months. If only I had legal standing. I think about Zeke's words and wish I had heeded them.

Chapter 14: What is a Stone Cold Freak?

I have called and invited Zeke out to dinner a couple of times over the past month and he has refused both times. He has invited me to lunch once and breakfast once and I accepted both invitations.

Finally I call and ask him what's going on. I come right out and ask the man if he's interested in seeing me again. I do cushion that question with "Don't you want to be my friend anymore or are you dumping me?"

Zeke gives what sounds like an uncomfortable chuckle over the phone and says he's having a hard time dealing with the situation with Dana and Dora. I find this strange because I'm the person dealing with Dana and Dora, not Zeke but I didn't call him to argue. I called because I want to see him and spend some time with him, a feat I have yet to accomplish with any consistency. I decide to throw caution to the wind. "I miss you, Zeke."

"I miss you too. Maybe, I'll stop by this evening, if that's okay."

"I'd like that. Can you stay for dinner?"

"Is seven thirty okay?"

"Perfect," I tell him a little embarrassed at my own joy.

I go to the market and grab up the items for a quick gingered beef stir fry. With the stir fry I do some brown rice, a tossed salad, and a sweet potato cobbler -- nothing fancy but delicious and simple. After getting all the ingredients together for my meal and the cobbler in the oven, I get my baby girl bathed and turn her over to her mother. I then take a nice relaxing bath, dress, and finish off my meal prep.

To my surprise, Dana, who is normally nowhere around when I'm cooking, joins me in the kitchen. "I'm having a guest for dinner. Do you want to join us or will you eat later?" I ask.

She gives me a smug look before speaking. "Must be a man. I thought so, the way you've been prancing around. Who's the dude?"

"Shantrell's brother, Ezekiel."

"Zeke Melancon?" Dana asks in a surprised voice.

"Yeah, do you now Zeke?"

"No, I know the name but I don't know the man. I guess I understand why you're so happy. I thought Brianna told me he was dating that uppity Deidra a few years ago."

"Yeah that was sometime back," I say as casually as I can.

"So, have you and Zeke got a thang going on, Cousin?"

Just the way Dana asks the question sounds downright nasty.

"No, we're just friends but he's good people."

"I hope he's not the reason you've been moping around here?"

"I have not been moping and like I said, Zeke and I are just good friends. Are you going to eat with us or not? If you are, please set the table."

How about my cousin goes and sets the table. Dana has not sat at the table with me one time in the entire month she has been back in my home, not once. I'm far too boring for her to waste time on but now that there may be a man present, she's setting the damn table. I know; I asked for this. I should not have invited her to join us but then she could have played dumb and said something embarrassing like, "Cousin Hannah, I can't believe you've got a man over for dinner," right in front of Zeke. I don't want the man to think I have no experience with men.

--

The dinner turns out well or maybe I should say the food is delicious. Both Zeke and Dana compliment me on the meal and rave over the cobbler which neither has had before. So, like I said, the food was delicious, even I thought so and I am my worst critic. The dinner, on the other hand, encompasses the entire dining experience and that is proving to be barely okay. Dana flirts with Zeke something awful. You'd think I was not at the table with them and I do my best to ignore her behavior. I'm not jealous; I'm just exasperated. I guess I can't blame Zeke for staying away. Dana is a piece of work and she's working the shit out of me.

When she makes no traction with the flirting she asks, "Didn't you used to date my Cousin Brianna's friend, Deidre? What happened there?

Zeke glances up from his cobbler and says, "The usual."

"So, you're free now?" Dana asks with a wicked smile and a gleam in her eyes.

To my surprise, Zeke looks at me with a smile and says, "No, no I wouldn't say that, not at all."

I can't help but drop my eyes and smile. When I glance over at Dana I notice her sucking in on her jaw as she studies Zeke. After a moment she looks over at me and gives a small shrug before turning her gaze back to Zeke. "You look familiar to me. I think I've seen you somewhere other than here in Seaside," she says to my guest.

"Very possibly, I couldn't say one way or the other," Zeke answers without giving Dana the benefit of a glance. He had started the evening very friendly but I can tell Dana is wearing on his nerves.

"So you work out there at the university, huh?" she asks.

"Yeah, I instruct economics"

"You like that? I bet the girls are all over you."

Zeke puts his fork down and leans back in his chair with a little chuckle. "No, I don't have too much trouble with that."

"Oh, you're kidding. I bet you just don't want to say anything in front of Hannah because she might get jealous. Hannah's not the jealous type. You don't have to worry about that. She'd never drop you over a little flirting." Dana gives me a sly smile and says, "Would you, Hannah?"

Zeke changes the subject before I can answer. "Listen, Hannah, I'm looking into purchasing a piece of property as an investment. I'd appreciate it if you'd take a look at it and maybe manage it for me if the sale goes through."

"When did you decide this?" I ask. "Do you plan on living in the house at all?"

"No, one of the professors in my department is leaving, going on to bigger and better things and he wants to get rid of this duplex for a really good price. When you get some time, I'd like you to look at it."

"Sure, I can do that. I'd be happy to."

Dana gets up from the table without a word and leaves the room. She doesn't say goodbye, nice to meet you, or anything appropriate. She's being her spoiled self-centered self.

Zeke looks toward her, shakes his head, and drops it. "I don't know how you're dealing with this, I really don't."

I play dumb. "What do you mean?"

"How's she doing with Dora?" he asks.

I look at him and shake my head. "Not the best actually; she doesn't have much patience for Dora. You know Dora likes a lot of attention and Dana doesn't like to give it. They are not crazy about each other."

"Wow!" is all Zeke says.

He and I go into the kitchen and get the dishes in the dishwasher and the food put away. As I wipe off the counter, Zeke comes up behind me and wraps his arms around me. "Did you really miss me?" he asks.

I turn and wrap my arms around him. "Very much, how about staying the night?"

"You know I'd love to do that but I'm not comfortable around your cousin."

"I know she's bratty." I say.

"Hannah, the girl just sat here and damn near propositioned me."

"What do you mean? I didn't hear a proposition!" I say in Dana's defense.

"That's because you're a woman and you weren't listening. I'm a man and I know when I'm being propositioned. Now, maybe it was just a test to see if I'd bite. She's dangerous that cousin of yours."

I angrily pull away. I'm not angry because of Zeke's allegation but because I know he will not stay the night with me and he hasn't invited me to go home with him. I wish I had the nerve to invite myself but I've already done that once and I don't want to have to always be the hunter. I want him to want me at least as much as I want him.

Zeke makes a couple of futile attempts to wrap me in his arms but I move away because I want more. He moves close to me as I stand at the kitchen sink, refusing to look at him. "Look, I'm not going to take you up on your offer to spend the night tonight but do you think maybe we can go out to dinner this weekend and maybe spend some time together?"

I feel my cheeks start to rise as I turn toward him. "Are you propositioning me?"

"Damn straight, I am." He leans in without touching me with his hands and kisses me long and hard. When we part, he says, "But if you don't want to come to my place and just want to go to dinner and a movie or something, that's cool. I just want to spend some time with you. I know I've been acting childish but I see now that you've got enough children to deal with and I don't need to add to your worries."

Zeke looks at me like he means what he's saying and really wants me to accept his invitation. I don't respond right away because I'm just too doggone elated.

"You wanna bring Dora with you? Maybe you guys should start coming over and spending a little time with me at my place. I'll clean up even."

I have to laugh now. "You'd clean for us?"

"Come on. It's not that bad, is it?"

I laugh harder and Zeke laughs with me. When the laughter stops, he gives me a look so sincere, I feel flustered. "I would. For you and Dora, I'd clean," he says in a near whisper with just the hint of a shy smile on the corners of his beautiful full lips.

I play down my own emotions and say, "Zeke, your place is kind of crowded. I mean, we'll come over this weekend if you want but I don't know if we'd be able to walk around in there with Dora's portable crib in the way."

The man puts some distance between us as he moves away to collect my kitchen garbage. "Well, let's do dinner. You bring Dora if you want. I'll leave that up to you. Let me know though because we might want to take her someplace that's child friendly, right?"

"Right," I answer in agreement, wishing the intimacy we were sharing had not ended.

After Zeke grabs up my garbage bag and says goodbye, I feel better than I have in days. Dana enters the kitchen as I finish sweeping up the floor and I'm surprised to see her but certain she will do her best to put an end to my euphoria. Dana usually hibernates in her room and watches reality television until I leave the front of the house, then she comes out to eat or watch television in the living room.

Dana returns to the kitchen and seems to be uncertain what she wants. She hesitates by the refrigerator for a moment and then says, "Oh, you guys have already taken care of the dishes. I came out to help you finish up. Is your friend gone?" Before I answer she asks, "Is there anymore of that sweet potato cobbler. That was really good, Hannah. You're going to have to teach me to cook."

"There's quite a bit more in the refrigerator in that Rubbermaid bowl with the red top."

"I think I'll have a little more," Dana says as she reaches in the refrigerator for the bowl. She helps herself to the cobbler but keeps an eye on me. "So that's Mr. Zeke," she finally says.

I know it's coming. "Yep, that's Zeke," I say with resignation.

"Humph, you know, I don't know how to tell you this, cousin, but he looks an awful lot like a guy I used to see on the streets who dated a friend of mine," Dana drops her bomb with a lowered chin and raised brow in wait for my reaction.

"Dated a friend of yours on the streets?" is all I can think to say.

"Yeah, you know. He was her trick, a john, you know."

This is the closest Dana has come to admitting being on the streets. She has always owned up to having a love of drugs and good-looking fast men but that's pretty much where her confessions ended before now.

I look at her with my mouth half open and try not to appear shocked by information I already know. What she says about Zeke doesn't faze me, initially. I pick up the bowl of cobbler and place it back in the refrigerator.

"I can tell you one thing; my friend Susie says he is a stone cold freak. I mean real freaky."

At this point I have to ask, "What is a stone cold freak, Dana?"

"Girl, somebody that wants to do everything to you or wants you to do everything to them, maybe both. She said he didn't mind shelling out the cash but that he was wild."

"Well, I guess he never hurt her if she dated him more than once."

"No, I don't think he did anything to hurt her. I'm just saying he was out there picking up hookers and Susie was one of the ones that would go bare back, no type of protection. I just thought you needed to know."

I want to ask Dana if she is sure it was Zeke but I just say, "Thanks for the heads up," and leave the room. She got me. She got me good. She says Zeke is a freak. He ain't got freaky with me. I mean I wouldn't want him to get real freaky but I could do a little more freak.

I wonder how much credence I should place on the story Dana has come up with about Zeke. My mother and Brianna would say, "Girl, don't believe anything Dana tells you," but still I wonder. Is Zeke the guy who has been hooking up with Dana's friend? Is that why I see him so seldom because he does hookers? I understand that men sleep with hookers but I don't want my man sleeping with no damn hooker.

I have to process this. My puritanical, Pentecostal, Christian side says it is a very bad thing for a man, especially my Zeke, to get freaky with a woman of the night. Now my liberal, open-minded, nonreligious side tells me, *Hey, he's got to get off somehow. Better he pay a hooker than screwing around with lot of different women who are looking for more than a one night stand.* I don't like this no matter how pious or freethinking I am.

Chapter 15: Have Your Own Babies

I have been looking forward to my evening with Zeke for three days now. For some reason, Dana insists on keeping Dora at home. I tell her I would really like to take Dora with me but she is adamant about keeping the child with her. I actually hate to go off and leave Dora with her mother so I call Zeke and change our meet up time to eight thirty. This gives me time to have Dora in her crib and on her way to sleep before I leave the house. Dana has no idea where I'm going and I don't want her to know. I probably should tell her I have a date with Zeke because then she might send Dora with me but I will not give her the satisfaction. When I walk out my front door and announce that I will not return until the next day, Dana is speechless.

I park my car at Zeke's place and we drive out to Phil's Fish Market in Moss Landing. The place is not fancy but the food is good. Zeke talks me into trying the raw oysters, a delicacy my father has been trying to get me to sample for years. I'm actually surprised at how easily they go down. The evening is nice and quiet and we get to focus on each other, something that can be hard to do with Dora in tow.

I drink a little too much wine and become slightly intoxicated, so much so that I ask Zeke if he's ever slept with a hooker.

Zeke looks at me and kind of laughs before asking, "Where the hell did that come from?" but doesn't miss a beat sucking down his steamed clams. When I don't answer, he looks at me again and the smile fades. "Oh, I know, that cousin of yours. That's what she came up with, huh. I knew she was working on something." Zeke shakes his head and slows down on the clams.

"What do you mean?" I ask innocently.

"She's the one that planted that seed. That's why you're asking me if I've ever slept with a hooker. I mean, am I supposed to believe that out of the clear blue sky you want to know if I've ever slept with a hooker. What, did you read some report about the propensity of men reaching middle age to sleep with hookers? Did you see a report on the evening news? What woman just wants to know if her man ever slept with a hooker, Hannah? Okay, just in case you don't know, I've dated a number of women and I've had a few long-term relationships and you're the first woman that's ever asked me if I've slept with a hooker. So, maybe you did just come up with that out of the clear blue sky but I have a strong suspicion that cousin of yours planted that seed. Now if I'm wrong, just tell me and I'll accept that." Zeke has put his fork down and is looking at me as he waits for an answer.

"This is not about Dana. I'm just curious," I whine.

"Damn, what did she tell you that you feel you need to confirm?"

"I told you, Zeke, this is not about Dana."

"Okay, well what do you want to know? Yes, I have slept with a hooker before. Is that it?"

"Recently?"

"Hannah! You won't tell me what she said but you're asking me all these silly-assed questions."

"I just want to know if you slept with one recently," I say.

"You mean since I've been dating you? No," Zeke says, indicating that he is finished with this subject.

"Are we dating?" I ask.

"What do you think this is, Hannah?"

"Don't patronize me, Zeke. I'm not your child."

He laughs again. "Okay, sorry, you got me on that one. But seriously, she told you something that's got you all curious about me."

"Sometimes I don't see you for weeks, Zeke."

"Hannah, no sooner than I met you, your cousin dumped the baby on you. Now don't get me wrong. I don't mind Dora. I don't mind her at all but you've pretty much had your hands full with Dana's child and two jobs. You don't have time for a man but I stayed away as long as I could, but I sure wasn't staying away because I have a thing for hookers. I haven't been with a hooker in years, not since I was drunk, stupid, and still in school. So what did she tell you? Did she say she saw me with somebody or worse? Was I one of her johns? Your cousin is a miserable person and she wants you to be miserable too. She can't stand seeing you look half way happy. That's why she doesn't stay around. She's got to do something to sabotage you or she has to get away from you. She can't stand to be around you and all the good shit flowing from you. She can't stand it."

"I doubt that," I say.

"You can doubt it all you want, sister, but that's what the hell's going on. You tell me when she's been around and you haven't been miserable. When was the last time you enjoyed her company? When was the last time she did something to please you? And then for her to come and drop Dora on you the way she did when she knows how much you have going on in your life. Sure, she didn't want to take care of the baby anymore but that's also to sabotage you. I'm not saying she doesn't love you. She loves you like she loved her mother. I bet you any amount of money your aunt left here because of her daughter."

I keep my head down while listening to this painful truth about my relationship with my cousin. Zeke watches me but he doesn't let up. "See, I can tell by the way you're not looking at me that I'm right about something I'm saying. She's trouble and you can listen to anything she says. I don't care. I've got nothing to hide. But do you really think I would admit something to you. Do you think if your cousin tells you I'm crazy and you come and ask me, I'm going to say, 'Yeah, Hannah, I'm crazy' or 'Yeah, Hannah, I like little boys.' I don't know why you waste your time listening to crap like that. You tell me one thing she has ever told you that was worth listening to, just one thing. So stop letting her yank your damn chain. I mean I can't see myself spending much time with you if this one is going to keep popping up like a bad penny and causing you all types of grief. I thought Dora was the only one that needed protection with this shit. Do I have to worry about protecting you too?"

I'm insulted. I have sat here and listened to Zeke lecture me and taken it because I realize I asked him a somewhat offensive question but I don't need him to talk down to me as if I'm his child. "I don't need you to protect me, Zeke. I can take care of my damn self."

"Well stop acting like you need protection. You let this, this, I'm not going to call her any names because she's your people. You let her come around and tell you some crap about me sleeping with hookers. That's the best she could come up with. Okay, I've slept with a hooker in the past. What's she going to come up with next, Hannah? Is she going to say I tried to hit on her, that I want her? That's the kind of crap women like your cousin do? And I have to be honest; I haven't wanted to deal with her. I was staying away because you had so much going on and you don't want me involved in your business. You don't even want me to comment. You tell me you don't need my protection but you do. Dora needs my protection. I need your protection. That's what people do when they care about each other, Hannah. We protect each other. We have each other's back."

I have no rebuttal. I know Zeke is at least partially right.

--

True to his word, Zeke's tiny apartment is immaculate. "I don't usually keep it quite as bad as you saw it the last time you were here. I guess that was the first and last time you were here. I was embarrassed. I'm glad you didn't run away screaming," he tells me with a laugh.

Zeke and I make love before settling in his bed to talk about all manner of things. We agree that we will not discuss Dana again, at least not tonight. I doze off for what seems like only a few minutes when I suddenly awake to a feeling of dread. I try to go back to sleep but there is a weight gripping my heart like I've never felt before. Zeke is sleeping hard so I creep from the bed and get dressed. I send him a text explaining that I've gone home and slip out the door without waking him.

It is well after one in the morning when I arrive at my home and I'm surprised to see an unfamiliar car parked in my driveway. That dark feeling of dread increases and I consider calling Zeke to come over before I go inside but talk myself out of it. The house is completely quiet when I enter and I find Dora sleeping peacefully in her crib. I breathe a sigh of relief and tell myself that all is well. Right at that moment I smell cigarette smoke and feel anger welling up inside me. I go to Dana's bedroom door and knock. I get no answer though I hear movement. "Dana?" I call out.

"What is it, Hannah?"

"Can I come in?"

"What do you want?"

"I want to come in."

"I'm sleeping," she replies

"Whose car is that in the driveway?"

She doesn't answer but I hear a deep exasperated sigh and some whispering. I open the door to find Dana lying in bed with a tall, bearded and heavily tattooed man who is smoking a cigarette. Dana looks concerned but the man looks at me as if I am a puff of smoke. "You need to put that cigarette out." I tell this idiot.

He glances back at me and says, "I'm almost finished and it will be out then."

I feel a lump of anger rising from my stomach into my chest. This is indignation. I am so pissed I would beat the brown off of him and the yellow off of Dana if I thought I could manage the ass-kickings. I look at Dana and tell her, "You need to get him out of here, now."

"Who the fuck does the bitch think she is?" the man yells at Dana. "You better tell her what the deal is before both of y'all end up looking stupid."

Now I'm so mad I do the dumbest thing possible. I turn and leave the room yelling, "I'm calling the cops. You need to get out of my house."

Before I get to my purse or the kitchen phone, the stranger has me by my hair and is squeezing tight. "You're not calling no damn body." Then to Dana he yells, "I thought you said it was cool for me to come here!"

"Hannah, he's only staying for a few days." Dana looks at me with pleading as if I would give any thought to letting this horrible piece of bullying trash remain in my house after this introduction.

The man loosens his grip on my hair and I pull free of him, making a dash for my front door. He follows me and I hear Dana yell, "Please don't hurt her, Travis!" I realize she is terrified and this scares me to no end.

The man grabs my arm with a hand that seems the size of a baseball glove but I somehow manage to shake my arm free before falling to the floor near the fireplace. He grabs me again and begins pulling me up by my arm. I reach for his groin with my free hand and I almost have it, but he reacts too quickly. This time in his haste to escape the pain of my grasp, he falls back and hits his head. I break for the door and manage to escape to the outside with him not far behind me. Once outside, I begin to yell at the top of my voice "Shantrell, call the police! Shantrell, Shantrell, help, help!" I know someone will hear me. I pray Richard, my neighbor on the opposite side, is at home and comes outside also. He and his two sons are massive men.

"Shut up, bitch!" my attacker yells but stops pursuing me.

I see Shantrell's front door swing open and she walks out with what I think is a 38 caliber pistol in her hand and Miss Mel is right behind her with a poker from their fireplace. Mrs. Richard Hernandez comes out with her sixteen year old son, Jose Luis, who is the largest of all the Hernandez men and an offensive lineman at Seaside High. Mrs. Hernandez doesn't speak much English but she does say in a loud agitated voice, "Llame a la policia!"

The fool still tries to step to me. I hear Shantrell cock the pistol. "You better step back boy because if you think I got this damn gun for show, you are crazy." Then to me she yells, "Move over here, Hannah." I move quickly in her direction.

The man knows he's out of his league at this point. He looks at Dana and tells her, "Get your shit. We're leaving." Dana turns to go inside without question or protest. He tries to follow her.

"Stay out of my house" I yell. At that moment we see a police cruiser with flashing lights turning onto our little street. I feel Shantrell hand me the gun and whisper. "Slip it to Mama but don't let anyone see you." I look at Shantrell and then at Miss Mel who looks me straight in my eyes. I slip the gun behind my back and Miss Mel takes it and goes inside their house."

"Good evening," Officer Ezell says. "What's going on here?"

Before anyone else can speak, my attacker says "Officer, I'm just trying to get my shit and be on my way."

I tell the officer my name and that I live in the home and that the man is an uninvited guest who refused to leave.

"I was invited. Her cousin invited me!" the thug protests.

"Is that true ma'am?" The officer asks me.

"Yes, my cousin is a guest in my home but I did not give her permission to have this man in my home. When I returned, just a few minutes ago, he was lying in the bed smoking a cigarette. I told him to put it out and he said he would when he finished. Then I asked him to leave and he refused. When I told him I was calling the cops he grabbed me by my hair and stopped me from using the phone. Then he tried to stop me from leaving my home. Tonight is the first time I have ever laid eyes on this man and I still don't know his name. My cousin had no right to bring this man into my home."

The officer pulls the man to the side and places him in the squad car while running a check on his ID. I remain out in the yard and watch Dana make two trips into my home and carry out her and the thug's possessions. I pray the officer finds outstanding warrants but after only a few minutes he releases the man from the squad car.

At that moment my heart drops as I see Dana coming out of the house with a bag over her shoulder and a still sleeping Dora on her hip. "No, you can't take Dora!" I shout.

Dana looks surprised for a moment.

"Wait a minute; what's going on here?" The officer asks with his hand facing Dana in the halt position.

I look at Dana and say, "Please don't take her, Dana. Please leave her here with me."

"Whose child is this?" Officer Ezell asks.

"This is my baby, Dora Grace Mechum. I have her birth certificate right here in my purse."

"Officer, she abandoned the child and left her here with me for months. I'm afraid for the baby's welfare."

"Is that true ma'am? Did you abandon the child?"

"No officer. My cousin offered to keep Dora because she knew I had no place to take her. I have a home now with my fiancée up in Berkeley. We're expecting our second child and I want Dora with us now."

The officer looks at me as if he is waiting for my rebuttal but I know his hands are tied. I still beg "Please don't let her take her. She abandoned her."

"Ma'am did you call Child Protective Services?" The officer asks me.

I don't even bother to answer the officer. "Dana wait" I walk up to my cousin and see what looks like hate in her eyes. I get close enough that no one can hear what I'm saying. "Please don't take Dora. I kept her with me and didn't call CPS because I love you and I knew you would want her back without a lot of trouble. I didn't want to put you through that. You're not ready to take care of her yet, Dana. Please leave her with me, please."

"If you knew I wouldn't want to go through a lot of trouble why are you giving me such a hard time now? We're going to be a family. I will make sure Travis is as much a father to Dora as he is to his baby. What you need to do is have your own babies and leave mine the hell alone."

Her words sting just as they are meant to but I'm still trying to get Dora back. "I've got more money for you. Aunt Alise told me to use my own judgment in how to give it to you. There's more than the five thousand I gave you."

Dana looks me in my eyes hard. "Is this more money that she left for me or Dora?"

"For you, strictly for you?"

"Then what did she leave for Dora."

"A house, you and Dora and the baby can live in. The house is in North Carolina." I lie about the location of the home.

"No money for Dora?"

"No," I lie again.

"How much more for me?"

"Fifteen thousand more." Another lie.

"Well you take good care of it. I'm sure I'll need it when I have the baby." Dana turns and walks away with a sleeping Dora on her shoulder.

"Did you get my shit?" The thug asks Dana.

Dana hands Dora to this nasty cruel man and says "Take her while I get the stroller." My cousin doesn't even look at me. She goes inside and returns with the stroller, which includes the car seat.

"Do you want to press charges against this man?" The officer asks me.

I should have the man arrested but I do not want to alienate my cousin any further and the look she gives me speaks volumes. I would concede nearly anything to keep Dora with me, but I cannot allow this man to remain in my home though I consider asking them to stay. That is the depth of my desperation. "No, officer, I just want him away from my home," I say quietly. I feel

Shantrell's arm around my shoulder. "Dana, you remember what I told you. If anything happens to Dora, you forget you ever knew my name. I get to make the decision. You remember that." Dana knows I'm talking about the remainder of the money her mother left her. When she looks at me, there is a bit less triumph in her gaze.

I stand and watch the car back out of my driveway and head down the road followed by the police vehicle. Not thirty seconds later Zeke pulls up and steps out of his car. "What's going on? I've been calling your phones but I get no answer," he says, clearly pissed off.

"Dana left and took Dora with her." Shantrell tells Zeke as he approaches us. "She had some asshole in the house who refused to leave and attacked Hannah. Miss Hernandez called the police. I could have handled that fool a whole lot better than the police and Dora would still be here with us."

Zeke is standing in front of me but I can't look at him. How many times did he advise me to report Dana to Child Protective Services? He takes my hand and starts walking me into the house. I pull away and hug Shantrell who is now crying. "Thank you for saving me, Shantrell. I was so scared."

"We'll get Dora back. I just know we will," Shantrell whispers in my ear.

I hug and thank Mrs. Hernandez and Jose Luis. Mrs. Hernandez tells me everything will be okay in a mixture of Spanish and English.

No sooner than I get in the house, I call Dana. She answers but hangs up immediately. Each call to her number after that goes straight to voice mail. "Stop trying to call her," Zeke finally says. The harder you try to contact her, the more she will feel like she has the upper hand. She has to think you're not that concerned about Dora. If she knows you want Dora more than anything else in this world, she'll keep her from you at all costs." He looks angry as he looks around at Miss Mel, Shantrell, and me. "Did anyone get the license plate number off the car?"

"Who had time to get a license plate number? That fool was crazy. He tried to ignore my gun," Shantrell declares.

"You pulled your gun?" Zeke shouts. What have I told you about that gun, Shantrell?"

"Be prepared to use it if I pull it. I had to. He was going after Hannah."

"I got the plate number when I pulled up but something tells me it's a rental," I say.

"We'll see what we can find out with that plate number in the morning. Maybe we can at least find out where they're living," Zeke says calmly now.

No one speaks a word after that until Miss Mel says "Hannah, if you need anything, you know I'm just next door. I think we need to stand and say a word of prayer for little Dora and her mother."

The four of us join hands as Miss Mel leads us in prayer. After a moment, Zeke pulls me into his chest and I hold onto him with all my might while Miss Mel completes her emotionally eloquent entreaty to God. I feel Shantrell and Miss Mel come up behind me and kiss me before taking their leave. Finally, Zeke takes me to my room and insists I lie in the bed. He covers me, locks up the house, and returns with a bottle of water for me. Zeke sits down in the arm chair next to the bed and doesn't say a word but he looks so angry. I wonder if he's angry with me for not heeding his advice. Look at all the trouble that could have been avoided if I had only gone to Child Protective Services. That agency would have more than likely allowed me to keep Dora with me but I was too busy protecting Dana's right to be Dora's mother. Dana relinquished that right when she left the baby with me. I am slow!

Chapter 16: Just a Kiss and a Cup of Coffee

I lie in bed and watch Zeke for what seems like hours. I watch him as he dozes off and wakes up. He repeatedly asks me if I need anything, then pleads with me to try and sleep. I want to slip from my bedroom and call Dana's number again but I know Zeke is right. Dana is more likely to bring Dora back if she believes I don't particularly want the child here.

I finally fall off to sleep some time after daybreak. Zeke is no longer sitting in the chair next to my bed when I awake but I hear voices out in the front of my home. No sooner than I sit up in the bed, my sister enters my room.

"When did you get here?" I ask.

Brianna sits down on the bed next to me. "Hi, baby. I just got here a little bit ago. Shantrell called me early this morning and told me about Dana taking Dora. I'm so sorry, Hannah." Brianna's voice cracks and I know she's fighting back her tears.

"I'm so scared for her, Brie. That man was mean, just plain evil," I say as I hold back tears of my own. "I should have listened to Zeke. If I had, Dora would still be here instead of out there with those people."

I hear a knock at my bedroom door and look up as Shantrell enters with my cell phone in her hand. "Hey, Hannah, your mother wants to talk to you," she tells me before handing me the phone and leaving the room.

I feel like a little girl again as I speak with my mother. It's so comforting to hear her voice. I tell Miriam about Dana leaving and taking Dora with her and how worried I am for Dora's well-being.

"Brianna called me and told me she and David were on their way down there. You need to do what you can to learn where Dana and Dora are living and make sure they're okay," Miriam advises.

"I'm not sure what to do, Mom."

"That's okay. You do what you can. Call and talk to your father and Christopher and let them know that Dana has taken Dora. We need everybody to work on this. Also call that lawyer of Alise's. She is one very smart lady."

"Okay. I'll call Caroline tomorrow and Dad and Christopher later today." I look at Brianna and know that it is time to tell all. "Mom, Dana's pregnant. She's about six months along."

Brianna's mouth opens slightly as she draws in air with shocked disbelief. My mother doesn't speak on the other end of the phone. I've always been Dana's staunchest ally in my family. By the time she was fifteen, Dana was so self-centered and spoiled that Brianna could barely stand to be in her presence. My mother loved Dana when she was a child but only tolerated her once she became difficult and would listen to no one.

My Aunt Alise tried so hard to compensate for the loss of Dana's father during the war in the Balkans that she stopped disciplining the child at a time when she needed the most structure. For years Alise never told Dana "no." By the time Alise decided to put her foot down, Dana was too strong-willed and out of control. In those days, I could cajole her with promises of shopping or some special event because she liked to spend time with me. It wasn't long before my lifestyle was too slow for Dana. I never went through the party stage. I have always been a homebody and would only go out if Brianna, Marshon, or Erika dragged me out. Dana was a different story. She started slipping out to house parties when she was thirteen and to clubs when she was sixteen. Always bright, she managed to graduate from high school on time but her grades weren't good enough for a four year school. Alise tried to talk her daughter into attending Monterey Peninsula College or Hartnell, the local two-year institutions. Dana declared that we should all be happy she had made it through high school and that she needed a break from school.

Within two months of her graduation, Dana had found a part time job and took off to the Bay Area. The job didn't last a good month but Dana loved the city and made it her home. She would come back to Seaside every few months when my aunt still lived on the peninsula. The first couple of visits Aunt Alise thought her daughter was home for good but then it would become clear that Dana was just taking a break, a vacation of sorts, from her hectic life of partying. She always had a story about a job she had lost or a roommate who had not paid his or her share of the rent, resulting in an eviction. Soon we all knew that Dana was on the streets and there was nothing we could do about it. It broke my aunt's heart that Dana chose drugs and being on the streets over family and a loving home.

About a year after Aunt Alise and Christopher moved in together, he took on a teaching position in his home town of Greensboro, North Carolina at Bennett College an all female historically black college. Alise pulled up stakes and followed him and we were all relieved to see her get out from under the pressure of dealing with Dana.

--

I have been in my room most of the day. It's nearly four in the afternoon when I venture out to the front part of my home. I find Brianna, David, Shantrell, Zeke, Budrow, and Mykol preparing to eat fried fish from a local seafood restaurant. I am starving and happy to indulge in a nice greasy meal.

After eating I go and take a long soothing bath. I emerge from the bathroom ready to sit with my friends and discuss what we can do to locate Dana and Dora. We brainstorm every action possible. I will talk to my aunt's attorney and ask her to recommend attorneys who practice family law in our area to include the Bay Area. Zeke and David will also ask their colleagues at the university to recommend family attorneys. Although it is after the fact, I will file a report with Child Protective Services. Zeke is certain he can attain the full name of Dana's boyfriend from the rental car contract. He will also visit the Seaside Police Chief and get recommendations as to the best course of action. Brianna will work on getting Dora's birth certificate and information on her father. Budrow volunteers to contact several of Dana's old Seaside friends to see if they have any information on where she might be staying. Mykol will talk to an old friend on the Berkeley Police Department and after we've gathered as much information as possible, he will contact another friend of his who does some investigative work in the Bay Area and attempt to hire his services, if needed.

It feels good to do something positive even if it is only making a list at this point; it's a start. After nearly two and a half hours, Budrow says his goodbyes and a few minutes later, Zeke declares that he is exhausted and needs some rest. The man stands up and walks out of the house without another word to anyone. I look at his sister who sits there looking at the door as if she can't believe her brother up and left so rudely. Zeke's behavior was weird and out of character. I refuse to look at my sister who I know is in full judgment mode.

No one says a word for a full minute until the doorbell rings. David opens the door to find Zeke standing there with a leather satchel. He walks in and gives a tired smile "Sorry, I meant to unlock the door before I went out. Listen guys, I don't mean to be rude but I'm about to pass out. David, Brianna, I hope to see you two before you leave tomorrow. Myk, I'll give you a call tomorrow afternoon. Goodnight all." With that, Zeke Melancon marches back to my bedroom and closes the door behind him.

I try not to look surprised but Shantrell stretches her face grotesquely to show her surprise and Brianna's expression is nearly as bad. I suppose I should be upset that Zeke would assume he is welcome to spend the night in my bed without an invitation but I'm too pleased to even pretend at being upset.

I make my way to my room as quickly as possible, leaving Brianna, David, Shantrell, and Mykol in the living room. Zeke is in the bed breathing hard and steady when I climb in beside him.

Just as I start to snuggle up next to the man, I hear a knock at my door. Brianna sticks her head in. "Can I come in?" she asks with a wicked smile and proceeds to come in without a response from me. "I wanted to say bye because we'll probably take off before you get up in the morning." My sister keeps her eyes glued to the nice specimen of man lying in my bed. She glances at me and gives me a silent but exaggerated "ooh" as her lips form an "O" and she points to Zeke's bare chest and abdomen.

I mouth back, "I know," roll my eyes, and grin real big. Then I say out loud, "Wake me before you leave in the morning and call me when you guys get in so I know you made it okay."

David pushes past Brianna and comes all the way into my room. "The old dog is sleep already? I wanted to tell him goodbye. That dude's out."

I smile at my brother-in-law who is so easy to love. "David, thanks so much for coming down with Brianna. I feel so much better having you two here."

"You're welcome, Sis. As soon as we get all this mess figured out maybe you can come up with Zeke for a few days. You haven't visited in a while and to be honest, I miss your visits."

"I'll bring her up, man. Just get out of here so I can get some damn sleep. Bye, Brie," Zeke mumbles, not bothering to open his eyes.

"Bye, Zeke and oh yeah, Hannah, I think Shantrell and Mykol are going to visit for a while longer."

"Okay, just tell Shantrell to be sure and lock up."

"Tell Shantrell to take her ass home and see about her kids," Zeke grumbles.

I kick him and shake my head at Brianna who winks at me and says, "You know I wouldn't front my girl out like that," as she closes my bedroom door.

I lie back down, turn on the television, and set the timer before falling fast asleep. Shantrell and Mykol are in the kitchen talking quietly and laughing two hours later when I get up to go to the bathroom. I have no idea what time they finally leave.

--

I awake to find Zeke looking me dead in the face. I lie still and wonder if I'm dreaming or imagining him. When he says, "Good morning," I know he's real. I don't answer. I'm happy he's here until I remember Dora's not and I don't know where she is or if she's being treated well. My eyes start to well up with tears. Zeke pulls me close and holds me until I stop crying. I felt so much better when we were making our list yesterday. Will any of those actions make a difference? It all seems so pointless but I know I can't sit still and wait.

"I've got to go in today. I'll make arrangements for someone else to take my classes for a couple of days. We'll put a dent in some of this stuff." Zeke rubs on my hair and consoles me before pulling away and using his thumb to wipe away my tears. We lie in the bed on our sides facing each other without speaking for what seems like a long while but is actually only moments. Before I can catch myself, I hear, "I love you, Zeke. I love you so much."

The man doesn't reply. Instead, he gives me the faintest of smiles and a soft kiss on the lips. "You want a cup of coffee?" he asks as he turns away and sits up on the side of the bed.

"Yes," is all I say, wishing I had not shared my feelings. I'm pissed, not angry, pissed. This man thinks it's okay to claim my bed in front of the entire world but he doesn't love me. I started this thing between us. Yes, "thing." That's what it is. I don't know what else to call it. I started it, but I did ask to enter his home and he invited me into his bed. So, now he feels it's okay for him to climb in my bed when he damn well pleases. God, why did I say those words? I'm so angry. No, pissed. I watch him as he returns with my coffee. It's just the way I like it. Dark with a touch of cream but not too sweet, like Zeke, actually. Oh goodness, help me.

Zeke sits down on the edge of the bed with his back toward me. "Listen, I was thinking, if it's okay with you, I'd like to bring some things over and stay with you for a while."

I want to say "sure" but instead I say, "That's not necessary, Zeke. I'll be okay here. I need some time alone."

He looks over his shoulder and studies me for a moment and I do my best not to let him see how pissed and hurt I am about his rejection.

"I wish you'd let me stay with you, Hannah. I don't think you should be by yourself just yet."

I make myself smile and boy is it hard. "I'm a big girl and I've got a good alarm system because I am a little scary," I tell him.

The discussion ends and I am in my house all alone one hour later. The feeling of despair that has been lurking the past two days draws closer and I move with purpose to fight it off. The call to Aunt Alise's lawyer, Caroline Gray, lifts my spirits a bit. She agrees that I should give Dana as little money as possible until she settles in a safe place and encourages me to file a report with Child Protective Services. Caroline tells me she will get back with me on the attorney recommendations after she's done some checking and talks to fellow attorneys.

I call and set up an appointment with Child Protective Services. Later in the morning, Shantrell shows up and starts picking up the house and pulling out cleaning supplies. "I noticed things needed to be freshened up some after we were all here yesterday. It's not bad and shouldn't take me long."

I try to talk her out of cleaning but she says she's already got her housework done and needs to stay busy. It dawns on me that I was not the only one to form an attachment to "Angel Baby" as Shantrell and sometimes Zeke call Dora. I accept the help and the company and I am pleased to have both.

--

Zeke makes no attempt to stay with me but he does take off work to help me with my list. Attorney Gray emails me the names and a bit of information on two family law attorneys in the area, but I select an attorney based on a recommendation from one of Zeke's colleagues. Zeke and I visit the Seaside Police Department and get advice on our best courses of action. Zeke and Mykol meet with a high ranking official in the Berkeley Police Department. Shantrell gathers a list of possible facilities where Dana might give birth but there are far too many to track on a daily basis. Brianna works up a flyer but we hold off on printing and distribution because I have a strong feeling Dana will contact me soon. I have money that belongs to her.

Chapter 17: The List

My mother comes into town on Friday evening for a quick turnaround trip. She says because of my Aunt Alise's illness she hadn't been able to get out to the coast to check on my grandmother. So Miriam is here to see about Granny and let the staff at the home see her and remember that she's still on the job as my grandmother's guardian daughter, a job she takes very seriously.

I'm glad to have my mother here but I don't want to be bothered. I think that's called ambivalence. I half-heartedly prepared for her visit. I've got fresh flowers in the guest room. I did a good sprucing up of the house to make sure things were up to an acceptable standard, her standard that is. I picked up a few of her favorite food items: a fresh basil plant, liverwurst, some Old World Black Bread, a package of Vermont Cheddar, and a couple of bottles of Chardonnay. I don't buy too many items because my mother loves to grocery shop and she'll want to purchase items from her favorite markets in Seaside and around the entire peninsula.

--

The timing of this visit from my mother is inconvenient as is everything in my life right now. For the past few weeks I've been dealing with an insurance claim on one of the properties I manage. The owner's of this particular house are working and living in the United Arab Emirates and I have their power of attorney to act on their behalf in regards to the home.

Most of the claims adjusters I deal with are professional and straight forward. I understand their hesitancy about working with me when there is a question of coverage. However, I do not speak for my clients but convey their wishes and find myself fairly short tempered when my homeowners or tenants are inconvenienced for no good reason.

A short six months ago I would stand in the bull's eye and allow the homeowners, the tenants, and the adjusters to throw daggers at me and I would barely flinch, no matter how unreasonable or unresponsive one of them might be. I no longer have the patience for wanton stupidity, the power hungry, or tantrums.

The adjuster on this particular claim obviously does not have enough to keep him busy. Yes, I find that hard to believe also since he works for one of the nation's largest insurance companies. For reasons I do not clearly understand, Mr. Peevey has decided to test me. I've dealt with him before, just over a year ago, and he was difficult as he wielded his power over the situation but this time I am out of patience.

Three weeks ago, my tenants returned home from a weekend trip to find every window in their home broken. The tenants immediately called the police and filed a police report and then they called me. I reported the incident to the insurance company and visited the property personally. Needless to say the tenants were angry, frightened, and distraught. The police had already taken the information for their report and left by the time I arrived.

I had no choice but to contact my clients in the Emirates in order to get information on the windows which were installed only three years ago. Based on the damages, the tenant spent two nights in a hotel and in order to mitigate the damages, I had Jay board up the windows with plywood until the company that originally installed the windows could get to them.

Mr. "Adjuster" Peevey has done everything but issue the $19,733.72 check to cover the new windows and the cost to mitigate the damages. He has investigated though. "Who knew you'd be away for the weekend?" "Who has a problem with you?" "Any problems on either of your jobs?" "Does your daughter hang out with a rough crowd?" "She's a pretty girl. Any bullying going on? Any altercations over boys?" "Do you get along with the neighbors?"

I guess we're just waiting for him to make an arrest before he issues the check. This crap has been going on for over three weeks and I've had my fill of it. Two days before my mother's arrival I spoke with Mr. Peevey's manager who told me she would need to talk to the adjuster and review the claim and would get back to me but I haven't heard a word and I am not a satisfied customer.

So it really is not the best time for my mother to visit. It is not like she will allow me to go about my business while she is in town. Miriam is what you might call a fireball but upon her arrival, she is more sedate than normal. There is no list and I am amazed. I pick her up at two thirty in the afternoon and wait the remainder of the day and night for the list but it does not show. Usually, my mother starts reciting what I call "the AD list" before we complete our hello hug but not this time. The AD list consists of the things she needs to **Accomplish** and the things I need to **Do** during her stay.

I find my mother far too quiet and I don't like it. I realize that the fireball comforts me. That's what I'm accustomed to. This quiet somewhat passive behavior has me thinking my mother is worried about something. I begin to worry also. Could she have come to town to tell me she's ill? For her to come all this way, she'd have to be really sick, sick like Aunt Alise. I need that damn AD list.

Brianna drives down and she, my mother, and I spend most of Saturday with my grandmother. I know the staff at the care home is glad to see us leave at the end of the day. Although my mother did not have an AD list for me she did, however, have a list for the care home staff. It was a checklist to be precise, one she had downloaded from an online site with a list of all the things to look for in and questions to ask the staff of your loved one's care facility. Miriam had addressed every issue on that checklist by the time we left my grandmother. I think Granny was even happy to see us get up out of there.

We get Brianna on her way back home early Sunday morning and I accompany my mother to Friendly Baptist Church. As usual, she tries to make me feel guilty because I don't attend on a regular basis and she does get upset when I tell her I find it hard to sit and listen to things I don't believe week after week. I'm surprised she doesn't ask me what exactly are these things I don't believe and I'm fortunate to avoid a heated discussion in which she will do all the talking and tear my behind to pieces.

After church we meet Miss Mel and Shantrell at the Breakfast Club and have a nice leisurely meal. "Where is that good-looking son of yours, Mel? I sure expect to see him while I'm here?" My mother tells Miss Mel.

"I'll tell him to stop by if he shows up this evening. He usually spends some time with us on the weekend. I didn't see him yesterday so I'm sure he'll be by today." Miss Mel responds.

Later in the day, I fight off each urge to peep out my front window in an attempt at spotting Zeke's vehicle next door. If I do see the vehicle, I'll start waiting for him to arrive at my door and be disappointed if he doesn't. I'm not surprised when he fails to make an appearance. This is my mother's last night in town and she manages to get quieter. I am aware of her watching me and certain she's now on alert to see how I feel about the absent Zeke. I want to say, "Don't worry about it, Mom. This is par for the course with me and Zeke," but that might cause the real Miriam to rear her opinionated head and tell me just how to handle Mr. Ezekiel Melancon. That is a lecture I can do without.

--

I don't sleep well and it has nothing to do with Dora or Ezekiel, well almost nothing. Mainly it's the doggone insurance claim. I spoke with Mr. Peevey's manager five days ago, but I haven't heard a word from her regarding the resolution of the claim. I should not have to spend my time and energy trying to get this company to pay out a claim they owe and will definitely pay out eventually. It makes no sense for them to inconvenience their customers in this manner. The problem is I'm not their customer and neither is the tenant. Their contract is with the homeowner but I am the homeowner's legal representative. I could call the homeowners and have them apply pressure but that makes me less effective as a property manager. It's my job to handle this situation and by the time I rise from my bed I've concluded I will handle it.

"Jess Gringham," how may I help you?" Finally, after fifteen minutes on hold, the director of Mr. Peevey's section comes on the line. To be fair, I didn't have to remain on hold. The person I spoke with offered to have the section director return my call, but I'm far to wired up to wait for a call.

"Mr. Gringham, my name is Hannah Jacobs and I am the property manager for a home which your company insures." My mother enters the room with two cups of coffee and sits one down in front of me. I nod a thank you but she doesn't leave the room, choosing to stand in the doorway and openly listen to my call.

The section director proceeds to explain their company policy of not discussing claims with property managers and I explain for the umpteenth time that I have a current power of attorney on file. I then explain the reason for my call. The director listens patiently until I complete my complaint and then proceeds to tell me that Mr. Peevey is one of his best claims adjusters but promises to review the case and get back to me.

"Mr. Gringham, I spoke with Mr. Peevey's manager, a Mrs. Chavez, five days ago. She said she'd get back with me also. I have not heard from her. My client carries a fire policy which includes the glass breakage endorsement. That endorsement covers vandalism. Your adjuster has had the police report for over two weeks. This situation is unacceptable. My clients paid a partial payment on those windows which was substantial and far exceeds the one hundred dollar deductible. They need their money and so does the small business that installed the windows. You represent a large profitable company and there is no good reason for the payout on this claim to take this long.

"I manage twelve additional properties insured by your company. Some of those homeowners switched from their old carrier to your company based on my recommendation. You see, up until last year, all of my experiences with your company had been very satisfying. I have no desire to inform the homeowners of my other twelve properties of the circumstances regarding the handling of this claim. I personally insist each of the properties I manage have the glass breakage endorsement. If that endorsement is useless, I need to advise my clients to get rid of it. Also, I need to find a company that will provide the coverage your company claims to provide but does not."

"Now, Miss Jacobs, I'm sure we are moving on this as quickly as we possibly can. Please, let's not over react," Mr. Gringham stutters.

"Mr. Gringham, if you think what I just promised is over reacting then listen to this. I have dealt with Mr. Peevey before and he was difficult and impressed me as sexist but maybe he simply does not care for me. In any case, this claim increases my poor view of the man. I'm sure he prioritizes claims based on the gender, age, and most likely the race of the person he is dealing with. So you need to know that I have thoroughly documented this entire claims process. If my clients do not receive the full and correct payment for this loss in their account within the next forty eight hours I will personally ask each of my clients insured with your company to switch carriers and I will write a letter to your executive branch with a very detailed description as to why they have lost thirteen fire policies on the peninsula in a matter of one month. Mr. Gringham, this conversation will be included in that correspondence."

"There's no reason to make threats, Miss Jacobs. Mrs. Chavez, Mr. Peevey, or I will call you today. Is it alright if we call this evening?"

"I would prefer you or Mrs. Chavez call. I don't want to talk with Mr. Peevey."

"Yes, ma'am, I understand completely and thank you for the heads up. It's customers like you that keep us on our toes. We will definitely get back with you this evening and if you have any further problems, you feel free to call me. That's what I'm here for."

"Thank you, Mr. Gringham. I appreciate you taking the time to listen and look forward to hearing from you later today."

I am exhausted when I put my phone down. I look and see my mother still standing there in the doorway. I had forgotten she was there.

"That was some power play, baby. When did you learn to play hard ball. You've changed, Hannah. It's good to see you throwing your weight around a little. Handle your business, baby, handle your business," Mom says as she turns to leave the room.

Chapter 18: Tag Team

I'm not sure why, but my parents are tag teaming me. Just three days after my mother leaves, I receive a call from my father who will be in town the very next day for a visit. I can't help but wonder what has brought this decision on but I don't question him, because I certainly don't want him to feel unwelcome.

When I pick my father up from the Monterey Regional Airport, he exits the terminal with the look of a man who has had a long, difficult, and unhappy life. I had been looking forward to seeing him but I feel only sadness now that he is in my presence. My father, William, and his, sister, Alise, were the only two children of my paternal grandparents. I can only guess at the pain my father may feel after the loss of Alise. Sister and brother were close and loved each other dearly.

The conversation from the airport to my home is a bit strained which is unusual because my dad usually does most of the talking. Like I mentioned before, I am not a talker. But today, Dad is quiet and has little to say. I finally ask, "What's wrong, Dad? You are so quiet."

"Oh, it's nothing really, baby. This whole situation with your cousin on top of losing Alise is worrying me. It was pretty disturbing when Dana refused to speak to me on the phone. I had no idea she felt that way about me. I tried to be there for her just like I was with you all, but Dana made it hard to love her and I guess I just let her go. I always figured you and Brianna were here for her if she needed you. I had no idea how much of a burden she would become. I know Alise did not expect you to have to deal with so much trouble from Dana either. She never stopped telling me how much she appreciated what you've done for Dana and her baby but she felt guilty too."

My father continues looking out the window on his side of the car. I know he is hiding his watering eyes and wish I could comfort him. He remains quiet for the remainder of the ride to my home. Once we settle down inside, I ask, "Why the sudden visit? Is there something you need to discuss with me and Brianna?"

"No. I had been thinking about coming out for a few weeks and since Dana left with the baby, I wanted to check on you and see how you are doing. I noticed how attached you and the baby were to the each other when you came to Greensboro. To be honest, I was only thinking about coming out until your mother called me. You know she never calls me because she figures her calls upset Tracy. So when she called and said she had visited, it was confirmation that I needed to visit, also. I didn't know about Dana bringing that hoodlum into your home until a few days ago. I'm so sorry we put you in this position, Hannah."

"Come on! I'm okay. I do worry about Dora, and Dana also, but I've got people helping me and I'm certain I will hear from Dana soon because I have money that belongs to her. You had nothing to do with this situation with Dana. I should have followed the advice one of my friends gave me and called Child Protective Services a few days after Dana left Dora with me. I was trying to protect Dana and that may prove to be to the detriment of Dora. You and Aunt Alise had no way of knowing Dana would have a child and leave her with me." I flippantly slap my dad in the shoulder, trying to get him to perk up.

He looks at me with tightly pressed together lips and shakes his head. "Hannah, when I think of all the responsibility we left you with. I mean, your grandmother, Dana, the houses, it was too much and yet you have handled it like a queen. All those years fretting over you and you were more capable than all of us." My father finally smiles.

I lean back on the sofa next to him and put my head on his shoulder as he wraps an arm around mine. "What do you want for dinner?" I ask.

"How 'bout I take you out," Dad says, sounding more upbeat.

"You're my guest. I'm supposed to feed you. Granny always said that you should not allow people to travel to your home without providing a good meal for them. She'd say the guest has already spent money traveling and has the expense of being away from home."

"Your grandmother was right but also she came up in a time when people had so few resources that we had to have certain rules of etiquette about food, not that many people paid much attention. I had a group of cousins that would visit all the time. No sooner than one would leave with two or three children, one of the others would show up with a family of three or more. My parents always provided the first few meals but after that they started making my cousins contribute. They never stayed long after my parents started asking them to help buy the groceries. Me and Alise always hated to see them leave because we loved having our young cousins around to play with." These memories seem to lift my father's spirits and I see the old gleam returning to his eyes.

"Thinking about your cousins makes you happy, doesn't it, Dad?"

"Actually, being here with you makes me happy. I was worried about you. Let's go eat. Where are you taking me?"

I know my stepmother dislikes exotic foods but Dad loves them. "When was the last time you had some good Thai?" I ask.

"Probably the last time I was here. We eat pretty simple food at home."

"Let's try Baan's. I like their food and the place is not too busy this early in the evening."

The drive to the restaurant is more animated than the drive to my house had been. My father is now going through his ritual of discussing all the sights of our little town as I drive down Obama Way, also named Broadway, to Fremont Boulevard. He comments on just about every old building on the drag. "I need to go into The Hair Company and get my hair cut while I'm in town. Is Old Willie still working there?"

"I don't go there for anything, Dad, but you can call and find out."

He goes quiet for a few minutes and continues taking in the sights. "I sure do miss Mom's. She had the best chittlins and sweet potato pie I've had anywhere. I would have thought one of her children would have taken that restaurant over."

I smile. "I'm pretty sure they all had their own professions. Do you and Tracy ever cook chittlins at home?" I'm being mischievous with this question because I know neither my father nor my stepmother like to spend time in the kitchen and only cook the most basic fare. I think, for this reason alone, my father still carries a slow burning torch for my mother.

"No, me and Tracy don't cook much of anything." My father doesn't realize I am kidding with him and the way he answers makes me feel sorry for him. I'm relieved that we've arrived at the little Thai restaurant. I know the food is good and a good meal will free our minds for a time.

The restaurant is nearly empty and we are barely inside when I spot Deidra at a table all the way in the back of the little place. No sooner than I recognize her, I zone in on the head of the person sitting at the table with his back to us. That head can only belong to one of two people, Budrow or Ezekiel Melancon and it is not Budrow. I now know what people mean when they say they were stunned. My father sees my stricken look and immediately follows my gaze. Once he sees Deidra, he yells out, "Hey, there's Dee," overjoyed at seeing his favorite of any of our old school friends. "Hey, Dee!" Dad shouts and waves as he moves with purpose toward Deidra and her dinner date.

Deidra looks up with mutual joy and returns the greeting. "Mr. Jacobs, how are you?"

I reluctantly follow my father to their table as I try to gather my composure and not look and act as if I'm a jealous wreck. Deidra rises from the table and I stifle a gasp when I see the top she wears under her opened cropped cardigan. The black bustier top is doing a lousy job of covering her breasts. I'm certain two thirds of the melon-shaped orbs are pushing out of the top of the garment. She looks good and very sexy. I hope this is not what she wears during her speech therapy sessions because if it is, I would think most of her male clients leave speechless. Deidra and my father embrace and she kisses him on the cheek as he pats her on the back. I glance at Zeke who appears to be caught completely off guard at seeing my father and me.

When my father and Deidra finish with the love fest and separate, Dad looks over at Zeke, who is now standing, and finally recognizes him. "Hey, man! I didn't know that was you." I can tell by my father's eyes that he is now aware of my discomfort. His eyes dart to my face and back at Zeke's so quickly, I doubt the others even notice his swift assessment. The last time my father saw Zeke, he had flown out to North Carolina to comfort me over the loss of Aunt Alise, now here he sits having dinner with a very seductive Deidra.

"You two know each other?" Deidra looks from my father to Zeke, glowing with a huge smile and clearly happy to see my father. Not waiting for an answer, she turns her glee on me. "Hey, Hannah. Girl, I haven't said a word to you. It's just been so long since I saw your dad. He hasn't changed a drop."

I smile but say nothing.

After shaking my father's hand, Zeke turns, looks directly in my eyes, and gives me a little smile. "Hey Hannah," he says as he searches my face. "Would you guys like to join us? We haven't ordered our dinner yet, just drinks?" Zeke pulls his eyes from me and looks at my father.

Dad looks at me but before he can say anything, Deidra says, "Oh please join us. It'll be so nice to catch up with you, Mr. Jacobs."

Now my father is completely in tune with my vibe and knows I have no desire to join this particular couple. "Look, we would join you but I just got here and Hannah and I need to talk a little family business, but I sure appreciate the invitation." My father smiles from Deidra to Zeke and back. "I'm going to be here until Wednesday morning. So give Hannah a call and maybe we can get together for coffee or breakfast before I leave. I haven't mentioned it to Hannah yet but I'm going to see if I can talk her into taking a drive up to Sacramento to see Brianna and the family." Dad could win an award for this performance. He looks over at me as if he is pleading for me to say yes about visiting Brianna.

Zeke has been watching me the entire time and asks, "You sure you don't want to join us, Hannah?" I get the impression he really wants us to join them but maybe that's what I want to believe.

"No, you two enjoy your dinner. Me and Dad need to talk. It's been awhile." I give Zeke a fake smile. "Try the chicken satay; it's the best in the area. Nice seeing you both."

"I've heard this food is delicious. Zeke has mentioned it to me a couple of times, so I couldn't wait to finally get here." Deidra gushes and hugs my dad again. "It's so good to see you Mr. Jacobs. I'll try to get by before you leave."

"It's good to see you too, baby," My father pulls free and follows me to a table all the way at the front of the restaurant, as

far away from those two as possible. I grab a chair facing the door.
I do not want to see them.

Once we take our seats my dad glances toward Deidra and
Zeke. "Deidra has changed quite a bit since the last time I saw her.
That was only a few years ago up at Brianna's place."

"Humph. Yeah she's changed alright. She's bigger."

"Bigger?" My father says looking confused.

"Up top, Dad, she had a boob job," I say, with my spiteful side
showing its ugly head.

Dad glances back toward Deidra and Zeke's table with both
his mouth and eyes open slightly wider. "Oh, oh, I didn't even
notice."

"Yeah, right, there is no way on earth you could miss those
girls. You'd have to have lost all your senses."

My father chuckles and then takes on a serious air. "You
okay?" he asks.

"I'm fine, Dad; I'm fine."

"You want to leave, baby? We can go somewhere else."

"I'm fine, Dad. Don't worry about it."

"I'm guessing you were surprised to see that guy here with
Deidra," my father says hesitantly.

"No, I wasn't expecting to see them here but it's no big deal,"
I fib.

My father reaches across the table and grasps my two hands,
which I have clasped together on the tabletop. He looks concerned
now and I can tell he's going into his protective mode. "Okay
Hannah, I'm just following your lead."

"It's no big deal, Dad, really it's not."

"If you say it's not, it's not." Dad looks me in my eyes and
smiles and I feel better.

Well needless to say, my appetite has diminished significantly.
My mouth was watering for Thai before we arrived but not now. I
can hear the shrill of Deidra's laughter over my shoulder and the
deep vibration of Zeke's baritone mumblings.

My father and I take the advice I dealt the cozy couple to the
rear and order the satay plus some steamed mussels for starters.
Then I go with the spicy chili basil with chicken and my father
orders the garlic and pepper with beef. As we talk and get deeper

into our conversation, I manage to take my mind off of Zeke. It helps that Deidra has stopped giggling. Once our food arrives, we eat quickly because I want to leave the restaurant before Zeke and Deidra to prevent the possibility of a long drawn out goodbye with the couple.

When we get back to my house, we call Brianna and tell her we plan to visit the next day but won't be leaving Seaside until about noon. This way she and her family will have time to attend church service and go out to lunch before our arrival. Brianna sounds happy that I'm bringing Dad up and she says she will have David throw some steaks on the grill.

Once we finalize our plans for the two day trip to Sacramento, I tell my father about the list of actions we plan for finding Dana and Dora and what we have learned so far. I give him a breakdown on what we've done and who has done what. Dad seems impressed with our efforts but a bit perplexed. "So the cat that's out with Deidra tonight is putting a lot of effort into helping you locate my nieces?"

"Yeah, I guess you could say that."

"Your mother told me that you were thinking about hiring a private detective to try and find Dana. That can be a pretty costly proposition. I've talked to Tracy and told her that I would like to pay those costs. Alise left me with some money, totally unexpected and to be honest, I don't need it. I will probably just invest it and, hopefully, watch it grow. I can't think of any better use for those funds than finding my nieces."

"Thanks, Dad. I'm trying to wait a while longer before we go that route. Like you said, detectives are expensive."

"Well just let me know if and when you decide that's the route you want to take. Now, what's going on between you and this guy?" Dad moves on to the next topic. "I was kind of under the impression you two were a couple when he flew his mother and sister out to Alise's funeral. I have to admit, I was blown away by the consideration he showed you and our family."

I think for a moment and have to admit, "Zeke's been here for me with all this craziness with Dora taking Dana. He's been a big help. From the very beginning he was the one who recommended Shantrell as a sitter and tried to talk me into reporting Dana to

CPS. I only took half of his advice but wish I had taken it all. Their whole family has helped me at one time or another. They've all been really supportive."

My father gives me a somewhat solemn look before saying, "I'm glad to hear that you've had good people close by with all you've had to deal with. I won't worry so much about you being all alone here. I know Brie is just up the road but I still worry about you."

"You don't need to worry. I don't feel alone, not anymore."

Dad nods his head as if he felt that last comment, then says, "I asked you earlier if it was a shock to see Zeke in the restaurant with Deidra."

"Well, Zeke and Deidra used to date, so maybe." I stop myself. I do not want to speak a situation into existence. "It was a bit of a shock but it's not like he and I have any type of a serious relationship. I like him. I'm not going to deny that I like him and sometimes I think he likes me too."

"Only sometimes, baby?"

"Yeah, Dad, only sometimes. I don't really know. Sometimes he's here and sometimes he's not. He hasn't said anything that would lead me to expect more."

"I'll be honest with you. When he showed up for your aunt's funeral, I thought he was ready to propose. He sure looked like a man in love to me."

I shake off my father's words. Dad loves me but I know he doesn't want to give me false hope. "You know Zeke's mother and sister live just next door. Shantrell and I have become very close."

"Listen, I don't want anybody mistreating my child. I was pretty impressed with that young man when he showed up in Greensboro. I'm not going to lie; I'm a little disappointed in him now."

I give my dad a dry smile. "You think you're disappointed."

"Ah, baby girl, I shouldn't be stoking your fire. Don't get your feelings hurt until you know what's really going on. Don't jump to any conclusions because I got the impression he was much more concerned with you than he was with Deidra back there at the restaurant."

There's a straw and I have to grab it and hold on. "You think, Dad?"

"That's what I saw. Whatever he says it is, if he says anything, take it for what it's worth. You know time reveals all. And I tell you one thing, Deidra couldn't call him out about the way he was looking at you. She kept laughing the whole time but that man asked you, specifically, to join them. His only thought was what you wanted, not Deidra. If she was offended by his behavior toward you, she knew better than to let him know it. So, you just work easy, baby girl. If he's for you, it will work out."

"So you don't think he's a low life?"

Dad chuckles. "I don't know enough about him, Hannah, to know what he is, I really don't. And I'm not here in town long enough to get a true feel for the man so it would be hard and unwise for me to judge him. I'm your father, so I'd like to sit down with the man and ask him what his intentions are.

"Dad!"

"I'm just telling you the truth but I understand. You don't feel you two have that type of commitment to each other so I won't ask him anything like that but I know you have sense enough to take the entire situation into consideration and make a good decision about him or any other man who steps up to you. Just give things some time."

"I will, Dad."

--

Granny gives my father a big kiss and holds his hand during our entire visit with her. She actually seems to recognize him and smiles nonstop though she does not speak. We stay with her until her lunchtime and leave her home headed to Brianna's.

Alise and LD act as if Santa Claus has come to town when they see their grandfather. They do love him dearly but the stash of twenties he will leave with each of them probably adds to their excitement. We arrive just twenty minutes after the family comes in from grocery shopping. Brianna looks tired and I know she's had very little time to rest. Just last week, she made that quick one day turn around trip to see my mother in Seaside. The week before she and David drove down because Dana had taken Dora and now

Dad and I show up on her. The fact that she went shopping for groceries on a Sunday is testimony of how swamped she has been.

Dinner will be the simplest affair possible with grilled pork chops, grilled asparagus, a tossed salad and some baked potatoes. I get the salad and asparagus prepared while Brianna seasons the chops and washes the potatoes. David and Dad go out back and set up the grill. After dinner is well prepped we sit and have a leisurely visit.

The conversation with family is pleasant and we manage to stay away from the subject of Dana but not Dora. Out of the blue, LD starts laughing about how funny Dora was on Fourth of July weekend when she was so excited about finding her balance and started walking around the yard. Alise and LD take turns mimicking Dora and LD goes so far as to plop down on his butt, clap his hands excitedly, and grin real big just like Dora did that evening. I manage to laugh along with the rest of my family. I don't even come close to crying when Alise hugs me later in the evening and says, "I sure miss Dora, Auntie. When is she coming back to stay with you?"

I hug her back, return the smile, and say, "I don't know, baby. That's up to your Cousin Dana. Hopefully, we will see her soon."

"Where do they live? Mom says somewhere near Oakland. Maybe we can go see them sometimes," LD speculates.

"Maybe when they get settled," I tell my young nephew.

"Okay, that's enough about Dora for now. You two need to get in there and finish up that kitchen. The floor needs to be swept and the counters need to be wiped down." Brianna dictates.

"I already wiped the counters, Mom," LD complains.

Brianna simply gives him "the look" and he turns and follows his sister into the kitchen without another word.

We adults settle back and enjoy more conversation. This is the best visit I've had with my father in years and I think Brianna feels the same because this is my father's first visit without my stepmother, Tracy, since they married a little over five years ago. Tracy is not a horrible person. She's not a bad person. She is, however, a bit jealous and wants to be considered in all things at all times. Brianna and I have to act like we love her as much as we love our father which of course is not the case. We do our best to make Tracy happy because we want our father to be comfortable and not stay away. As much as Tracy requires from Brianna and I, she gives back to my brother, Bill. She fawns over him like he is royalty and gets slightly upset when we treat him like he is a mere commoner like the rest of us. The funny thing is, Bill likes her no more than Brianna and I. Sadly, the three of us only tolerate Tracy.

Brianna and the family leave me and Dad at home with each other on Monday morning. Brianna takes the afternoon off work and we take my father out to Thunder Valley Casino for a little black jack. My father loves to gamble and he and Brianna always slip off and spend a few hours in the casino whenever he visits. I seldom accompany them but this time I decide to try my hand at the slots. We leave the casino up three hundred and forty five dollars, with Brianna being the only one who lost money. Dad spends most of his winnings taking the family out to dinner.

--

Miss Mel and Shantrell come over and keep me and my father company the evening before he leaves. It is at this point that I realize Zeke has not called my number since I ran into him at that restaurant with Deidra. He hasn't called to explain why he was out to dinner with his old flame. He hasn't made an effort to see me or talk to me. I haven't heard from him and I haven't called him either. I'm proud of myself because when I walked out of that restaurant I thought, *Just wait until I get a hold of him.* Then I thought, *You don't have a reason to get a hold of him. It's not like he's committed to you in any way.* I expected him to call me. I thought he'd call and try to feel me out, try to find out if I was upset with him or something but I got nothing, not a word. That's okay though. It's going to be alright. My dad said that it's going to be alright and I know that however things turn out, it'll be just fine.

The Melancon women laugh and talk and flirt with my dad hard and he enjoys their company to the fullest. He and Miss Mel talk about old times and although they did not know each other well they knew many of the same people and participated in many of the same functions and events. They laugh so hard at one point that Miss Mel gets off the sofa and gets on her knees when Dad tells a story about a mutual friend who had a reputation as a drunk. They talk about how they used to party and the dances they used to do. Miss Mel says she remembers my father as a jealous man and Dad doesn't deny it. "I think I might have run Miriam off being so jealous but I'm not jealous anymore because I don't want to run off this one I've got now," he jokes.

The conversation takes on a serious note for a moment when Miss Mel mentions Shantrell pulling the gun on the thug to protect me. My father had not heard the details of the altercation and he takes on an angry air during the retelling. Miss Mel realizes she has stepped in it and is telling more than she should. Old girl does an admirable job of emphasizing the victorious side of the story and by the time she tells my father about Shantrell telling the thug not to move and then how we passed the gun behind us to keep it out of the sight of the policeman, Dad is laughing along with her.

After more than two hours, Miss Mel gets up to leave. She gives my father a big long hug. They may not have been friends before tonight but they are buddies now. My father tries to talk her into staying a little longer but she says Zeke is stopping by to pick up dinner and she needs to pack it up for him.

"Well, tell him I said hey," my father tells Miss Mel as she makes her way to the door.

"I sure will and you have a safe trip."

Shantrell stays a little longer laughing and talking with Dad and me. When she leaves, my father looks at me and says, "That girl ain't married?"

"No, Dad, she's not married; she's divorced."

"Wow! That girl there is something. I can't believe nobody has snatched her up."

I look at my father like he must be losing his mind. "Well, I'm not married!" I say passionately.

My father's face turns serious when he says, "Yeah, well, Hannah, you're kind of quiet. I imagine men realize they have to go easy with you. You seem like you'd be very particular. I would think most men would be a little intimidated about approaching you. They would spend a lot of time trying to figure you out. That girl there, she's an open book. She's a live wire. I can't believe nobody – well, I guess she'd have to be careful. You can't just jump up and marry anything that comes along just because they like you. She's a beauty ain't she?"

"She is pretty isn't she, Dad?"

"She's a beauty," my father says just above a whisper as he shakes his head and thinks about the woman who just left my house. Then he looks at me and says, "No prettier than you are though, girl."

"I don't worry about that kind of stuff, Dad"

"I imagine you don't and you shouldn't. I'm so glad you got such good neighbors, Hannah."

"I am too. They have been a big help to me and it's nice to have friends so close by."

By the time I drop my father at the airport the next morning, he is in a much better mood than the one he harbored when I picked him up four days earlier.

Chapter 19: Dick Work

I receive a call from Zeke the day following my father's departure from town. If I didn't know better, I'd think he had been waiting out my father's visit before contacting me. As much as I would like this call to be of a romantic nature, it is better than I could have hoped. Zeke tells me he bribed an agent at the rental car company and has Travis's full name, a driver's license number, and an address. I'm overcome with joy and cannot hide it. Zeke advises me to temper my expectations but I cannot.

"I was thinking about riding up on Sunday and checking the address out. What do you think?" Zeke asks.

What I think is that I can go up there today but I don't want to sound overly anxious. I take down the information and tell Zeke I will get back with him. I call Erika, the one person I know who knows the East Bay well, to ask her if and when she will have time to ride up to Berkeley with me. I explain that I'd like to check out the address and we might need to spend the day. Erika tells me she might be able to take off the very next day, that Friday but if not, she says she's free on Saturday.

So come early Saturday morning, two days following the call from Zeke, Erika, Marshon, and I drive to the Berkeley address Travis used on the rental car contract. We park close enough to the home to see anyone arriving or leaving. The house is situated in a nice neighborhood where all the yards are well maintained and the houses are updated with fresh coats of paint, new siding, upgraded roofing systems and more. The neighborhood is definitely upper middle class.

We sit for several hours before we see any movement from the home. A middle-aged white woman, who looks nothing like anyone we would expect, exits the home at about one thirty in the afternoon. My heart sinks because I am certain Dana and Dora are not living in this home.

We discuss the situation and decide to use the direct approach. I march up to the door and knock. A tall slender black man, who looks to be about my parent's age, opens the door with a pleasant smile on his face.

"What can I do for you?" the man asks.

"Hello, sir. I'm looking for a Mr. Travis Ransom."

A frown washes across the man's face. "I'm Travis Ransom," he says, displaying no trace of the pleasant man who answered.

I hope Dana's Travis has not stolen this man's identity; if that is the case, this will be a dead end. Then the slowly illuminating lights of my mind become strong and bright. "Mr. Ransom, is it possible that you have a relative named Travis also?" I ask.

The man's face goes stone cold and he starts to close the door on me. Without thinking, I yell, "Please help me, sir!"

My outburst is effective. It stops the man from closing the door on me. "What do you want with Travis?" he asks belligerently.

I try to explain in as few words as possible that I'm not looking for Travis and don't want to cause him any trouble. I tell the man that my cousin left my home with Travis a few weeks prior and that I am very worried about the young child they had with them.

"Is it your child?"

"No sir, she's my cousin's child but Dana left the child with me for months without a word. She showed up about six weeks ago, pregnant with another child. She got angry with me and left with Dora and I haven't heard from them since. My cousin can be fairly irresponsible and I just want to make sure she and the baby are okay. I'm particularly concerned about the child."

The man looks at me doubtfully so I babble on. "My cousin's mother died about two months ago. She lived in North Carolina but she and Dana had not been in close contact for years. Now, my father, my sister and brother, and I are the only family Dana and Dora have besides each other. We would be letting my aunt down if we didn't do our best for them, especially for the baby."

"You say your cousin's pregnant again and she's with Travis."

"The last time I saw her she was with Travis, at least that's what she called him."

"Travis and I don't see each other but his mother hears from him every once in awhile. He stays somewhere over in Frisco. If you leave me your number, I'll call you if I hear anything."

"Oh thank you, Mr. Ransom." I pull out a business card and hand it to the man and wonder if I should tell him more. "I don't know if it means anything to you but my cousin is about six months pregnant. She told me that Travis is the father of the child she is carrying. Do you know if he mentioned becoming a father to your wife?" I see what I believe is hope in the man's face.

"No. I haven't heard anything like that. This would be a first," the man says and ventures a smile.

I smile back and reach to shake his hand. "Thank you for talking to me Mr. Ransom and please call me if you learn anything that will help me find my cousins."

"I'll do that, Miss." He looks at my card before continuing. "Miss Jacobs," he says with a courteous nod.

I walk down the walkway of the Ransom home with hope. I know this man wants to help me. He wants to know if he will soon be a grandfather by way of the son who has most likely caused him so much disappointment. This is a strong connection to Dana and thus Dora. I hope to hear from the Ransoms very soon.

I get back to the car and relay my conversation with Mr. Ransom to Erika and Marshon who share my excitement. "Hot damn we did some real private dick work here, didn't we ladies?" Marshon boasts. We decide to celebrate at Rick and Ann's, one of Erika's favorite eateries, before heading back home.

Once we place our orders, I step outside to call Zeke. I'm a little nervous because I never got back to him about Sunday and I have left him out of my plans all together. I know this is a slight and I regret the way I've handled it but I did not want to wait until he had the time to come up to Berkeley and check out the address even if it was only one more day.

"Hey," he answers his phone and does not sound at all thrilled about the call.

"Hi, guess where I am?" I say, trying to sound happy about a situation that I'm certain will piss him off.

"I don't think I can. That might take all day and I don't have that kind of time I'm in the middle of grading." There is no joy in Zeke's voice and I consider telling him to call me later when he's not so busy but I know it's best to take my medicine and get it over.

"I couldn't wait so I got Erika and Marshon to drive up to Berkeley with me this morning. I met that guy's father. His parents live at that address."

There is dead silence on the phone. "Zeke, you there?"

"So did you get everything you need?" he asks with even less excitement in his voice. I think I may have really screwed this up as far as Zeke is concerned.

"Well, he couldn't give me any information but says his wife talks to the son once in awhile. So I left my name and number and he promised to contact me if he gets any info on Dana and Dora."

Zeke does not say another word so I continue. "Well, I just wanted to tell you what happened and thank you again for getting that information for me. It was a big help," I mumble.

"Yeah," Zeke responds.

"I'll let you get back to work," I say as my throat begins to tighten with fear. I wonder if Zeke is too angry to talk to me, is he back with Deidra and finished with me, or simply finished with me. He is so cold.

"Take care," he says and the phone goes dead.

When I get back to the table my friends look at me with anticipation. "What did Zeke say?" Erika asks.

"Not too much. I think he might be pissed with me. I didn't tell him I was coming up here. He offered to drive me up tomorrow and I told him I'd get back to him but I never did."

Marshon asks, "Why didn't you want him to drive you up here? Are you tired of him already?"

"Of course not. I don't spend enough time with him to get tired of him. I didn't want to wait one more day. If you two hadn't come with me, I would have come alone. I can't stand this sitting around waiting for something to happen when I can take some action. I just hope he's not too angry. He did not sound happy."

"What did he say?" Marshon asks as she bites down into some cornmeal pancakes.

I look from her to Erika and say, "Basically, nothing. He asked if I found everything I wanted or needed or something like that and that was it. I thanked him again and he said yeah and for me to take care."

"That doesn't sound good. Oh, you hurt his wittle feelings. He'll get over it; just give him some time. He's a big boy," Erika advises.

I sure hope Erika, who is usual the cynic of our group, is right about Zeke. I don't want to lose him as a friend.

--

Two weeks later all hope is gone as I lie in my bed with the covers pulled up to my neck. There has been no sign or word of Dana and Dora. Not one ray of hope beams down through the dreary days of my life. My allies have stopped calling daily to check in and I haven't heard from Zeke since I ditched him for my girlfriends on the Berkeley trip.

I can think of no further action in the hunt for my cousin and her child. We've decided to hire a private investigator if we have no additional information in the next two weeks. We've posted hard copies of the flyers around the Bay Area and asked all our friends to post them on their Facebook pages. I have little faith in the web. We sent out messages to Dana on the web when Alise died and had no luck.

I lie in my bed and think about the hopelessness of all this. I'm having a hard time focusing on anything but my search. The ringing of my doorbell only upsets me. I don't want to be bothered, not even with Shantrell who always makes me feel better. I don't want to feel better. I don't think I'll answer. My car is in the garage so there is no tale-tell sign that I'm at home. I lie very still hoping whoever is at my door goes away and after another minute, I'm certain they have. Then the damn doorbell rings again, urgently this time, like three rings in a row, as if the asshole knows I'm in here. I am not answering.

My cell phone starts ringing. It's Zeke. I refuse to answer. Now the person at the door starts to bang, hard. I give in and go to the door. Sure enough, it's the man I love. "I got you a present," he tells me. He hasn't called me in over two weeks and I thought for certain he had dumped me but here he stands telling me he has a present for me. I see nothing in his hands. I don't respond but step back so he can enter the house.

"Why are you closed up in this house so late on a Saturday? It's a beautiful day out, a little brisk but it feels good once you start moving."

I walk into the kitchen, open the frig, grab a bottle of water, and kick the door closed as I take a drink. "I'm wondering what happened to the present I don't see," I tell him with all the snarkiness I feel.

"Get dressed and I'll show it to you. Come on. Get dressed." Zeke takes his usual half seat on a barstool looking way to upbeat in my opinion.

"I'm not going out today." I plop down on the sofa with my bottle of water. I look at my house slippers and the horrific pajama bottoms, remnants of a pair I've had since high school, and I know I look a mess but I don't care.

"Come on, Hannah. Don't spoil this for me. It took me forever to find the perfect one for you."

"What is it, Zeke?"

He looks at me and smiles that perfect smile of his. I wonder if his teeth are false. They are far too perfect. Damn if he doesn't get better looking every time I see him. What's that Janet Jackson said in that song, "That's the Way Love Goes."

"It's a surprise. Get dressed. It won't take too long," Zeke pressures me.

"It better not." I rise to do as I'm bid, all the fight gone.

"You know those little stretchy pants you wear to walk in? Put a pair of those on and some sports shoes."

I stop and turn around. "Are you kidding me! What's going on, Zeke?"

"Come on, babe, let me surprise you. Don't you like surprises?" Zeke pleads as if his life depends on my cooperation.

"Not anymore." I think about Dana leaving Dora with me and what a surprise that was, and then Dana's creepy boyfriend, my aunt's illness and death, Bradley's marriage, and lastly Zeke having dinner with the pair of boobs called Deidra. No, I've had my fill of surprises. If I never have another surprise I would not be the least bit upset. No more surprises for this girl.

Zeke gives me a look of sheer exasperation. He's tired of trying to cajole me and pacify me. Before he showed up at my door, I thought he was tired of me all together and worried I would not see him again, at least not on an intimate level. How much will it hurt me to spend some time with him on his terms? Not at all. I love the man, even if he doesn't love me. Maybe I should make an effort to show him I love him. Well, I won't go that far but I will try to be more cooperative.

I turn and head to my room and get a pair of the little stretchy exercise pants he talked about from my drawer and put on my newest cross-trainers. I run my fingers through my hair. They get caught but I get them through several times for good measure and then I put on a hair band. Zeke looks at me as if I'm dressed for prom night and he's my date when I enter my living room. Sometimes I think he might really have a thing for me.

We jump in his FJ Cruiser and he heads south through Monterey and around the bay into Pacific Grove. Twenty minutes after leaving my house, we stop at Lover's Point. I smile for the first time today when I see Shantrell and her boys. Not far from them, I spot Mykol who throws us a wave. Zeke takes my hand when we exit the vehicle and walks me over to a brand new sea green lady cruiser three speed bike. "Would you ride with me? I had Shantrell and the boys break it in for you."

"Whose bike?" I ask, not sure Zeke means that the bike is mine.

"Yours, this is your present. Come on let's ride a little ways together."

I try to maintain my bad mood but I'm too excited about my new bike. I haven't ridden in years but can't wait to give it a go. Memories of Brianna taking Dana and I on bike rides add to the upturn of the corners of my mouth.

Shantrell scoots up to me. "We're going to have a picnic when we finish riding. I picked out your helmet. Yours has pink daisies and mine has purple tulips. I just rode your bike around a couple of times but other than that I haven't been on a bike in forever so I can't go far. The boys come out here and ride with Zeke and Buddy sometimes."

While me and Shantrell stand around like a couple of old ladies, Zeke, Mykol, and the boys take off and leave us. Shantrell jumps on her bike to hurry after them. I'm wobbling as I get started and finally yell after Shantrell to not leave me. I don't want to be out here riding alone because the kind person who dragged me out here abandoned me. Maybe this is my payback for not taking him to Berkeley.

Shantrell stops and waits for me to slowly peddle up to her. "You okay?" she asks with a grin.

"I'm fine but stay close until I get my riding groove going."

So Shantrell and I ride along at a leisurely pace and take in the scenery we know and love so well. By the time we return to the cars we have ridden a little more than seven miles and I am so proud of myself. I have to admit it was a lot of fun. Not long after we return the guys ride up also. Within five minutes they head off in the opposite direction. I know Shantrell wants to follow them but she stays behind with me. I'm still breathing hard and sweating although it's a cool sixty degrees out.

"I hope they don't go too far," I tell Shantrell.

"They won't. That brother of mine is so competitive, Myk too. I think we made them change their game plan. We need to build our stamina so we can keep up with them. Did you see those sisters checking them out when we first started out?"

I laugh and tell her, "I was puffing too hard to see anything."

I devour my second bottle of water and start on a third. Shantrell looks at me and says, "Baby, you're going to have to get in better shape to keep up with Zeke. He's a sports junkie. I think that's why he and Buddy get along as well as they do. Buddy's a junkie too. They both prefer to play sports than to watch them. Buddy is going to be mad when he finds out we were out here riding today and he missed out."

"Where is Buddy? I haven't seen him lately."

"His new woman has him working two jobs. This is a first and I don't know how she managed it but he's doing it. I think he might actually like Niecy for more than what she can do for him financially or maybe he's just tired of changing up women every six months."

Shantrell and I sit and look out at the water, play with our phones, drink water, and talk. We then move to Mykol's car, where Shantrell uncorks a 2012 bottle of Sterling Merlot and we enjoy some truly smooth grapes. When the inconsiderate men we

have "thangs" for show up along with Caliel and Jameel it has
been well over ninety minutes from the time we all initially took
off on our bikes. All four are hot, sweaty, happy, and Zeke is
cramping. Shantrell and I sit and watch them get water and
casually look at Zeke as he hobbles around and groans. I really
don't care; I'm toasted. I think Sterling might be lying about that
13.5 percent by volume. Eventually, Shantrell produces bananas to
help with Zeke's cramping. He limps back and forth past me and
guzzles water and eats a couple of bananas. I continue to ignore
him because, like I said, I'm toasted and could care less about his
cramping hamstring. He should be happy he beat Mykol to their
stopping point by a good five seconds. Of course Mykol, who is a
year or two younger than Zeke, is not cramping and Zeke's cramps
are giving Mykol great satisfaction.

Finally, Zeke's cramps subside and he's able to sit still. He
gives me a dirty look which I ignore. It's the Merlot. Damn it's
good!

We pull several coolers from the back of Shantrell's car and
spread blankets on the ground before settling in on The Point to
enjoy the picnic she has prepared for us. Shantrell has herb roasted
chicken legs that she marinated for hours before roasting; flat
bread sandwiches made with prosciutto, cranberry pecan goat
cheese she blended, and spring mix; Old Amsterdam Gouda, fresh
dill slices, vegetable chips, sourdough bread, and several types of
homemade cookies. An elderly couple watches us hard with smiles
on their faces. Shantrell puts a sandwich, a chicken leg, cheese, a
pickle slice and two cookies on a plate and offers it to them.

"Oh, we just had lunch not that long ago. We couldn't take
your food," The lady protests as her husband reaches for the plate.

"I'll be insulted if you don't," Shantrell tells the couple."

The woman laughs and says thank you as she graciously
accepts Shantrell's offering.

Mykol shakes his head with a smile, impressed with the picnic
and Shantrell's way with people. I've seen Shantrell pleased
before, many times. She is a woman easily pleased but Mykol's
presence makes her happier than I've ever seen her.

It has gotten cooler so we won't be out much longer. The boys
finish their food and walk out near the water. Shantrell and Mykol

stretch out on a blanket facing each other and talk quietly. Zeke and I are sitting on our own blanket but he watches Mykol and Shantrell more than he watches me. It occurs to me that Shantrell is a major concern to him. She's so buoyant that I never thought Zeke might worry about her. I know he does not want Mykol or any man messing over his sister but Mykol is making a play for Shantrell, hard, and she is playing just as hard and caught up with the big fine fine fella.

I lie on the blanket and watch all that is going on around me. I stare at the people walking around the Point. I see Jameel and Caliel running playfully along the water's edge and Shantrell and Mykol smiling and gazing at each other. Out of the corner of my eye the elderly couple is still nibbling on the food Shantrell shared and smile happily. I can see Zeke keeping a watchful eye on his nephews but never losing sight of his sister who is a wise woman more than capable of taking care of herself. I see the watercraft gliding along in the Bay and peace settles in all around me. I wish I could lie here on this stretch of beach forever and just let the world keep on moving along at a nice leisurely pace like the world I see before me at this moment. My troubles seem so far away.

If Zeke was hitting on me like Mykol is hitting on Shantrell right now, I'd be a truly blissful creature, at least for the time being. I probably should have shown more concern about his cramping hamstring. Although he is ignoring me, I'm grateful. The bike ride was just what I needed, a good dose of exercise. I still haven't thanked him properly for the gift. I'm beginning to feel that I may take Zeke for granted. The blues that was shrouding my world has lifted and the day seems bright. Before Zeke showed up at my door, the only thing I had to look forward to was a visit with my grandmother and, to be honest, those visits often deflate my spirit instead of elevating it.

I lie quietly with my eyes closed and before I know it, my party is rustling around me and gathering up our picnic fixings. It's starting to sprinkle on our outing and we're calling it quits. The bikes are mounted and or partially disassembled and loaded inside the vehicles. The boys want to ride with their uncle and me but Zeke declares he is taking me to see Granny so they need to go with their mother. To pacify them, he vows to visit before he goes home. Jameel and Caliel seem to think this is a special treat and are satisfied.

Zeke is such a ladies' man. When we get to the care home, he silences his phone and remains completely engaged with my grandmother. She finds him interesting. Having just seen my father a couple of weeks earlier, I question if she can distinguish the two men from each other. She watches Zeke closely and I have to stop her from touching his face any number of times. Zeke just sits still and allows her to watch him and touch him. Since she can't get to his face as much as she wants, she settles for holding his hand. I don't mind that she ignores me. Hell, I've pretty much been ignored all day. She seems content having Zeke in her presence and that makes me feel good about him.

Later when we arrive at my home, Zeke unloads both our bikes and puts them in the garage before we head next door to Shantrell's home. Miss Mel quizzes everyone about our picnic.

"Why didn't you come out and join us, Miss Mel? It was fun. It sure took my mind off of things," I say.

"It was too cold out there for me today. Maybe I'll join y'all the next time. I thought you guys would have been back long before now. How is your grandmother doing, Hannah?"

"She's good after your boy here paid her a visit. She liked Zeke, hardly noticed me at all." I smile, recalling how content Granny seemed.

"Yeah my boys have that effect on women, especially Zeke." Miss Mel laughs and then asks, "Where is your friend, Zeke? He's not stopping by?" Miss Mel keeps her eyes on Shantrell as she asks Zeke the question.

Shantrell ignores her mother as she sets out trays of food she left in the refrigerator for this evening's meal.

I head into the kitchen and wash my hands at the sink before snatching up one of those goat cheese and prosciutto sandwiches along with a handful of chips.

"I don't know where Mykol is. You'd have to ask your daughter. I'm sure she knows." Zeke tells his mother.

Shantrell actually blushes and pushes Zeke in the shoulder. "He'll be over later." She tells Miss Mel still not looking at the woman.

Chapter 20: A Performance Worthy of Applause

It is well after eight at night by the time Zeke and I enter my home and I'm not surprised to find a number of messages on my answering machine. Another call comes through as I sit and listen to the messages from the previous calls. My body actual convulses as if I'm having a seizure when I hear Dana's voice on the line.

I manage to keep my cool and "Hello" is all I say in response to her greeting.

"How's everything going with you, Hannah?" she asks as if she left my home under the best of circumstances. Zeke watches me, guessing by my reaction that I'm on the phone with Dana.

"I'm fine," I answer and put the phone on speaker. "How about you?"

"Getting bigger every day. I think this is going to be a big baby." Dana sounds like she might be smiling.

"Do you know if it's a boy or a girl?" I ask.

"I don't know. I prefer to be surprised. Travis wants me to find out. He's hoping for a boy but I'm not particular either way."

I have no response for this. I have never been pregnant and have no experience on which to base an opinion and could care less what Travis wants.

Dana gets to the reason for her call. "Well, I need to get some things for the baby and Dora. Would you wire me some money?"

"How much do you want?"

"I need to buy a crib and a stroller for two and Dora is outgrowing all her clothes. I guess about the same amount as before."

"I'll mail you a money order or deposit it in your bank account. I have the account number here on the last statement that came in the mail."

"I had to close that account. Those people were trippin' so I have no way to cash a money order that large."

I feel desperation rising in my chest and Zeke can see it in my eyes. He moves in front of me and lays his hands out flat as he lowers them slightly, signaling for me to calm down.

"Give me an address and I'll bring the money up to you. I can also bring up all of Dora's things. She has quite a few things here that you should be able to use for her or the baby. No sense in buying things you already have. You could use that money for something else."

Dana hesitates and I hear her talking to someone in the background. She's got her hand over the mouthpiece so I can't quite make out what she's saying. I wish she had muted the phone because it sounds like she's arguing with the person. Dana's calm is gone when she returns to the phone. "Hannah, would you please just wire the money. I need it right away."

"There is a three thousand dollar limit on the amount of money I can wire you and it will cost two hundred to wire that much money. I knew you'd be calling so I already checked. I can bring the money up tomorrow, the full five thousand. Just give me an address."

"Just a minute," she tells me impatiently. This time Dana mutes the phone and I mute mine.

"I guess she needs Travis's okay," I say to Zeke who doesn't respond but is watching me intently.

"Okay, Hannah, you can leave the cash with Travis's mom. Her name is Sarah Ransom and her address is..."

My mind goes blank for a moment. I don't hear the address Dana gives me so I ask her to repeat it. It is the address for the Ransom family so there is no need to write it down. I suddenly realize that it is Saturday night and I have no way of getting such a large sum of cash until Monday. "Dana, I spoke to soon. I forgot it's Saturday and the banks won't be open tomorrow. I'll have to come up on Monday."

"But I need money now," Dana yells at me and her desperation comes through.

"I'll wire you as much as I can get my hands on tomorrow. Will I be able to see you if I come up on Monday."

"I don't know, Hannah. Our schedule is kind of up in the air."

"Then I'll go ahead and wire the remainder on Monday and Tuesday."

Dana is quiet on the line and I'm sure she doesn't know if she should be relieved or disappointed that I don't insist on seeing her and Dora. "So, you're not coming up after all?"

"No. I'll try to drop off Dora's things sometime in the next few weeks so you'll have them. Is this the address where I should leave the things?"

"No, I'd better call you with an address for that. I don't think Sarah will want the boxes at her house," Dana says so quietly that I feel sorry for her.

"Well, figure out when would be a good time for me to come up and I'll bring Dora's things and let me know what you need for the baby and maybe I can get Brianna to come along with me. You know she's a sucker for babies. She bought Dora all kinds of stuff," I laugh. "And don't let this baby be as old as Dora before we get to see him or her. I'll wire the money to Dana Marie Mechum and use Dad's first name as the verification question. I hope you realize these money wires are going to eat up your money fast. I've got to go. Kiss your little girl for me. Bye, baby."

I hang up and take a deep breath in order to ward off the tears. Zeke looks at me and nods approvingly. I know I've surprised him almost as much as I've surprised myself. He starts to applaud my performance. It is as if God came down from the heavens and whispered Zeke's very words in my ear. "If she knows you want Dora more than anything else in this world, she'll keep her from you at all costs."

I smile at Zeke but there is water on the rims of my eyes when I ask, "Why are you clapping?"

"You didn't ask about Angel Baby. You did good."

"I remembered your words and I know now that you were right. The more Dana believes I want Dora with me the more determined she will be to keep her away."

"I was afraid you were going to break down and cry for a moment there but then you just flipped a switch and became cool as a cucumber." Zeke walks over to me and gives me a hug.

"It occurred to me that my goal is not to take Dora from her mother but to protect her. Even if I find out where they are, I can't go and steal Dora away from Dana. Dana would have to give up her parental rights willingly and freely. Tracking them down won't do much good." As I'm saying these words to Zeke the harshness of the situation comes into full view. I have wanted Dora as my own. My aunt's words to me fed into those feelings but Aunt Alise was a sick woman and not thinking clearly. Dora is Dana's child. My goal should be to help Dana become a responsible parent who provides a decent home and security for both her children.

Zeke pulls me over to the sofa and maneuvers me onto his lap. This is the most romantic gesture I've had from the man in weeks. The bike was thoughtful but far from romantic. He wraps his arms around my hips and looks at me with what seems like relief. "I'm glad you realize that. I was wondering when you'd accept that reality."

I give him a peck on the forehead and rise from his lap.

"Where are you going?" he asks.

I don't bother to answer his question. "Why didn't you tell me you believed I was wasting time trying to find Dana? I've had everyone so tied up with this when it really served no purpose. God, I'm so slow."

"Don't say that. You are not slow in any way!" Zeke shouts and looks angry. This reaction to my words leads me to believe I'm not the first person he has heard call me slow. I'm embarrassed. I cannot bear the thought of Zeke feeling sorry for me. I don't want him to think I'm inept, so therefore need his guidance and protection. For the first time in a very long time I feel inadequate, as if I don't meet the standards for a man like Zeke. I feel slow and incompetent. Suddenly, Deidra pops into my head and I feel hopelessly jealous.

I'm tired and want to climb back in the bed and cover my head. I miss Dora so much but she's not mine to miss the way I do. I long for her deep in my core. I worry for her during the day and in the wee hours when I'm all alone but she's not mine. "I'm going to take a shower." I tell Zeke.

"I wish you'd sit here with me for a while," he says.

Zeke looks nearly as sad as I feel. I start to sit next to him, but, once again, he pulls me onto his lap. I don't resist but I feel so unhappy and it shows. Zeke takes my chin in his hand and turns my face to his. He kisses me nice and deep. I feel his arms wrapping around me and pulling me closer. I enjoy the closeness. "Why won't you let me comfort you, Hannah?" he asks as we pull away from each other. "I worry about you."

"You do comfort me when you're around."

"If you'd let me, I'd be here for you. I know you can take care of your own business but I need to make sure you're okay. I know how much you love that baby. I know you worry about her and miss her. I want to be here with you. Every time I think about you over here alone, it bothers me. Each day I want to be here with you more than I did the day before."

"You want to protect me. I've got an entire family of protectors, Zeke."

"I want to be with you, just until some of this confusion over Dora passes. Don't send me away."

I pull back and look at him and wonder who's bullshitting who here. Could Zeke and I actually be getting our signals this mixed up? I'm tired and want to shower and go to bed. Once again I tell him. "I'm going to take a shower."

"Can I stay?" he asks.

"Sure, if you want."

--

Zeke is nowhere to be found when I leave my bathroom. I peep outside and his SUV is gone. "What the hell?" I ask no one out loud. I wonder where he went. This relationship is getting stranger by the minute. I consider calling him but I'm not up to a word game with Zeke so I grab a glass of that marvelous Merlot Shantrell introduced me to, guzzle half of it down, secure my house, and head off to bed.

Just as I start to get cozy, my doorbell rings and I must admit I am relieved. Zeke enters the house with his satchel. "I needed to get a change of clothes so I don't have to rush off tomorrow."

"I wondered what happened to you."

"Why didn't you call me?" he asks and I feel like this is a test.

"Why didn't you tell me you were leaving?" I'm tired and testy.

Zeke makes a sound that is a cross between a grunt and a chuckle, shakes his head and heads off to the shower.

I sit in my bed feeling pissed and not sure why. I'm not being nice to Zeke. I feel like cursing him out. I'm sick of him. I finish my wine and wait.

When Zeke enters the room he stands on the side of the bed and asks, "Why are you being a bitch with me, Hannah?"

Damn it if I don't feel the tears starting to flow. I had no idea they were coming. I'm a fucking wreck and I know this man is going to dump me if I don't get my shit together. Hell I hardly see him as it is.

Zeke lies down beside me and tries to take me in his arms but I push him away. No sooner than I push away from him I know he will misread this and think I don't want him with me but how do I tell him that I hate the way he has to comfort me. I want to be fun and giving and not so damn pitiful. I want him to enjoy me and to laugh with me like I heard him laugh when he was with Deidra at the restaurant. I heard him laugh in a way he hasn't laughed with me in weeks. How do I tell him all these things without telling him how much I love him? I love everything about him. Here I am so pathetically pitiful. Who would want me to love them and more importantly who could possibly love me back when I'm like this?

I go into the bathroom and wash my face. I look in the mirror at the braids on each side of my head and remind myself of that little girl who fell off the monkey bars and hit her head, knocking herself unconscious all those years ago. I did nothing to make myself attractive for Zeke tonight. I have on a nightgown that used to belong to my grandmother. I always loved this gown so I sleep in it when I feel particularly lonely for family. I have so many beautiful pieces of sleepwear. Why did I put this gown on?

I take the braids down and brush my hair together and twist it up into a knot at the crown of my head. I remove the gown and rub my body down with Marc Jacobs Daisy Dream body lotion before going into my jewelry case and putting on the earrings Zeke gave me for my birthday. This is the best I can do closed up here in my bathroom. All my beautiful lingerie is in my dresser drawers out in the bedroom. I do dig in an old makeup case and find a smidge of one of my favorite lipsticks, a matted melon. I look in the mirror and think I look pretty good, sexy even. So what if I'm ass-naked.

I walk out of my bathroom with my head held high and hope Zeke doesn't think I'm severely bi-polar. He smiles at me and sits up straighter in the bed. I walk around to his side and climb up on the bed and straddle him. The look of surprise on his face is priceless but he's all in. "Hi," he says.

I lean forward and kiss him. He kisses me back as he reaches around and grabs my butt and holds on. Our mouths open wider and it's as if we are both trying to taste all we can of each other. After a moment, Zeke pushes me off him and on to my back as he crouches over me with short kisses on my lips. He quickly places kisses down my neck, chest, and breasts, before lying next to me and slowly rubbing each breast in turn. His hand begins drifting to my belly button and delicately rubs my stomach. "You changed for me," he says in such a low voice I can barely understand his words.

"I didn't actually change." I say with a chuckle.

"Yeah you did. You came out a different person."

He pushes me to turn over onto my stomach and begins to run his hand up and down the length of my body as he watches and traces kisses along his hands path. Zeke pushes on my legs to part them as his hands travel up my inner calf to my thighs. I feel his fingers barely touching my pubic hair and then he pulls on them very gently just before he touches me. One finger gently rubs up and down until my body opens on its own, allowing his finger to glide inside me with no resistance. He runs his finger along every opening and I grown and spread my legs wider with each new touch.

I turn over, ready for Zeke to enter me but he has other things on his mind. Zeke kneels in front of me and kisses his way down my belly to my thighs. He kisses and then gently pulls on my hairs with his teeth before kissing the very spot he had been rubbing with his hand just moments before. "I don't think you should do that, baby. I'm ready to burst," I plead.

"So burst in my mouth, he tells me and kisses my slit several times with closed lips."

This is like torture. I know what's coming and I want it badly. I feel his tongue gliding in just between those lips and I can't get my legs far enough apart. First he uses only the very tip of his tongue to run the length of my lips, just inside the opening and then he goes deeper. "Oh, hell." I say as I grab the sheets. "You'd better stop." But Zeke keeps going, just a little deeper but not too deep, not too hard, not too fast. I swear he's enjoying this more than I am. He runs his tongue unto the little nub and kisses it very gently and dips his tongue down inside me repeatedly. I try not to give in but before long I know it is a losing battle. The sensation is too good and it can't possibly last. Before I know what's happening, I tighten my thighs on the sides of his head and hold his head in place as I yell, "Please don't stop, please!" and he doesn't. Once I'm completely drained I push his head away or he would keep going.

Zeke wipes his face on my sheets before reaching into my nightstand and grabbing a condom. I had no idea he had stashed them there. I lie there drained as he climbs over me. Somehow I find the energy to push him onto his back and change our positions, causing Zeke to smile with joy as I glide down onto his hard body. I love it when he groans deep in his chest as he enters me. "Damn, Hannah, you are so damn delicious." He moans. I don't know where I find the stamina after my bike ride today but I crouch over him and use all my leg strength to glide my body up and down on his until he starts squeezing my butt so hard I have to tell him, "Not so hard, baby."

Zeke loosens his grip for a moment then grabs me even tighter as he starts to release. "Okay, okay, okay. I'll let go. Just give me a minute." And it actually takes him a full minute to finish. He holds onto me and each time I attempt to move he tells me. "Not yet." I believe this has to be the longest orgasm in the history of man.

Chapter 21: Tom and Jerry

We sit in my bed buck naked with me sitting between Zeke's bent knees and leaning back against his chest. "Why do you watch Mykol and Shantrell so hard? I get the impression you don't want them together."

"It's not that I don't want them together. I just don't want my sister hurt. She's a softie. I'm sure you've seen that soft underbelly of hers. All that hair and makeup can only cover so much."

"What makes you think Mykol would hurt her? He's no longer into Deidra, is he?"

"No, but Deidra is still into him."

"What makes you think that?" I sit up, lean forward slightly, and look over my shoulder so I can see Zeke's face with a look of dismay on mine.

"She told me. I've become her confidant of late. She wants to get back together with him."

"Why is she telling you this instead of Mykol?"

"I think she may be afraid of the rejection. She asked me if he was seeing anyone else. I wasn't sure about him and Shantrell at the time. She even started crying. I didn't know what to do with her but pat her on her back and send her on her way."

My face is getting more and more contorted. I slide around a little more to get a better look at this man. "When and where was this?" I nearly shout.

Zeke can tell by my reaction that he has told me too much but he keeps talking. "She stopped by a few days ago. She didn't stay long. I was on my way out to a class."

"I'm jealous."

"Jealous? Why?"

"I don't like her stopping by your place. I don't like you meeting her out for dinner. What was that about any way? If she wants Mykol why not talk to Mykol. This play on Cyrano de bergerac is bullshit. I've known Deidra a long time. Timidity is not a trait she is familiar with."

"I think she just wanted some advice, babe. She's tried to approach him but he's given her the cold shoulder."

"How long were you and Deidra together?" I ask.

"About four years." Zeke says as he rubs me on my back, trying to calm me down.

"Marriage was never discussed?"

Zeke laughs. "I think I was too broke for Deidra with all my family obligations. She's kind of high maintenance but we hung in there as long as we could."

My body stiffens as I wonder if Zeke would still be with Deidra if she'd have him. I want to ask but think I may not want to hear the truth. Is Deidra slowly reeling him back in? I'm so tired of this roller coaster ride with Zeke. This man is a college professor but doesn't recognize when he's being played. If Deidra wants Mykol back all she's got to do is call the damn man and not waste time crying on Zeke's shoulder. And Zeke, who considers himself such a critical thinker, is too dim-witted to recognize game. Who is the slow one here?

"You've gone quiet on me. What's wrong?" Zeke asks.

I turn back around and lean against him once again. "I've told you that I don't care for this situation with Deidra supposedly crying to you about her relationship with Mykol."

Zeke kisses me on the shoulder. "You care that much?" he asks.

"Yes, I do. Have you told her to talk to Mykol?"

"I have, several times."

"And has she?" I ask.

"Not yet, at least not as far as I know."

I start to leave the bed but Zeke grabs my arm and pulls me back against him. "Where are you going?" he asks.

"To sleep," I say in a huff."

Zeke leans forward and kisses my shoulder again. "Stay up with me awhile longer. We don't spend much time together. Are you very tired?"

He's aroused but I don't care. I'm tempted to say, "I'm tired of us," but I don't mean that the way I know he would take it. "I feel like we're playing some type of cat and mouse game," I say, "and I'm tired of that."

Zeke moves his arms from around me and I turn so I can see his face. His maleness which had been poking me on my buttocks just moments before is wilting. I guess this is the effect relationship gibberish has on the male of the species. Zeke is pissed. It's clear he wants a night of sex and me broaching the subject of "us" is a serious damper on his desired goal. He runs his tongue across his teeth and sucks on them before asking, "Who's the cat and who's the mouse?"

"I consider yelling, "I'm the fucking mouse!" but think better of that. I mean, who the hell wants to be the mouse. "It's just a manner of speech, Zeke. I feel like we're just playing with each other and I don't like it."

"So stop playing with me."

"I'm not playing with you!" I say indignantly.

"So, I guess you are the mouse," Zeke says calmly with emphasis on the "you are." He looks at me with a hint of anger and no trace of a smile.

I get up from the bed, grab my bathrobe and put it on. "That was just plain mean, Zeke. Maybe you should go," I say without thinking and getting angrier by the minute.

Zeke makes no attempt to move. He just sits there and looks at me. "Why are you starting up with me tonight, Hannah? What do you want me to say?"

"I want you to say goodnight and leave my house." I say once again but Zeke continues to look at me without moving.

"Are you playing with me, Zeke? Am I just someone to occupy your time when you get bored with everything else in your life?"

"What do you think, Hannah? Listen, I'm not leaving. I'm not sure what has pissed you off to the point that you want to start up with me like this but I'm not leaving and I'd appreciate it if you'd come back to bed. Like I said earlier, I don't get to spend much time with you and I want to tonight."

"What about every other night? Why tonight?"

"Because you act as if you could care less if you see me most of the time. Even when I'm around, your mind is somewhere else. I feel like I'm a bother when it comes to you. I'm sure not a priority. I just try and get time with you when I think it might be safe. I stay away so you won't send me away so quickly when I come around."

I'm astounded by Zeke's words. How can he possibly think I don't want him around? I told the man I loved him and all I got was a cup of damn coffee for that. I can't help but stare at him, speechless.

"You know, Hannah, you talk about cat and mouse and playing games but I'm sure I've told you more than once or at least indicated that I don't like the whole game thing, never had the patience for it. So, you're telling me to leave now. You're telling me that I've made you so uncomfortable that you need me to leave or do you call yourself punishing me by making me leave?"

This is a question I am not prepared for. Do I want him to leave? He sounds like if he has to leave it may be awhile before I see him again, if ever but he's challenging me and I don't want to back down to the challenge. I look at Zeke and think for a moment which is something I should not need to do if I really want him to go. I should be able to say, "Yes, I want you to leave." If I don't want him to leave, why did I tell him to go? I feel my anger dissipate. "I'm not trying to play games, Zeke. It's just this whole thing with you keeps me confused."

"This thing with me keeps you confused! This thing with me keeps you confused!" Zeke repeats. "I'm just trying to stay out of the way here. I'm just trying to protect myself. You're talking about this whole thing with me and I'm thinking this whole thing with you. I'm trying to be supportive and stay out of your way. I'm giving you some space and you're confronting me about Deidra. You know what's going on between me and Deidra is not important to you right now. Me and Deidra – please!"

"Why would you say what's going on between you and Deidra is not important to me? Why would you think that? This is my whole point. I don't know what's going on between me and you. You show up once in awhile. I only see you sometimes. Why would you think I have so much confidence in our relationship that I wouldn't care what's going on between you and Deidra?"

"There's nothing going on between me and Deidra, Hannah! Deidra is interested in Mykol!" Zeke shouts.

"No she's not because if she was she would be eating dinner with Mykol, not you. She'd be stopping by Mykol's place, not yours!" I shout back.

"Okay, okay, you've made your point and it's a good one. Deidra and I lived together; we were a couple. I should not be her sounding board, her shoulder to cry on, or any of those things. I will take care of that. I would not like it if the table was turned so you're right on that score. I just think it's pretty jacked up for you to start all this serious talk when you know I'm just trying to spend some nice quiet time with you."

"I don't know how you expect me to keep quiet about Deidra. The last time I saw you the two of you were sitting up in a restaurant together. You knew my father was in town visiting and you made a point of staying away. Do you know how embarrassed I was when you were a no show after we saw you in the restaurant with her? My mother came to visit before that but you were nowhere to be found."

"Hannah, if you wanted me to come over you should have invited me. I get tired of trying to guess what you want from me."

"Why do I need to tell you I want to see you, Zeke? When have you ever asked me out or invited yourself over that I've turned you down? Never."

"Never, my ass. The week after Dana took Dora, I tried to stay with you and you turned me away. You knew I planned to take you up to check out that address and you went without me. Didn't even bother to discuss it with me before you took off with your friends. You could have at least had the courtesy to tell me I wasn't needed."

"I'm sorry for that. I was wrong." I finally sit back down on the bed, more tired than ever.

I'm sorry too but you pissed me off with that "cat and mouse" shit. I've just been trying to spend time with a woman I like and want to be with but as much of a priority as you are to me, Hannah, you don't have time for me most of the time. So I ask you again, who's the cat and who's the mouse?"

I don't respond. Zeke's a damn good debater. It seems the harder I try not to be difficult, the more difficult I become. He said he likes me, not loves but likes. That's a good thing. My father always told us to make sure we like any person we date because it's hard to spend a large amount of time around a person you don't like, no matter how attractive he or she may be. I suppose love grows from liking a person first.

Zeke watches me and I can't help but look at him. He's tired too. Neither of us says anything for a moment. Then Zeke asks, "So, do you still want me to leave?"

"No, I don't want you to go. Please stay."

Chapter 22: Blick Cissoko

I'm surprised to answer my phone and hear my Aunt Alise's long time boyfriend, Christopher on the line. I have spoken to him only twice since my aunt died and I am glad to hear him sounding less burdened than on those two occasions and during the last days of Alise's life. After the perfunctory greetings and casual conversation, Christopher asks if I have any additional information about Dana and "the baby," as he and my father consistently refer to Dora. You'd think she is the only baby in the world. I tell him there has been no change since the last time he and I spoke which was the day following Dana's last call for cash.

"I had a very interesting call earlier today and I wanted to tell you about it," Christopher says, immediately piquing my curiosity. "A young man by the name of, I'm not sure I'm saying this right but I'll spell it for you, Blick Cissoko, called me. Do you have something to write with so I can spell that name for you?"

I grab a pen and Christopher spells the name before giving me more details. "This guy wanted to speak to your aunt and of course I explained that would not be possible." Christopher's voice trails off as if these words are difficult to speak before he goes on. "He apologized and told me that he was looking for Dana and he sounded quite desperate to contact her. I felt sorry for him, actually. Anyway, he says he and Dana spent some time together a couple of years ago but lost touch with each other when he left the country. He returned not that long ago and found some documents belonging to Dana in the apartment he sublets. That's how he got this number and Alise's name. I thought you might want to talk to him, Hannah. He might know something about Dana that could help you find her."

The last thing I want to do is have an encounter with one of Dana's johns. Nearly every day I remind myself that I am no longer looking for Dana and Dora. Christopher sounds so excited and I can tell he thinks this information may help my efforts at finding them so I agree to call the man. I even manage to sound excited and pleased about the information.

I don't call right away but the more I ignore the phone number I've written on the whiteboard on my refrigerator, the more the name Blick Cissoko along with his phone number glares out at me. Two days after receiving the call from Christopher, he calls again and I curse when I see his name and number on the caller ID.

"Hannah, that guy called me again. He says he's on the peninsula and is hoping he can talk to you before he heads back up to the Bay Area."

"What's he doing down here?" I ask with an eerie feeling creeping up my spine.

"He says he's been down there since the day after we spoke. I'm afraid I told him that you live in Seaside and he's been waiting on your call."

I apologize to Christopher and promise to call "the john" right away. I hang up and go into the kitchen and look at the number on the refrigerator. Dana must have put a whippin' on this guy. I hope he's not weird or something but I will reach out to him and hopefully he will stop pestering Christopher.

At first I think I must have the wrong number because the person on the line sounds British. The richness of his voice leads me to believe he is black. I don't say "Sorry, I must have dialed the wrong number," but instead ask, "Is this Blick?"

"Yes, this is Bleak. Is this Hannah, by chance?"

"Hi, yeah, this is Hannah. My uncle tells me that you are looking for Dana. I wish I could help you but I have no way of contacting her."

"Yes, I understand. Christopher explained that no one in your family knows how to get in touch with her. He thought I might be of some assistance but I don't really know much about Dana's friends up in the Bay Area. She and I dated for some time and occasionally she would come and stay with me. She lived with me for about three months before I went back to the UK. That was nearly two years ago. I've been back and forth several times but I've failed to find her and I simply wish to make sure she is okay and not in need of anything. She was not at her best the last time I saw her."

I get the impression that this man, Blick, is genuinely concerned for Dana, but I can't help him. I wonder how Dana felt about him. Did she like him or was she using him for money like he was using her for sex. He definitely got caught up with some emotions surrounding Dana that were more than sexual. As I listen to him, I feel a connection and I want to meet the man. "Are you available for coffee, Blick, Bleak? I'm sorry; could you tell me how to pronounce your name?"

"Yes, please don't worry about the pronunciation. Most people say "Blick" but it is actually pronounced "Bleak." It's a nickname. Yes, I am available to have coffee at any time you designate."

"There's a Starbucks in Seaside on the corner of the1500 block of Canyon Del Rey and Del Monte. Can you meet me there in an hour?"

"Gladly, 1500 block of Canyon Del Rey. I'll see you there and thank you for taking the time to meet with me, Hannah?"

--

I sit in the Starbucks and look around in wait for the man I spoke with thirty minutes earlier. I am here way ahead of time but I want to see him when he walks in. I want to observe him and make sure this is a man worthy of my time. I'm nervous but not quite sure why. For the last three days, since Christopher told me about the call from Blick, I've been in a fog. I feel like I'm moving in a dream world and I need to know why I am feeling this way or at least do what I can to clear my head.

The store is pretty full and there are two other black women seated at nearby tables drinking coffee, one alone and one with a friend. The lady sitting alone looks middle-aged but hopefully, Blick doesn't know my age. Of course, if he has my last name he could pull me up on Facebook and see my photo but I doubt he'd go to that much trouble, after all, it's Dana he's looking for, not me.

When I first sat down, my head popped up every time the door opened but now I've decided to play it cool and try not to look like I'm expecting anyone. Finally a very slender, tall, dark man enters the store. He glances around quickly and hones in on me immediately and waves. Damn, I can't believe he picked me out so quickly. I wave back and he heads in my direction. This man is piss-your-pants gorgeous. He could model clothing for the world's finest clothiers. I tell myself to close my mouth and after doing so, I give him a tight-lipped smile.

"Hannah?" he says once he arrives at the table.

I nod and use my hand to point to the chair across from me indicating for him to have a seat. I saw that in the movies somewhere. I feel like I'm being less than friendly but I'm nervous and don't want my voice to crack. I need to get a grip. Everything about this guy says money and I mean lots of money, but then he takes off his shades and my heart flips. Oh no!

"I see you already have a coffee. Would you like something more," he asks.

I speak for the first time and thankfully my voice is full. "No, thank you but please get something for yourself. I'm in no hurry."

"Are you certain?" he asks with a soft warm smile.

I return the smile and nod.

Blick heads to the counter to order his coffee. My mind is no longer in a fog but it is all over the place. How did Dana get caught up with this man? I guess his family would question how he got caught up with Dana.

The man returns with his coffee in hand. "Hannah, I want to thank you once again for meeting with me. I have been at a loss for so long now. I know it is likely too late for me and Dana but I must make sure she is okay. If you don't mind me asking, when was the last time you had contact with her?" Blick makes himself comfortable in his seat.

"It's been a few weeks but like I told you over the phone I have no way of contacting her."

"So, she is well?" he asks and then stares at me.

"As far as I know, Dana is fine."

We sit and look at our coffees for a moment and it is apparent he wants more than to learn about Dana's well-being. "I can see the resemblance. You and Dana are clearly closely related. May I ask why you decided to meet with me?"

"I want to know about you and Dana. When and where did you meet? How long were you two together? What type of relationship you had? You obviously care a great deal for her and I guess I'm just curious as to why."

Blick looks embarrassed and keeps his eyes on his coffee as he moves the cup around in his hands and then looks over his shoulder in an attempt to make sure no one is listening to our conversation. "Do you know about your cousin's life up in San Francisco?" he asks.

"Not much, but I know she was doing things she did not want her family to know about."

The man nods his head, looks at me, and leans in closer. "I was in the city for six months working a new job with a tech company. I am a technology marketing specialist and I travel a lot for my work. I know you probably hear about people who say they have no time to settle into relationships but that has been my situation. In any case, I attended a company sponsored event one evening and Dana was there also. I had no idea she was working but I was attracted to her. We seemed to hit it off well and I thought she was, without a doubt, the loveliest woman I had ever met. You can understand how difficult it was for me when I realized she was." Blick hesitates and looks around uncomfortably before asking me, "You understand?"

I simply nod, and ask "When was that?"

"Oh, I'm not certain. Is that important?"

"I'm just trying to figure out some things about my cousin?" I tell him.

"I'd say it was very possibly June 2012. I had only been in country about two months when I met Dana. A month later she came to stay with me in my sublet. She understood that I would be leaving and going back to London but I thought we would stay in touch. Three months later, when I left, she was not doing well, seemed to be under the weather or something. I called every few days but after about a month, her phone was down. I looked for her when I returned but to no good outcome. Fortunately, the people I sublet with had kept some of my things but since it was nothing of consequence, I hadn't really gone through the items. That's where I found the paperwork that had the name Alise Mechum and the phone number. I tried the number and thankfully got Christopher on the phone. He has been very helpful. I am sorry for his loss."

I look at this man and try to think. I don't have much time to make a decision about how to handle this.

"Would you like another coffee?" he asks.

"I would. I'll have a tall Americana, if you don't mind."

"Certainly, I'll be right back."

While Blick is away from the table I try to think clearly. The fog is gone so I should be able to sort things out in my head but before I know it, he is sitting before me again. "I think you should know that Dana is pregnant," I say bluntly and watch for Blick's reaction.

"Oh, is she married or in a serious relationship?" Some of the peace has left the man's face.

"Not married as far as I know but in a relationship and I guess you could say it's serious."

"BLICK, two tall Americanas!" the barista calls out.

Blick leaves the table and collects our coffees. When he returns, he asks, "Is she happy, Hannah?"

This question makes my heart ache. "Let me show you something." I pull out my cell phone and find the video of Dora running around my yard when she first started to walk. I press play and hand him the phone.

Blick watches the video and smiles at first but then becomes solemn. When the video stops he hands me the phone and asks, "Whose baby is that? She's beautiful."

I flip through my pictures and find the most recent photo I have of Dora and hand the phone back to Blick without answering his question. He accepts the phone and studies the photo closely. "She looks like you," he says as he looks up at me, "and Dana. Is this Dana's child also?"

I nod. "This is Dora. She was born in July 2013."

Blick looks back at the photo and puts his free hand up to his face and rubs his chin. "She's my daughter isn't she?"

"I couldn't say," I answer. The truth is, I won't say but I am certain I am having coffee with Dora's father.

--

The argument Zeke and I had a couple of weekends ago forced us to sit down and talk about what we want from each other. I managed to not use the word "love" but I told Zeke I wanted to see him more often. I explained how much I miss being with him when he stays away. He just smiled in disbelief and repeated what he said about staying away to stay out of the way. We both acknowledged that we were not doing a good job of communicating what we wanted and things have been so much nicer since that talk. Now I see Zeke so often that I'm afraid he may get bored with me because, honestly, the more I see this man the more I want to see him.

For the first time in a long time, years actually, I am enjoying a steady relationship with a man I like, trust, and who excites me. I pray I don't mess this up and that what we share grows into something long lasting, maybe even permanent. I tell myself not to call or text him too often, to give him some breathing room. The great think is that if I don't reach out to Zeke, he contacts me no matter how busy he is.

I know I have to work on being a bit more open and honest with the people in my life. I really want to tell Zeke about Blick but our relationship is going so smoothly that I don't want to upset the applecart. Is that the saying? I don't want to hear what I think Zeke will tell me about Blick, which is to stay away from the man. I've only seen Blick the one time but I am certain Zeke won't like that. The problem is that the more days that pass the more I feel I need to talk about Blick with Zeke. I've heard all the advice about having an open and honest relationship so I've made up my mind to tell him because it's really no big deal. I just hope he won't be too upset when he learns I've been keeping this tiny insignificant secret. I mean everybody has secrets, right?

Chapter 23: His Sister's Keeper

My mother, stepfather; Eugene, and I will spend Thanksgiving at Brianna's home in Sacramento. We will leave Brianna's that weekend and my parents will visit with me and my grandmother before returning to North Carolina.

I asked Zeke to join my family and me for the Thanksgiving holiday but he was reluctant about leaving his family. I'd like to spend the holiday with Zeke and his family also, so I called and got an okay from Brianna to extend an invitation to the Melancon family for Thanksgiving dinner. Now that I have my sister's okay, I call Zeke and ask if the rest of his family would consider spending their Thanksgiving with my family at Brianna's home in Sacramento.

"Wow! How much arm twisting did you have to do to get Brianna and David to agree to that? We're talking about five or six more people. I would hate for them to go to so much trouble," Zeke says.

"It won't be a lot of trouble, especially if we go up a day or two ahead. Then Shantrell and I can help prepare the dinner. My mother and stepfather will be there already."

"I don't know, Hannah. We would all need a place to stay and that can get expensive."

"I've found some nice vacation rentals online and they're not too pricey. There are several good sized houses not that far from Brie's place. I wish you'd consider asking them. I understand if they'd prefer to stay at home but I think it could be a lot of fun if you all came to Brie's for dinner. The kids get along well together. I know your mother goes on her senior excursions but when was the last time Shantrell got away, other than for my aunt's funeral? Would you be willing to come up if your mother and Shantrell agree to join us?"

"This could cost a lot of money and you know I'm not a wealthy man?" Zeke complains.

"I know but would you at least look at the houses. I've sent you a link. I'm more than willing to help pay for the house."

Zeke laughs. "You mean like we could go Dutch on the rental cost? You'd probably dump me a week later. No, that's okay.

You've got a place to stay free of charge. I'll talk to my mother and sister to see what they think. I'll let you know."

Not two hours later, Shantrell greets me outside my front door before I make it inside. "Do you think Brianna would mind if I bring Mykol along," she asks me excitedly. "He's supposed to eat Thanksgiving Dinner with us and I can't go off and leave him here all alone."

This is a good sign. Shantrell is all in as long as Mykol is included and I'm certain Brianna will say, "What's one more mouth on Thanksgiving Day?"

My neighbor barges ahead as if all has been settled. "Girl, Buddy is so relieved that we will be going to Sacramento because Niecy's family always gets together on Thanksgiving and I think he and Niecy have been arguing about how to satisfy both their mothers. I know Mama would be highly pissed if Buddy didn't at least spend a few hours with her on Thanksgiving but I think Niecy wants to spend the entire day with her family. I was hoping they'd invite us over but they're a large group in a small house and real clannish. So do you need to ask Brianna about Mykol?"

"I'll ask her but I'm sure it won't be a problem. Is it for sure your family will come if Mykol comes."

"I don't see why not. Zeke says he wants to go but doesn't want to leave us. Mama told him not to worry about us but when he told her Brianna had invited the family, you could have knocked her over with a feather. She's excited about visiting with your mother and getting away for a few days and I am too but I did invite Mykol to Thanksgiving dinner at our house."

"Do you think Mykol will want to come with us?"

"Oh, I'm sure he won't mind. He's real easy to get along with. I wish my husband had been half as easy as Mykol is; we'd still be married," Shantrell smiles with pleasure at this reflection.

While Shantrell and I stand in my kitchen and discuss our Thanksgiving plans, Zeke, who does not care for texting, sends me a text message that reads, "It's a go for Thanksgiving! Thx much!"

I don't tell Shantrell about the confirmation I received from Zeke because I have questions. Has he found a house? I wanted to help him pick one out but maybe he asked his mother or sister's advise or maybe he chose one on his own. Some of the homes were beautiful and not very expensive. I hope he didn't go with one of those tiny flat-roofed ranch houses. Let me stop. I've talked the man into taking his entire family out of town for Thanksgiving and now I want to select their accommodations. I can see why he sometimes keeps me at arm's length. I don't need to have my opinion about everything and if I do I should learn to keep it to myself.

So, as hard as I try to not get involved with the specifics of the Melancon's stay in Sacramento, I simply cannot resist the urge when Zeke shows up at my home later in the evening and asks me to help him select a house. The smile on his face tells me that he knows I'm jonesing to have input in the decision. But I am not a selfish being. I like the whole team thing sometimes, so I say, "Can Shantrell look at the houses with us?"

"You're really trying to make me blow my budget for this trip aren't you? Next you'll be telling me to just leave it to you, Shantrell, and my mom. Okay, call Shantrell but not my mother. That woman's taste are entirely too rich."

Once Shantrell arrives, her first doe-eyed question to her brother is "Do we have a limit on how much we can spend?"

Zeke gives me a "See what I mean" look and turns his attention back to Shantrell before answering her question. "Hell yeah there's a limit, Shantrell. I'm not made of money. Is Buddy coming along or not?"

"He's not coming. They're going to Niecy's mother's house but Mykol is coming with us. At least I plan on asking him to come."

Zeke actually looks disappointed. I'm not sure if this is because Mykol may join us or Budrow will be absent or both. Zeke is still reserved when it comes to Shantrell's involvement with Mykol. The fact that Miss Mel and Shantrell's boys make as much of a ta-do over Mykol as they do over Zeke may not help Mykol's cause. The disappointed look could be about Budrow because he and Zeke are good friends even though they don't always get along.

I set my laptop up on the kitchen counter and Shantrell and I go to a vacation rental web site and start scoping out the homes while Zeke goes into the kitchen and makes coffee. Rather than look over my shoulder, Shantrell uses her phone and Zeke uses his tablet. For some time no one comments on the properties for rent until Zeke says, "You two are awfully quiet. Make sure you look for places that aren't too far from Brianna and David's place. We need at least four bedrooms and two baths."

As soon as Zeke tells us what he's looking for in a rental property, Shantrell comes over and points out a home to me. It's one of the ones I've been looking at but the price seems high. We look at the pictures together on the laptop and try to drum up the courage to ask Zeke to look at this particular property. I really wish he would let me help him pay for the place although I tell myself I'm staying at Brianna's.

We hear Zeke from behind us asking, "Which one are you looking at, Shantrell?"

Shantrell signals me with a light tap on my back and answers, "The Lumber Mill House. It's nice."

"You think your mother would like it?"

"I think she would if she could have the master suite," Shantrell answers with a laugh.

I plug in the neighborhood and confirm that the house is within a reasonable driving distance from my family.

Zeke comes over and looks at the pictures on the laptop. "That's cool and the price is right. I'll email the owner but you might want to pick one or two more in case we don't get this one. Try to stay in that price range, okay."

"Okay, Zeke," Shantrell answers her brother with so much humility I have to look over my shoulder to make sure she's okay. She looks me in my eyes and gives me a little happy smile and I know she is doing all she can not to jump up and down shouting for joy because the house is fabulous.

--

During the days leading up to Thanksgiving, Brianna calls me two to three times daily to discuss her big Thanksgiving. In addition to me, my mother and stepfather, and the Melancons, David and Brianna's other dinner guests will include David's parents, Leticia and Joseph; his sister, Rosemarie; and Rosemarie's two children, Michele and Damion.

"This is the largest number of guests I've ever had for dinner. I mean I've had parties with finger foods and I guess we have had a couple of barbecues with more people but this is the biggest Thanksgiving. I'm excited about cooking for all these people. You will be here on Tuesday, right?" Brianna asks excitedly.

"I'm heading out early Tuesday afternoon. I hate to leave Granny but they have a nice dinner at the home. I'm staying here and spending Christmas with her," I vow.

"Maybe we'll come down for Christmas this year," Brianna says.

I've heard this before but I would never try to hold my sister to a promise of come to Seaside for Christmas. She has told me a number of times that she and David prefer to remain at home with the children during the Christmas holiday season.

Brianna and I have gone over her menu repeatedly but she keeps adding and changing out things. She has expressed a desire to impress Miss Mel and Shantrell who are excellent cooks. I've told her any number of times that Thanksgiving will be wonderful and I'm in the process of reassuring her once again.

After more assurances, Brianna moves on to another subject. "Ooh, I've been meaning to tell you, my best friend called me a couple of days ago."

"Who, Deidra?"

"Yes, and she is not very happy right now. It was not easy talking to her because she started asking me about our plans for Thanksgiving. I know she wanted an invite. It was awkward. I started to just go ahead and invite her but that would be entirely too messy. I just didn't know how to not invite her so I pretended to have an important call and got off the phone. I feel horrible about that but I didn't want to tell her that her last two boyfriends would be at my house for dinner with their new women. My girl would not want to show up under those circumstances, at least not by herself."

"Ooh, that is messy. I'm sorry, Brie."

"No need for you to apologize, baby. It's not your fault. Things like this happen. Even if she was seeing someone, I don't think it would be a good idea for her to come with Zeke here. She was way too into him. Does she know you two are a couple?"

"I don't know. You didn't tell her?"

"No and she never asked. To be honest I have avoided the subject. She's tried to hint about you guys a couple of times but I played dumb. Anyway, she hasn't called me back and I hope she doesn't until after Thanksgiving. I'll probably invite her up for New Year's so if you're planning on coming up at the same time, please leave Zeke at home."

"Seriously?"

"Yes, seriously."

--

I try not to watch Shantrell as she paces back and forth out on my patio. I wonder if she's talking to Mykol or Zeke because she's been waiting for a call from Zeke for two days and has not heard from or seen Mykol in a couple of days either. Zeke is having Shantrell's business plan for a daycare center evaluated by a colleague. Brother and sister have been working on the plan for months now. When they started on the project, Zeke was doing the majority of the work, but in the end every detail and calculation were the result of Shantrell's efforts. Zeke thinks it's a masterful plan. Considering his own apparent bias, he recommended they have the plan evaluated by his colleague who works with small business startups and Shantrell agreed.

The exhilaration that should accompany the prospect of starting a new business has been dampened by the absence of Mykol. Over the past few weeks, I have observed Mykol's SUV parked in front of the Melancon home nearly every evening except for the past two nights. At first Shantrell was worried something might have happened to the man, but Zeke confirmed that Mykol was showing up on campus for his classes. It's sad to see Shantrell so unhappy especially during this time when her mind should be blossoming with ideas for a new business.

I try not to stare as she comes in from the patio but I can't help but notice that she is moving at a very deliberate pace. This is not at all like Shantrell who is usually so vibrant. Shantrell has never impressed me as a person unsure of herself. I have only known the confidant energetic woman who lights up every room and brings a smile to nearly every person she meets.

Shantrell picks up her apron and puts the strap over her head before tying the strings in the back. Normally, I would not notice such mundane tasks, particularly by Shantrell who does everything quickly, but today she's moving as if each motion is monumental. She has come over to help me prep the pies I'm donating to a local church for the Thanksgiving meal they will serve the elderly and needy on Thanksgiving Day. I'm baking the pies off early Tuesday Morning before heading off to Brianna's for Thanksgiving. The church has assured me they will have adequate refrigeration for the pumpkin and sweet potato pies. The pecan pies have so much sugar in them that they never go bad.

"I talked to Mykol just now. His mother and sister are coming to town to spend Thanksgiving with him, so he's not going to make it up to Brianna's with us," Shantrell says.

I don't know what to say. My friend is hurt and I'm at a loss. My mother is coming out in me because I'm trying to think how I can fix this situation. Maybe Mykol could bring his family up to Brianna's also. I make myself stop the problem solving and try to think what, if anything, I should say to Shantrell. Finally, I ask, "You okay?"

"I'm fine, baby? It sure puts a damper on my Turkey Day but there will be other days. That's what I get for looking forward to such a good time. Something always happens. It's better to just take each day as it comes."

--

"Listen here, Little Sister, I hope you and your people are not bringing a bunch of mess to my house," Brianna tells me harshly over the phone.

"What are you talking about?"

"I just got off the phone with my girl Deidra and she tells me that she is spending Thanksgiving with Mykol."

"What did you say?" I heard Brianna clearly but I want to doubt my hearing.

Brianna goes on. "I asked her if they were back together but she didn't answer the question. She said Mykol's mother and sister are visiting with him for Thanksgiving and she's having Thanksgiving dinner with them. What in the world is going on? I thought Mykol was coming up here with Shantrell?" Brianna complains.

"He was but he called and told her he wouldn't be able to make it because his family is coming. Oh goodness! I hate this for Shantrell. This is exactly why Zeke didn't want her messing with Mykol. He was worried that Mykol might start back up with Deidra. I can't believe Mykol would do this. Should I tell Shantrell? Oh, God! Should I tell Zeke? I think he'll be more upset than Shantrell."

"I don't know what to tell you about Zeke but I wouldn't tell Shantrell just yet. There may be more to this than we know. She's probably already feeling bad enough," Brianna advises.

"You're right about that. I'll just leave it for now. I wish you hadn't told me," I whine.

For some odd reason I feel responsible for the fact that Mykol will be a no show on Thanksgiving and will be spending it with his old girlfriend. The entire situation is casting a dark cloud over what was such a promising holiday. I want to run and hide when I spot Zeke's SUV next door. I'm certain he will stop by, mainly because I don't want to see him today. Shantrell is driving up to Sacramento with me tomorrow so we can help Brianna prepare for her big Thanksgiving. Zeke, Miss Mel, and the boys are driving up Wednesday morning and at this moment I would be content not looking Zeke in the face until Wednesday afternoon.

My doorbell rings as I'm standing in my kitchen contemplating grabbing up my purse and keys and leaving my house. Sure enough it's Zeke and he's not hiding the storm brewing inside him.

"Did Shantrell tell you Mykol backed out of going up to Brianna's?" Zeke says as he enters my house without even a how do you do.

"Yes, she did."

Zeke takes a half seat at a bar stool and looks at me as if he's waiting for me to say something more but then tells me, "Well, I ran into Deidra at the gas station a few minutes ago. She tells me that she's spending Thanksgiving with Mykol." Zeke seems to be watching me even closer and I do my best to hide the fact that I already know about Deidra and Mykol, so I deflect.

"Why would Deidra tell you something like that? She has to know Mykol is seeing Shantrell by now."

"Not necessarily, unless she saw them together, and why shouldn't she tell me she's spending Thanksgiving with Mykol. I told you she wants to get back with him."

"Did you tell Shantrell that Deidra is spending Thanksgiving with Mykol?" I ask.

"Hell yeah, I told her. That's my sister. You expect me to keep something this important from her."

I stand in front of Zeke with my arms crossed and my lips pursed in disgust. Something about this is not right but I can't put my finger on it. Why after all these months would Mykol suddenly decide to drop Shantrell and go back to Deidra? He and Shantrell have become downright boring they love on each other so much. Don't get me wrong. They don't do a lot of mushy kissing in public but they are so steady with each other. They consider each other in everything and Mykol can hardly keep his hands or his eyes off of Shantrell. I was certain he loved her and she loved him. Why would Mykol play such a cruel game?

"Maybe you should have waited until after Thanksgiving to tell her, Zeke. From what Shantrell has told me, she doesn't get much time away and she was looking forward to this little trip. She's been so excited. Why spoil her holiday? She was already feeling down because Mykol wasn't coming with us. Now she's heartbroken. That information could have waited."

Zeke sits there with a deep scowl on his face but does not respond to my comments or speak at all. The man sits there and reflects. Finally, he says "Damn, I blew that, baby. I always tell myself that I want to protect my family and here I probably went and added to her hurt feelings. She was trying to smile and pretend that Mykol's change of plans was no big deal and I yelled at her as if she did something wrong. Shantrell usually sets me straight when I get out of line but she hardly responded to me at all. Man, I can be an asshole."

Zeke gets up to leave. "Is there anything you need me to bring up on Wednesday? Text me if there is. I probably won't see you until we arrive because I've got to get some paperwork out of the way this evening. Call me before you leave tomorrow and I'll see you when we get there. Thanks, Hannah. I've got to go and talk to Shantrell." Zeke gives me a hug along with a quick kiss on the mouth and leaves as abruptly as he entered.

Chapter 24: A Diaper?

The Aldridge home is full of fat happy people by the end of the day on Thanksgiving. Brianna has shown every other cook in the house that we ain't got nothing on her in the kitchen. She served the traditional classic candied yams, collards greens, dressing with giblet gravy, and roasted turkey along with nuevo fare such as fresh cut French style green beans with sausage and bean sprouts, brandy glazed carrots with fresh thyme, vegetable dirty rice, and stuffed roast pork. This list is a mere sampling of the fabulous spread Lady Aldridge served her guest. So you may understand why, when the children started yelling, "Can we play games now?" the grown folks said, "Y'all get somewhere and sit down for a little while."

The end of the day and late into the evening does find ten of us squeezed in around Brianna's dining room table playing a somewhat physical game of Spoons. We've already put Jameel, LD, and Caliel in check several times since we started the game. The first check came after Jameel knocked his chair over and almost knocked me out of mine in an effort to grab a spoon after getting four of a kind. Then LD dove so hard for a spoon he slid across the tabletop and wound up looking straight up into his mother's face at the other end. Brianna tried to look upset but had to laugh along with the rest of us. The final straw was when Little Caliel, who already had the letters s, p, o, beside his name got so angry about not winning a spoon that he pushed his older brother. Hearing Shantrell's raised voice, Zeke came into the room and started barking at his nephews but we made him leave and go back into the TV room and watch football. Shantrell then told the boys, "If you three keep this up, you will not play the next round. You're taking this too seriously. It's supposed to be fun, not a riot."

The boys are now behaving better and showing some sportsmanship but, honestly the tamer the game has become the less fun it is. We move on to a noisy game of Turkey Day Bingo that Alise has put together for us and it proves to be nearly as fun as Spoons. Zeke and my stepfather, Eugene, have abandoned the television set and come in to observe our play. After the first round, Eugene declares he wants to be the caller. Brianna and I smile at my mother because we know Eugene just wants to be close to her. Mom smiles back at us and tells Eugene that he had better make sure she wins a round.

When my cell phone begins to ring, Zeke picks it up from a side table, looks at the name on the caller ID and furrows his brow before he hands me my phone. He makes a point of grasping my hand with his to get my attention as he passes the phone to me and then looks me in the eyes with a question in his. When I see the name "Blick Cissoko" on the caller ID my heart begins to beat quickly and I can't hide my nervousness. I haven't spoken with Blick since we met at the coffee shop although we text each other occasionally. I told him I'd call if and when I heard from Dana.

I consider letting the call go to voice mail. It is Thanksgiving after all but I go ahead and take the call. With hopes of distracting Zeke from his curiosity about the name on my phone, I ask him to play my bingo card while I take Blick's call.

"Sure," Zeke says but gives me a look that lets me know he's more interested in the call than ever.

I find a quiet room so I can hear the soft spoken Blick. He apologizes, says he hopes he hasn't caught me at a bad time, and asks how my Thanksgiving is going before asking me about Dana. I tell him there has been no change but I hope to hear from her soon. "I thought about something I might be able to do to help but I won't bother you with that today. It sounds like you are at a party. Please, once again, accept my apology for calling today. We don't celebrate Thanksgiving and I forget what a big day it is for Americans. May I call you next week to talk to you about my idea?"

"That'll be fine, Blick, and there's no need to apologize about the call. I'll talk to you next week. Call anytime."

I end the call and hear my mother yell, "Turkey Day Bingo!" as I walk back into the room to Zeke's curious stare.

As we end Miriam's winning round of Bingo, Brianna declares it's time for a second kitchen cleaning. We make our way to that part of the house and Brianna puts coffee on so we can make more of a mess. David's mother, Leticia or Miss Tish as I call her, pulls one of her homemade turtle cheesecakes from the refrigerator and it's not long before the kitchen is full of people vying for various types of dessert.

"Shantrell, you've got a call. What's up with your phone?" Zeke enters the kitchen holding his phone in the air. He looks from me to Shantrell. "Looks like I'm playing operator tonight."

"My phone is off. Who is it?" Shantrell says gruffly.

Zeke looks like he doesn't want to answer the question, so Shantrell repeats it.

"It's Mykol. He says he's been trying to get you since yesterday but keeps getting your voice mail."

Shantrell is serving dessert and is cool as can be when she says. "Tell him I'll call him tomorrow." She doesn't bother to look at Zeke when she says this and I know Zeke wants to say, "Tell him yourself," but there are too many people around who he does not know well, so he is not his usually abrasive self. Also, I don't think Shantrell will talk to Mykol even if Zeke puts the phone up to her ear at this point. With a look of exasperation, Zeke turns and leaves the room, taking his phone with him. Miss Mel, Brianna, and I have not moved from our spots or closed our mouths since Zeke said, "It's Mykol." Now the three of us look at each other and at Shantrell who keeps on serving dessert and ignores us all together.

After all the kids and men have whatever decadent sweet they choose to indulge in, we ladies take seats in the kitchen and have tiny tastes of each dessert along with our coffee. Miss Mel does pretty well sticking to the almost sugar free sweet potato pie. She has "Sugar," you know. She does taste a tiny piece of the marble cheesecake off of Shantrell's plate.

I'm surprised to see David, who had a plate with three good-sized pieces of dessert on it when he left the kitchen, reentering fifteen minutes later. Surprise hardly describes my emotion when I see Mykol entering the room right behind him with Zeke bringing up the rear.

"Happy Thanksgiving, everyone," Mykol says as he looks around the kitchen and then settles his eyes on Shantrell.

Once again, Miss Mel, Brianna, and I have our mouths open but this time we turn our heads from side to side as we look at Shantrell, then Mykol, then Shantrell again. Shantrell's mouth is closed but her eyes are open wide like saucers as she stares at Mykol.

"Happy Thanksgiving, Shantrell. Do you think I could have a word with you in private please?" Mykol asks.

"Where are your mother and your sister?" Shantrell asks so quietly that she seems to be in a state of shock.

Mykol gives a little disgusted smile. "They're fine. They're at my place."

"In Seaside?" Shantrell asks.

Mykol doesn't answer but puts one hand up as if he's about to say something then drops it down by his side. He stands there and looks at Shantrell, who does not move. At this point, Zeke and David seem uncomfortable and leave the kitchen. Brianna walks over and speaks into Shantrell's ear for a moment and then steps away and looks at the woman. Shantrell has dropped her eyes and pursed her lips, though only slightly, more in defeat than disgust.

"Hey guys, let's give them some privacy," I say. It is as if the other ladies present suddenly realize we are not watching television and no, this is not a soap opera. We all shuffle out of the kitchen, leaving Mykol and Shantrell alone.

"What did you say to Shantrell?" I ask Brianna as we leave the kitchen.

"I told her that we don't want to ruin everyone's Thanksgiving with a messy situation. Mykol doesn't look like he's mad or hostile. Just go ahead and talk to him and see what he has to say. As you could see, she wasn't very receptive. They're going to be alright. That brother didn't drive all the way up here to tell her he's sorry for deceiving her. I guarantee you that."

"I hope not," I say.

Miss Mel has been listening and adds her thoughts on the situation. "I told Shantrell something was not right with this whole picture, the mother and sister suddenly deciding to visit and then that girl going to Mykol's for dinner. He likes Shantrell way too much just to decide to go back to that girl so suddenly. I mean he and Shantrell didn't fallout with each other or anything. I'm so glad he came up here to get this mess straight."

--

After everyone other than the overnight guests left Brianna's, I had planned to slip off and climb into the bed with Zeke but my mother, Brianna, Miss Tish, and Rosemarie want to sit up in the kitchen and discuss Shantrell and Mykol until there is not one word left to say about the couple that hasn't been said repeatedly. Then they start quizzing me about Ezekiel. This means I have to sit through not only a barrage of questions about our relationship but more advice than I can bear. I would turn off the tap of wisdom if it flowed from Brianna or my mother but Miss Tish is the well from which the insight flows. So I sit and listen, smile and nod. Finally, at about one in the morning, I can take no more and head off to my bed on the sleeper sofa in the study. I've slept on this sleeper before and it's okay but I'd be so much happier in the bed with Zeke.

--

Miss Mel has declared that her vacation rental is entirely too fabulous for her not to utilize the kitchen so she is hosting brunch the day after Thanksgiving. She made everyone promise to come with a big appetite, emphasizing that we can eat the holiday leftovers for dinner but must eat with her for brunch. We arrive to the smell of fresh homemade biscuits, grits, bacon, turkey sausage, three different types of quiche, pancakes, and fruit salad.

Zeke is nowhere in sight but shows up just moments later with containers of fresh squeezed fruit juice. He enters the kitchen where a number of us are getting the magnificent spread out on the counter, gives a wicked smile as he cuts his eyes from Mykol to me and says, "Hannah, could I have a word with you in private, please."

At first I assume he is serious until David cracks up laughing and points at Mykol. Who looks a bit put out and tells Zeke and David. "Hey, you two laugh all you want; I ain't too proud to beg."

"Yeah and drive hundreds of miles to do it," Zeke continues to poke fun at Mykol."

"Did you wear a diaper, man?" David asks in jest.

"A diaper?" Mykol repeats, looking confused.

"Yeah you know, so you wouldn't have to make pit stops." David, Zeke, and Mykol crack up in laugher at this and most of the rest of us smile. Shantrell just blushes.

David's father finally says. "Leave the man alone. It takes a big man to admit when he's wrong." I don't believe Mr. Aldridge knows why Zeke and David are teasing Mykol but he clearly feels Mykol does not deserve the ribbing.

"Were you wrong, man?" Zeke asks Mykol with a serious look but still joking.

I walk over to Zeke and take him by the hand and ask, "What do you need to talk to me about?" I attempt to look clueless and Zeke looks surprised by my question. I lead him out of the kitchen as our family members yell out oohs, ahs, and uh ohs.

Once we are out of the kitchen, Zeke takes the lead and walks me into the room where he sleeps. In the room with the door closed, I ask again, "So what do you need to talk to me about?"

Zeke smiles and kisses me, a nice deep wet kiss that frankly leaves me swooning. When he pulls away he surprises me with, "Who is Blick?"

I can't hide the shock that comes over my face. I had forgotten all about his reaction to Blick's call the day before. I thought Zeke had forgotten the call also. I head toward the door and say, "I'll tell you about it later."

Zeke pulls me back and smiles but the look in his eyes clearly says he's not in a playful mood. "How about just telling me real quick right now so that I won't spend the rest of day wondering,"

"Are you jealous, Zeke?"

"Should I be?"

"No," I say adamantly.

"So, who is he?"

"He's an old boyfriend of Dana's," I say, knowing this will only cause more questions.

"An old boyfriend or a john?"

"An old boyfriend who wants to get in touch with her."

"So why haven't you told me about this guy? I hope he's not like that Travis guy. You might want to stay away from any old boyfriend of your cousin."

This is the very reason I did not want to discuss Blick with Zeke. I knew he would discourage me from having any contact with Blick and I appreciate his concern but I will not cut the man off. I believe he is Dora's father and that connection is entirely too strong to disregard.

"Can we talk about this when we get back home? I'm starving," I say.

"Sure, but please don't try to shut me out on this, Hannah; I mean it."

I just smile and nod. I feel some power over Zeke and I like it.

The smile is still on my face when I exit Zeke's room.

"What were y'all doing in there that's got you walking around with that sly smile on your face, missy?" Brianna asks.

"Just talking. I wish I had the nerve to get my swerve on with my family just on the other side of the door."

"Come here." Brianna takes me by the arm and pulls me into a corner of the study. "I just had a call from Deidra and she is not doing well."

"What's going on?"

"She says Mykol was not happy when she showed up at his house yesterday for dinner. His mother invited her and he had no idea she was coming. She says Mykol's mother is ten times worst than Miss Mel. Frankly, I don't see a problem with Miss Mel but hey, I'm not dating her son." Brianna throws her hands up in the air and looks at me as if she expects me to comment.

"Miss Mel is cool. I don't know what the problem was with her and Deidra but what happened yesterday?"

"Mykol had taken Deidra home to Phoenix with him a couple of times and I guess his mother was impressed with her pedigree. It seems Mykol's mother is a bit of a social climber and thought she was about to get a daughter-in-law from an influential family. She has been calling Deidra periodically every since the breakup, trying to mend fences or something like that. Anyway Deidra says Mykol was cool throughout dinner but was not happy or interested in anything happening at his house yesterday. She said he kept trying to get someone on the phone and got more agitated as the day went on so she pulled him to the side to talk. He came right out and told her that he is seeing Shantrell now and that it is serious between them. Deidra is so unhappy. I hate this shit. I need to go and spend some time with her but I feel like I'm in the middle."

"Did you tell her Mykol came up here?" I ask.

"No, she had no idea that Shantrell and the family were here. I'm off next week. That was supposed to be my me time but I think I'll ask her to meet me in the city so she and I can spend a few days together. That's when I'll tell her about Mykol driving up. Of course that may mean I'll have to tell her about you and Zeke also but I really think she already suspects you two are a couple. At this point, I'm almost wishing the Melancons had not moved next door to you," Brianna says and I know she is serious because Deidra is her girl.

--

My stepfather, Eugene, volunteers the men to take care of the kitchen cleanup after brunch and all the men agree though some only grudgingly. They make the boys help by sweeping and carrying the garbage out. We ladies sit and relax out on the huge patio near the fire pit. We can hear the men laughing and arguing inside. Although it was Eugene's idea for the men to clean the kitchen, he and Mr. Aldridge are clearly only supervising. The ladies get a serious laugh out of this.

After the kitchen is cleaned, Brianna and the seniors take off for the casino. Zeke, Mykol, and David head back to Brianna's to watch sports and chill. The boys tag along with the men with plans to shoot hoops outside in Brianna's driveway. Shantrell, Rosemarie, the two girls, and I head down to Old Sacramento to be tourists.

The night finds us all back at Brianna's eating more food than we should and making another big mess to be cleaned by someone. Alise pulls out her karaoke machine. Initially, only the kids, Brianna, and the seniors are bold enough to belt out a tune but before long every person in the room reaches for the mic. Miss Tish definitely should have gone into show business. She sings the Emotions' hit "Come on Back" with my mother and Miss Mel singing backup. They are actually good. They went out of the room and practiced a few moves beforehand and put on quite a performance. Brianna and David forbid Alise from doing Beyonce's "Drunk in Love" so she does "Put a Ring on It" instead, which is cute. David is the worst with -- oh my lord – Color Me Badd's "I Wanna Sex You Up." I don't know how he managed it but he talked Zeke and Mykol into singing background. They clearly did not practice. Zeke and Mykol's background vocals are a hot mess but I laugh too hard at David's falsetto and the fact that he only knows the chorus. He puts on his glasses but still squints at the lyrics and cannot keep up with the lead. Like I said, it is a hot mess. I'm glad Alise pulled out the machine because we have a blast with the karaoke.

Chapter 25: A Place of Refuge

Saturday evening finds me driving back to Seaside alone. Miriam and Eugene will drive down early tomorrow and visit a couple of days. Zeke protested when he realized I would be traveling alone. I put a quick stop to that. I have been making this drive alone for nearly fifteen years now. Shantrell offered to stay back with me but I could tell she wanted to ride with Mykol and he wanted her with him. Zeke offered to put his mother and the boys in the car with Shantrell and Mykol so that he could follow me but I refused his offer. He was not happy with my decision but accepted it. I am a big girl and I will not allow him or anyone to cripple me.

I always enjoy the solitude of the drive between Seaside and Sacramento. I listen to good music and think about all sorts of things. Tonight's drive is not allowing much time for reflection. Zeke has tried to keep me on the phone with him. He's not the best phone conversationalist. I hate it when a person calls me and then has nothing to say but hangs on the line. There has to be some type of phone etiquette that dictates that the person who makes the call is responsible for keeping the conversation going and should end the call when there is a lag. I think Zeke actually calls me and starts grading papers. I'm usually so pleased to hear from him that I just sit on the phone and listen to him breathe and think. Tonight I end the call with him because I want my quiet time in the car and he is yet again unhappy with me.

Not ten minutes later the phone starts chiming again. I curse, certain it is Zeke or another of my family members, but it turns out to be a private number. I answer to the sound of a barely audible Dana. "Happy belated Thanksgiving, Cuz."

"Hey, baby! How was your Turkey Day? Good I hope." I sound so much happier than I feel at this moment.

"It was okay, but we didn't have any turkey," Dana says, still speaking very low. "How was yours. I called the house several times. When I didn't get an answer I figured you were at Brianna's. It took me a while to find your cell number. You know I always call you at home."

"I wish you'd give me your number so I can call and talk to you sometimes. I don't know why you feel the need to be so distant and secretive," I tell Dana.

"I change numbers so often. Every thing's so crazy here. Did you have a good Thanksgiving? Was Uncle William or Aunt Miriam and Uncle Eugene at Brianna's? I'd love to see them."

I've never heard Dana say she wanted to see my mother or father. She must be having a hard time. "Mom and Eugene were there this year. You know Dad and Tracy don't do all the big eating holidays. They like to keep it healthy."

"Boy, what I wouldn't give for a big holiday feast right now. Anyway, Hannah I need to get a little money."

"How much do you want me to send you?"

"Just a thousand. I need you to hold on to as much of that money as possible."

I am tempted to tell her that I can only hold on to as much as she allows but I don't bother because I am determined to give her no more than the twenty thousand she believes my aunt left her. The remainder will stay in an account, waiting for her to come to her senses. I just hope that's sooner rather than later.

"Dana, I met an old friend of yours. He's been trying to find you."

"An old friend of mine?" Dana sounds surprised by this information.

"Yes, a guy by the name of Blick Cissoko." I hear a gasp on Dana's end of the phone but I continue. "He says you and he dated a few years back. He returned to the Bay Area not long ago and found Aunt Alise's name and number on some papers you left amongst his things. He called Christopher and Christopher thought I should talk to him."

Dana is quiet on the line and I think she may be crying. When she doesn't say anything, I say, "Dana?"

"Hannah, let me call you later. Now is not a good time. I promise to call you in the next day or two. Dora is good. Don't worry about her. Love you."

This call from Dana leaves me down right puzzled. The mention of Blick's name made her cry, she tells me she loves me, gives me Dora's status, and drops the subject of money. Dana must have some very strong feelings for Mr. Blick Cissoko. I pray her feelings toward the man are good and that he is not another Travis Ransom, Jr.

--

I receive a call from Blick early Monday morning as I'm sitting down to enjoy coffee with my parents. I leave the room so that I can speak to him in private, causing my mother's antennae to rise from her skull. I feel her eyes burrowing into my back as I leave the room.

Blick is soft spoken and kind as usual when he tells me that he has contacted a private investigator to find Dana.

"I don't think you need to hire an investigator to find Dana. She called me two nights ago and I told her you have been looking for her. She promised to call me in the next couple of days. Give it some time. The reason I can't tell you where to find Dana is because she does not want me to find her. I feel like she may be having a change of heart but that's her decision. Dana is not missing, Blick. She simply has not wanted me and my family to know where she is and that is her right. I'm hoping that she will change her mind now that she knows you want to see her."

"How did she sound? Is she well?" Blick asks anxiously.

"It was a quick call but she seemed fine. I'll get more information when she calls me back; I promise."

"And the little girl, she has her with her? She's okay also?"

"Yes, she told me that Dora is doing fine. How are you doing?"

"I am very anxious to learn about Dana and the child. I want to be sure they are okay. I am willing to hclp Dana in any way I can but I must be honest. I want to see her and I want to meet the child."

"I understand. I promise to call you just as soon as she calls me back."

"Will you do me a favor, Hannah?"

"If I can," I say tentatively, dreading the man's request.

"Will you ask her to see me, please?"

"I won't ask her to see you but I will tell her that you want to see her."

--

Dana's call comes right on time. She calls on Wednesday evening after I have finished a day's work and put my parents on their flight back home. "Hannah, I've left Travis but I can't come home because he will look for me there," she says excitedly.

Oh shit! I do not want to deal with this fool and if he thinks Dana is here, he's going to bother me. I may be a big girl but this scares me. "Where are you, Dana and is Dora with you?"

"Of course my baby is with me. Do you think I'd leave her with that asshole? I'm not that crazy, Hannah. We're in Santa Cruz. I know Travis will call every hotel on the peninsula looking for me and if he can't find me by name he'll describe me. He'll pay for information. He's done it before and often. He has no reason to think I'd be in Santa Cruz."

"Why did you leave him?" I ask, not really caring why.

"I guess when you said Blick was looking for me, it gave me hope that I might have somewhere else to go."

This breaks my heart. Why doesn't Dana feel I would offer her refuge? I'd help her get a new start where ever she decided to live. "You could have come here, Dana. I'd help you in any way I could," I say quietly with hurt feelings.

"He would have followed me and harassed me and threatened you and Dora and anyone else he thought I loved. But hearing that Blick is looking for me makes me want to try and start over somewhere else. I just want to try. I know I may not be able to make it with Blick. His life is too different from mine but I want to give Dora and my baby a chance."

"When did you leave?" I ask.

"This afternoon. Travis will probably be out until late tonight. Hopefully, he won't miss me until much later. I told him that my phone was out of minutes but you would be sending money tomorrow. So he hasn't been calling me. I need some cash, though. I only have enough money to pay for a couple of days here."

"Do you want me to wire you the money?"

"No!" Dana says vehemently. "Travis has an in with a MoneyWire representative. He can find out when and from where money was sent, who sent it, who picked it up and where they picked it up. I still have a bank account but not the one you and I set up. I did close that account but immediately opened another one online. I wanted Travis to think I was out of money because he takes every cent I get my hands on."

Dana gives me the bank account information so I can deposit money into her account. I feel sick to my stomach by this situation. I am afraid for Dana and Dora, myself, and everyone close to them. Maybe I watch too much television but I fear that Travis may be a desperate man.

I hang up the phone and dial Zeke. "Hey, baby, what's going on?" He sounds busy and I know he's swamped with all the end of term requirements but I need him.

"Can you come over here and stay with me?"

"Why? What's up?"

"I've heard from Dana and frankly I'm afraid to be here by myself. She's left Travis."

"Where's Dora?"

"She has Dora with her?"

"I've got to gather up my papers. It'll probably be an hour before I can get there."

"That's fine. Thanks, Zeke."

I stand in my living room and recall Zeke saying he does not do complicated. I'm sure he feels our relationship is one of the worst he's ever had and it is nothing if not complicated. I realize that I am afraid for Zeke and every person I have a personal relationship with. I call Zeke back and tell him not to bother about coming to me. I'm coming to him.

--

I make the forty minute drive to Santa Cruz early the next morning. I use Zeke's SUV just in case Travis has already made it to our area and remembers my car. Chances of this are highly unlikely but possible. I don't call Dana until I am well on my way. As I speak to her, I hear Dora talking in the background and my heart flutters and eyes fill with tears. This is the first time I have heard her voice since the night I put her to bed two months earlier and came home to find Travis in my home. How often I have wished I had let him spend the night. Maybe if I had been friendlier or nicer when I asked him to put the cigarette out he would have left the next day with no problem – maybe. I quickly stop this line of thought. I can't turn back the hands of time and doubt I would have let the man remain in my house if he had been reading the good book.

The door opens to a small overpriced boardwalk motel suite. Dana looks worse than ever but I can't focus on her. I give her a quick hug and make my way to Dora who sits on the bed playing with Dana's phone. I stand next to the bed and watch her for a few moments until she looks up at me with those lovely deep-set brown eyes. She has grown so much. "Hi Dora," I say.

"I," she says and looks back down at the phone.

"Do you remember me?"

The child looks back up at me and then looks at her mother. Dana says, "Do you remember your other mother, Dora, Cousin Hannah? Remember?" She sits down on the bed and lifts the child onto her lap. Dora leans into her mother's bosom and shyly peeps up at me.

"Can I hold you?" I reach for her and she comes to me without hesitation. I try to hold back my tears but the spigot is open and I can't turn it off. Dora feels much larger in my arms than I remember. I hold her against me as she lays her head on my shoulder.

I sit down at the little table in the room and take in the decor which is eighty's drab. My heart feels so heavy. "What do you want to do, Dana?" I ask, not able to stop the tears from streaming down my face.

"I've got to get away from here. I guess I need to leave the state. I thought about North Carolina but Travis knows too much about my family there. I'm sure he knows Christopher's address. I just don't want to go anywhere that he might look for me. Oh, Hannah, I've messed up so bad and I miss my mother. I don't know why I didn't try to spend more time with her. I had no idea how much I loved her. She was my Angel. Next to you, she was my greatest ally." Dana's tears bring an end to mine.

"Where would you like to go?" I ask.

"I don't know. I wish I could migrate to another country," she says with her head hung low. Suddenly, as if she recalls something hopeful, she looks up with her eyes glowing and says, "Tell me about Blick? Is he as fabulous as I remember?"

I smile. "I don't know how you remember him but he is a pretty hot guy. He really wants to see you Dana. I told him about Dora."

Dana jumps up from the table and moves away before turning around. "No Hannah, you shouldn't have told him. What did he say?"

"He thinks she's his child and I do also. She has his eyes."

"Oh god!" Dana sits back down with her head hanging and the tears flowing again.

Dora sits on my lap watching her mother cry and it is obvious this is a scene the child is accustomed to. What I wouldn't give to get them both in a safe and happy place with the snap of my fingers. I want to take them home with me and take care of them but it's not safe.

"He is Dora's father. I didn't put his name on her birth certificate or anything. I was so afraid he wouldn't accept her. He comes from a wealthy family. I fell in love with him, Hannah, an honest hard working man, but I knew it wouldn't work, not with my history.

"I want so much for Dora. When we left you, she was so sad and clingy with me. I took good care of her and we bonded all over again, didn't we girl?" Dana smiles at Dora, who surprises me with a, "Huh."

"I called about a safe house for you guys, just to get some information," I tell Dana.

"No, no way! Those places are not safe. The guys find out where the women are way too often. One of the girls I used to work with got hurt really bad messing with a women's shelter."

"They do some good work, Dana. It's something to consider until you get settled permanently. You can't just stay here."

"I need a few days to think and then I'll know what to do. I wish I could see Blick. It would be so nice to see him again but I don't want him to see me like this. I know I look horrible. I could see it in your eyes."

I can't deny her claim but I try. "You're pregnant and tired. Of course you're not at your best."

"I haven't been at my best since Blick left me."

We visit for a while longer before going out to get a bite to eat. I take them to a nice fresh food restaurant because Dana says it's been a while since she had a well prepared meal. After our lunch we go to the bank and then to the market to buy up groceries. Dana and I talk more easily than we have in years. She feels like she did when we were girls. All her barriers seem to be down and she speaks freely.

I help Dana put away the food when we get back to her little motel suite. I know I need to leave so I can get home before dark but I dread leaving my family in this depressingly drab place. I tell Dana I don't know if or when I'll be able to visit again but I will call every day. Dora starts to cry when I leave and this breaks my heart. Dana looks as if she wants to cry also. I must find a way to get them to a safe place.

--

Zeke is all packed up and ready to go to my house when I arrive at his apartment. We discuss dinner and decide to order take out because we're both exhausted and just want to get to the house to rest. Zeke goes to pick up the food from Baan's and I go to the market to grab a few essential. I feel a little leery about going to my house alone. Zeke asked me to wait and let him go to the market with me but I told him I was tired and wanted to get home as quickly as possible. Travis has certainly figured out that Dana has left him by now and my home is the first place he will look. I wonder if he has already stopped by. I don't notice any strange vehicles parked near the house and I keep a watchful eye as I pull into my driveway and on into my garage. I grab my mace before I get out of the car even though I'm certain no one entered the garage after I pulled in.

Once I'm inside my home and have the alarm set, I feel better. I left all the curtains and blinds drawn shut when I left last night so no one could walk around my house and peep in my windows. If Travis came by, hopefully he assumed I was at work. As I put away my things, the doorbell starts to ring with urgency. I know it's not Zeke because he only rings once unless I don't answer, none of that rude impatient ringing for him.

With my stomach in my throat I ask, "Who is it?" without bothering to look out the peephole.

"I'm looking for Dana. Is she here?" the identifying response comes.

I start to think how to answer and then tell myself not to hesitate. I know my storm door is locked and I'm certain the man does not have a gun at the ready so I open the door and say, "What are you doing here and what do you mean you're looking for Dana? Where the hell is she?" I glare into the cold cruel eyes of the one man on earth I hate.

"That's what I want to know. She left yesterday and I haven't seen her since."

"Did she take Dora with her?"

"How the fuck do I know. They're not at my place. I thought they might have come here."

"Well they're not here and I told you to stay away from here. I'll call the police if you come back here again and I mean that."

"Didn't Dana call you for some money a few days ago? Where did you send it?" Travis watches me closely, hoping he can discern something from my answer.

I want to say, "None of your goddamn business," but I sense the man getting angrier by the second. I feel relief when I see Zeke pulling up into my driveway. "You'd better go," I tell Travis as I stare directly into his eyes. He turns his head toward Zeke, most likely attempting to assess the threat level Zeke imposes. I'm sure his initial assessment changes once Zeke rounds his vehicle with one hand behind his back.

"What's going on, Hannah?" Zeke asks with a look on his face that scares me more than the threat caused by Travis.

Travis starts moving quickly down my walkway as he says, "I'll be in the area until you hear from Dana. I'm sure you'll let me know when you do."

Zeke starts toward the man, yelling, "Hey man, hey!" but Travis moves quickly and heads up the street and out of sight. Zeke turns back toward me but the anger is still on his face. "I can't believe you opened that damn door, Hannah. What the hell were you thinking? What if he had a gun?"

I don't answer but stand there and watch as Zeke returns to his car and grabs up his satchel along with the bags containing our dinner. I realize that I am trembling but I'm not sure if it's fear, anger, or both. Neither Zeke nor I eat our dinner. We do share a bowl of crème brulee ice cream.

The next morning Zeke and I go to the Seaside Police Department to file a police report and I start the process for a restraining order against Travis.

I'm terrified. I'm afraid for everyone I'm close to. I'm especially afraid for Zeke because it is clear he will take Travis on if given the opportunity. I don't want Zeke hurt in any way because of bad decisions made by me or Dana. I'm afraid for Dana and Dora because Travis looked like a cornered animal. He does not want to lose his meal ticket nor does he want to lose his power over one of his ladies. Dana most likely makes him a good bit of money when she is working. Every time I think of a place for my cousin and her children, I worry that this worthless piece of shit who calls himself a man might find them and do harm to not only Dana and Dora but to the people who provide refuge for them.

Chapter 26: Not Again!

After several nights with very little sleep, Shantrell offers me an Ambien. I take the pill and soon find myself dead to the world. I awake at quarter past ten the following morning to Shantrell shaking me and demanding, "Wake up sleepy head."

I sit up in the bed and try to figure out the exact why, who, what, when, where, and how going on around me. Why is Shantrell in my room waking me up, what day is it, where is Zeke and when did he leave? How did I manage to sleep so long and who drugged me? I drag out of my bed as Shantrell goes into the kitchen to make coffee. Ten minutes later I enter the kitchen still dragging and plop down in a kitchen chair. Shantrell sets a much appreciated cup of coffee in front of me.

I sip and begin to come to life when I notice the light blinking on my answering machine. I jump up without thinking and push the button to retrieve the messages. Sure enough Dana's is the first voice I hear. "Hannah, I'm in trouble. I'm bleeding bad. Hannah, please pickup."

"Oh shit," I hear Shantrell say.

I slam the phone down and push the caller ID button but the number comes up as anonymous. I run in the room and grab my cell phone from my purse. I have messages on my cell also. I listen to the first message which is Dana telling me that she's cramping and beginning to spot. I get her number off my cell and dial her back but get no answer. I go back out front and tell Shantrell, "I've got to go."

"I'll come with you. Let me go tell Mama to make sure she picks the boys up from school."

"Please hurry, Shantrell!"

While Shantrell goes next door, I call the motel office and ask if they have information on Dana. The desk clerk tells me that an ambulance took Dana to one of the area hospitals but she's not certain which one. I ask about Dora and learn that a policeman took Dora away from the motel. My heart starts to pound so hard that it feels as if it could push through my chest.

I call Brianna and tell her about Dana. Brianna says she will call around to the Santa Cruz hospitals and call me back with the information on Dana's location.

Shantrell is back when I hang up the phone. She insists on taking the wheel, declaring I'm in no condition to drive. We make it to the motel in forty minutes flat, just as Brianna calls with the information that Dana is at Watsonville Community Hospital. I go into the motel office and identify myself as Dana's cousin. I tell the woman I need to find Dora and get to the hospital to check on Dana and ask her to not allow anyone else in Dana's room. Thankfully, the woman seems understanding and tells me to let her know if she can help in anyway. Those words are like music to my ears.

Shantrell navigates to the hospital while I call the police department and attempt to find Dora. The police department puts me in contact with Child Protective Services. I am still on hold with that agency when we arrive at the hospital. Shantrell drops me near a front entrance. I jump out of the car with the phone to my ear, still on hold. The information desk attendant sends me to labor and delivery. I get on the elevator and lose my phone connection. When I get to labor and delivery I try to calm myself as I explain to the nurse behind the desk that I am looking for Dana Mechum.

"If you will have a seat over there, someone will be right with you, miss."

"Could you please just tell me if my cousin is okay? I've still got to find her child."

"Your cousin is in surgery. Please have a seat, miss. I can't tell you anymore than that."

I sit down and attempt to calm down before calling Child Protective Services again. Shantrell arrives and I tell her that Dana is in surgery and we must wait and speak to her doctor in order to get her status.

I move away to an isolated corner of the waiting area to place my call to CPS. Once I get someone on the line, I explain that I am looking for Dora. After a great deal of soft talking and more time on hold, I learn that Dora is in their custody but they will not release her to me. They are attempting to contact the child's stepfather, a Mr. Travis Ransom. This is a blow of the greatest magnitude. I cannot believe that Dana actually married this man. This means CPS may allow Travis to take Dora.

I tell the Child Protective Services representative that Dana ran away with Dora and was staying in a motel suite in Santa Cruz in an attempt to hide from Travis Ransom. I explain that my cousin is afraid of the man and I have strong reasons for believing he is an abuser. The CPS worker tells me she has already attempted to contact Travis but will not release Dora to him or me. She says she will wait for Dana's instructions on the placement of the child. I end the call, not knowing if I should feel better or worse. Shantrell watches me with something bordering on fear in her eyes as I approach. She knows the call to CPS has gone badly.

"Are you here for Ms. Mechum?" A tall graying female doctor asks as I take my seat next to Shantrell.

"Yes we are?" I answer anxiously.

"Please step over here with me." The doctor says.

Shantrell and I follow the doctor into the empty hallway. "Are you both family?" she asks.

"We're her first cousins. Her mother is deceased and she has no siblings. We're the closest family she has other than her one-year-old daughter," I answer, not bothering to mention Travis. After all, I don't know for certain he is Dana's husband.

"Well, you're the only ones here," the doctor declares before proceeding. "Your cousin is out of danger. She lost a lot of blood and we'll need to keep her for a day or two. I'm sorry but the baby was delivered stillborn, a little boy about thirty two weeks gestation. We had to give her some blood but she was alert enough to sign for the transfusion. She'll be out of it for a few hours but I expect her to start regaining her strength in a day or so."

"Are there any medications or special instructions for her?" I ask.

"That will all be in her release orders. She'll just need to take it easy for a few weeks but it is important that she follow up with a gynecologist as soon as possible."

"Doctor, what happened? What caused the miscarriage?" I probe further.

"Honestly, I can't say for sure but it doesn't look like she's had any prenatal care."

"Will she be able to have more children?" Shantrell asks.

"I can't see why not but she needs to get with a good GYN and keep her exams up to date. My best guess is that she'll be fine?"

I thank the doctor and ask if it's okay to contact her with more questions.

"That'll be fine. I'll be looking in on her for the rest of my shift and I'll be back in tomorrow." The doctor shakes our hands, gives us a small tight-lipped smile, and takes her leave.

I enter the recovery room to see Dana who is still quite groggy and not up to talking. I give her a kiss and hold her hand. "I'm so sorry about the baby, Dana." I can think of nothing else to say.

Dana does not respond but looks away from me as tears stream down her face. I stand there quietly holding her hand as she holds mine tightly.

Once Dana is settled in a room, I ask her if she's okay with Shantrell coming in to sit with us. Dana nods her approval. Shantrell and I sit quietly with her for a while before I realize that I am on the verge of starvation. Shantrell and I eat in the cafeteria but barely talk. Eventually, Shantrell works up the nerve to ask about Dora and I tell her that Dora's situation is up in the air for right now and explain that CPS will not turn the child over to me. Once again, I don't mention Travis. The possibility that Dora may end up in his care is too painful to consider.

I finish my meal without tasting the food because I hardly knew what I was eating. It's not that the food was bad but because my mind was somewhere else altogether. I feel anxious to get back to Dana's room. Shantrell takes off for home but plans to return later in the evening. I ask her to call Zeke and update him on the Dana and Dora Saga.

Before returning to Dana's room, I stop by the hospital's Social Services Office. I have to wait a good thirty minutes but get in with a Mrs. Gonzales who seems very receptive. I explain Dana's situation and that Dora is with CPS. Mrs. Gonzales tells me she will visit with Dana before she leaves for the day and take action based on the information Dana provides. When I get back to Dana's room, I find that she remains in a near stupor but I still tell her about my visit to the social worker. I explain to Dana how important it is for her to tell the social worker that she wants me to take care of Dora while she is in the hospital. Sure enough Mrs. Gonzales arrives to interview Dana later that afternoon. I leave the room and give them time alone, praying that Dana's lethargy does not cause the social worker to decide that Dora may be better off where she is.

I feel encouraged when the woman shakes my hand, smiles, and tells me, "I'll get right on this," as she leaves Dana's bedside. I feel even better when Dana tells me that she told the woman to please have CPS bring Dora to me immediately. "She said they probably won't bring her until tomorrow morning but I let her know I was not happy with the delay. I told her that you are the only person I want looking after my child." Dana gives me a weak smile and dozes back off into oblivion.

Zeke and Shantrell drive over later in the evening to bring me my car. After they get an update on Dana they ask about Dora. I tell them about my visit to the Social Services office and that CPS will most likely bring Dora to the hospital the next morning.

I think Zeke may feel that I've left him out to the loop once again but this is not about Zeke. He tries to hide his irritation with me but he cannot. Every time we make eye contact he turns away but stares at me when I'm not looking at him. Shantrell sits with Dana while Zeke and I sit in the waiting area and ignore each other. Eventually he moves next to me and takes my hand, holding it with no warmth. "You look tired. It's been a rough day. Let's go get you a room so you can get some rest tonight."

"I think I'll sleep in the room with Dana tonight. She's still pretty weak. I'd be afraid to leave her."

This does not sway Zeke's decision to get a room. He leaves and returns thirty minutes later, considerably more relaxed. Before he and Shantrell depart for home, he wraps me up in his arms and holds me for a moment before handing me the hotel room key. "Okay, I got you a room at the Holiday Inn Express. It's not even three miles away. Tomorrow, when Dana is better, please go and get some rest. Shantrell packed you an overnight bag. I'll be at your place and you can contact me on my cell if you need me for anything."

--

Dana sleeps through the night but is wide away with her color back by six the next morning. She even has a tiny bit of life in her eyes. After she has her breakfast and I have my coffee, I ask her about her marriage to Travis Ransom. Without looking at me, she tells me they married just a month earlier. "Travis was on such a rampage. He kept saying that he knew I was going to try to leave him and that was the reason I wouldn't marry him. I was scared to death, just terrified for me and Dora. I had to marry him, Hannah."

This marriage will make it more difficult for Dana to free herself from Travis. I manage to hide my fury over this horrible mess of Dana's life. I speak so calmly, I can hardly believe the words are coming from my infuriated mind. "Dana, you know that if anything happens to you, most likely, your husband will become Dora's legal guardian. Blick would have to prove that he's Dora's father and fight Travis in court for custody."

Dana gives me a faint smile and sits up a little straighter. "No," she says. "Blick would have to deal with you. Travis let down his guard after we married. I visited a free legal clinic and did a will. I mailed copies to Uncle William and Christopher in sealed envelopes along with letters telling them to open the envelopes if anything happens to me. I name you Dora's guardian and the executor of my estate, what little estate I have left." She smiles at me again, grabs my hand, and kisses it.

I squeeze her hand in return and don't say anything for a few moments because I don't want to cry. I love Dana more at this moment than I have for a long time. Finally, I say, "I'm so sorry about your little boy. We'll have to make arrangements for him. Did you name him?"

"Oh god!" Dana says as she turns her head toward the wall. "His name is Travis, Travis Ransom III, poor little fellow." Dana looks back at me and goes on. "I should have taken better care of myself. I didn't do any drugs, Hannah, I swear, not while I was carrying my baby and not with Dora either. I took good care of myself with Dora. She was born strong and healthy, a little early but healthy." Her tears are welling up again.

"I know, Dana. Now you've got to rest and get yourself well."

"Have you talked to Blick? Did you tell him about me being in the hospital?"

"No, I haven't called him. I thought I'd wait and let you call when you're ready."

"I think I want to see him. When they were rushing me here and I was so afraid I was dying, you, Dora, and Blick were the only people I wanted to see before I left. I want to see him, Hannah. Will you call him for me?"

"I will but you're not dying, baby."

"But I want to see him now, as soon as possible."

--

Brianna arrives at the hospital just before the hospital Social Services representative, Mrs. Gonzales, calls me to come to her office to meet the Child Protective Services representative with Dora. Brianna accompanies me to the Social Services Office where we find little Dora sitting on the floor playing with a doll that is not one of her own. When she sees us, she simply looks away. I'm certain she is confused by the different people coming in and out of her life and the abandonment. I pick her up immediately and want to tell her that I will never leave her again but I have little control over that situation, instead, I hug her close and then give her a big smile. I then give Dora to Brianna who does the same. The child sits quietly in Brianna's lap while I complete some paperwork for the social workers.

After leaving the Social Services Office, the nurse allows us to take Dora in to see her mother for a few moments. Dora's response toward Dana is the same as it was toward Brianna and me, disinterest. I realize that I have not seen Dora smile once since I met her and Dana in the small Santa Cruz hotel room. This hurts my heart; I wish I knew what her little mind is thinking.

Brianna stays at the hospital with Dana while Dora and I go to the hotel room. I scrub out the hotel tub and put her in the bath with me. Dora plays with her toys in the water and after a short time she begins to share the toys with me. After our bath we both nap for a while.

I make the call to Blick as Dana requested. He sounds appropriately concerned about both Dana and Dora. He is clearly as excited about seeing Dana as she is about seeing him and asks if he might be able to see Dora also. I explain that is something he needs to discuss with Dana.

Brianna comes to the room a couple of hours later and she and I, along with Dora, go over to the motel to collect Dana's things and pay any additional charges. Zeke and Shantrell arrive at the room in the late evening. They sit and fawn over Dora like she is the Christ child. I savor this softer side of Zeke. He gets right down on the floor with Dora and watches her and talks to her so gently. It's not long before he coaxes a smile out of her. I love this man!

I pack up a bag of Dana's clothing for her to wear from the hospital. Shantrell and Zeke stay behind in the hotel room with Brianna and Dora when I leave to spend some time with Dana. I find Blick sitting on her hospital bed holding her hand and talking to her. They both smile and welcome me but before long I can see I'm just in the way. Dana tells me that the doctor says she will be released the following morning and I confirm that plan with the nursing staff.

Dora is lying in bed sound asleep next to Brianna when I return to the hotel room. I immediately move the child into the bed with me. My sister just smiles and understands. I have my first drug free good night's sleep in days in that hotel queen sized bed with my little cousin cuddled up beside me. When I awake, I lie in the bed and watch Dora sleep, pleased to have the child back with me. All three of us sleep in until well after eight in the morning. I take Dora down to the hotel breakfast and try to feed her some eggs and cereal but she insists on feeding herself.

My sister convinces me that the best option is for Dana and Dora to go home with her to Sacramento until Dana makes a decision as to where she wants to settle down. I must admit I feel so much better knowing they will be with family instead of closed up in some hotel room hiding out and I am certain Dana will not object to the temporary arrangement.

Brianna remains in the hotel with Dora when I leave to pick Dana up from the hospital. I'm surprised to find Dana's hospital bed completely stripped when I enter the room and she is nowhere in sight. I see a nursing assistant coming down the hallway and ask about Dana. "Oh, she was released earlier," the lady tells me.

"Are you sure because I'm here to pick her up?"

"I'm pretty sure but you can check at the nurse's station." The woman smiles at me before moving on down the hallway.

I swallow hard and march up to the nurse's station. "I'm here to pickup Dana Mechum," I announce.

The nurse looks up from her busy work. Recognizing me, she furrows her brow thoughtfully as she reaches for Dana's chart. "Ms. Mechum was released over an hour ago," she says matter-of-factly.

"Do you know who picked her up?"

"I'm sorry but I didn't see her leave but someone had to pick her up or we would not have released her. She's on some strong medication."

I turn away from the desk and just stand there. Where could Dana have gone and with whom? I cannot believe she's done this again. Could she have taken off with Blick? Did Travis show up and make her leave with him. I go into the bathroom and before I know what's happening I find myself rushing into a stall to release my breakfast. This is all too much for me. Dana is killing me. I feel myself aging by the second.

I dread telling anyone what is happening. Maybe she's somewhere waiting for me. I go to the hospital cafeteria and look around in an attempt at staying off the inevitable. I've got to look at Dora who already seems so detached from everyone. I have to tell Brianna, Zeke, and everyone else that Dana has done the unthinkable, yet again. I walk slowly out of the front of the hospital and out to my car, hoping all the way that I see Dana sitting somewhere waiting or that she calls out my name. My thoughts bounce all over the place as I make the short drive to the hotel. I sit in the car and think. What if Travis did show up and forced her to leave with him?

I enter the hotel room and tell Brianna. "You won't need to take Dana and Dora home with you. Dana wasn't at the hospital when I got there. They said she left an hour earlier."

Brianna, who was in the process of gathering up her things to leave the room, stops and looks at me but says nothing for a full minute. "Who do you think she left with?" she finally asks.

"I'm not sure but I'm guessing Travis or Blick. I tried Blick's number but the call goes straight to voice mail. I really don't believe it's him but I could be wrong."

"I thought this whole situation had really made a change in her. I swear I could see a real change of heart. She seemed so different," Brianna sounds nearly as pathetic as I feel. She looks at Dora for a few minutes. The baby is now watching us closely as if she senses there is a problem. "Come here, Dora," Brianna calls the child over to her.

Dora gets up from the floor and paddles over to Brianna who picks her up and holds her close and kisses her. "I love you, Dora. Give me a hug." The baby places her head on Brianna's shoulder and does as she is bid. "I can take off a few more days and take baby girl here home with me." Brianna says as she rubs and pats Dora's back.

"No. If I haven't heard from Dana by tomorrow, I will notify Child Protective Services. I want Dora with me. I can work from home. I'm not letting anyone take her from me again without a fight. She needs an advocate."

Chapter 27: What's Best for Dora

This time I do what I believe is best for Dora. I go and talk to my lawyer who advises me to file a report with Child Protective Services. With the previous report I filed and the fact that Dora was turned over for my care while Dana was in the hospital, I find myself in immediate temporary custody of Dora Grace Mechum. No one but the authorities can take her from me for the time being.

The evening after I left the hospital and brought Dora home with me, I received a call from Blick. He had been in the air travelling to Chicago when I tried to reach him earlier by phone. He confirmed what I had suspected, Dana is not with him. He told me he was certain she would not have freely left the hospital with Travis. Blick said he'd be back in San Francisco in a couple of days so I gave him permission to come down and meet Dora for the first time. After Blick's call I realized that I had been hoping, in some small way, that Dana had left with him. Of course that would have made both Dana and Blick negligent parents, still I preferred Blick to the alternative. I wonder what kind of hold Travis has over my cousin.

After Child Protective Services, I make a futile attempt to file a missing person's report. Once I give all the particulars of Dana's disappearance, the Seaside Police tell me I'll need to file in Watsonville and that most likely Dana will not be considered missing because she has taken off so many times before.

All my allies are quiet. Some are speechless and others are too angry to speak. I'm sure Zeke falls in the later group. He has been staying at the house with me and Dora but not doing much talking, at least not to me. He talks to Dora a lot.

A few days after our return to my home, on an early Saturday morning, Zeke takes off without a word. This is the day of the scheduled visit from Blick, who arrives around noon, just in time for lunch. Shantrell joins us and we sit and eat tuna fish sandwiches. Blick watches his daughter and smiles. He makes repeated attempts to engage her but it's obvious he's not accustomed to children. His effort is commendable, however. I let him take Dora in the back yard for a while and she seems fine with him. Dora has become so aloof that she would likely behave this way with anyone.

I tell Blick about the temporary custody order before asking him about his thoughts on a relationship with Dora. He tells me that before Dana resurfaced with Dora he had hired an attorney to advise him. "I need some time to think about what is best for Dora and what will also work for me. She's such a quiet little thing. Is she always so distant?"

"Now she is. She didn't used to be. I think she has had too many drastic changes in her life, different people coming and going," I explain.

"I see. I hope we all can work together to make her safe and do what is best for the child."

"That's all I want." I tell him. Blick stands there and observes Dora as he nods in agreement. I believe we begin to form a bond as we both consider what will be best for the little girl.

--

After Blick's visit, I take Dora out with me to check on a couple of properties. I'm relieved to see Zeke's car in the driveway when I return. I no longer feel afraid that Travis may show up at my home because Dana is most likely with the man and she is the one he wants, not Dora.

Miss Mel, Shantrell, and Zeke are sitting in my living room when I enter the house. I speak, happy to see them all. Shantrell gives me a weak little smile and gets up and takes Dora from my arms and heads to the back of the house. The move is so sudden that it surprises me. I don't understand why she is taking the child away?

Miss Mel does not smile or speak a greeting, neither does Zeke but he does stand up and start talking. "Hannah, I went to see the Ransom's up in Berkley today."

I stand still and look at Zeke as a cold chill rushes over me. "What is it?"

Zeke looks at me with wet eyes and says, "Dana and Travis were in an automobile accident the day they left the hospital. They drove off a cliff on Hwy 1. Neither of them had on their seat belts. They didn't make it. I'm so sorry, baby."

I look at Miss Mel who pats the seat beside her. I obediently walk over and sit down next to the woman and let her wrap me in her arms. I don't want to cry and I try so hard not to but after a moment I wrap my arms around Miss Mel and weep until I simply can't anymore. My poor cousin, why did this happen to her? There was so much tragedy in her young life. Zeke tries to pull me from Miss Mel but she brushes him away. I lay my head in her lap and she rubs my hair. I really want my mother or Brianna right now but Miss Mel will suffice.

"Zeke, will you call Brianna," I ask.

"Shantrell called her right before you came in. She'll be down tomorrow," Zeke tells me.

--

All of my family, including Christopher, comes into town for Dana and her baby boy's memorial service. A number of her old high school friends and a few friends from the city also come to pay their respects. There is very little joy making or happy remembrances shared between family members. It is hard to focus on the joy Dana brought to our lives with the last ten years of her life being so destructive but every time I look at Dora, I see cause for joy. I'm thankful Dana had a child. Dora brings smiles to each of our faces and it is clear she is beginning to feel comfortable with us once again. My niece, Alise, never leaves Dora alone and by the time Alise leaves for home, she's calling the child "Mini Me."

Christopher, my father and mother, and Brianna are all so very sad. They each express a great deal of guilt over Dana's death. Each tells me the same thing, though using different words. They say they should have done more or wish they had reached out to Dana or not been so judgmental. They all say they feel like they let either Dana or Aunt Alise down. I wish I had the energy to console them but all I can offer is a few feeble words of encouragement. I truly believe only Dana and Travis are responsible for the tragic end to their young lives.

Blick is silent. I think he feels robbed of the love of his life but he is a young man. I'm sure he will love again and hopefully he'll have the chance to share life with the next person he loves. Right now, Dora is the only person he has a smile for.

--

"Is this Hannah Jacobs?" the person with the unfamiliar voice asks me over the phone two days following Dana and Baby Travis's memorial service.

"Yes, this is Hannah."

"Hannah, my name is Jasmine. I have a message for you from a friend. I wasn't sure if I should deliver the note or not but something tells me it's important."

"Who is the message from?"

"It's a written note. I haven't read it. Could we meet somewhere or I could bring it to you."

"I don't understand. You say you have a message for me but you don't know who it's from."

"I didn't say I don't know who it's from. Please, could you just let me bring you the note?"

"You can bring it to my house, if that's okay."

The mysterious caller agrees, I give her my address and she tells me she'll be at my house in an hour.

One hour later to the minute, an old Mercedes E500 pulls up in front of my home and parks. I watch the young woman approach my door and recognize her as she gets close.

"Hannah?" she questions as I open the door for her.

"Yes, come on in, Jasmine, and have a seat."

The young lady looks nervous as she sits down across from Brianna and pulls on the bottom of her short skirt in an attempt to make it longer to cover some of her exposed thighs.

"This is my sister, Brianna." Brianna and Jasmine look at each other and nod. Jasmine smiles but Brianna does not.

"Can I get you something to drink?" I offer.

"Ah, no, no thank you. I'm fine." The young woman reaches in her purse and says, "Like I said I started not to give you this. I just didn't want to get involved and I wasn't sure what it could be about. I need my job at the hospital and they fire people for a little of nothing. I probably shouldn't have accepted the note. The lady was a patient and she was leaving the hospital. I entered the room and her husband was rushing her to hurry and get dressed. She complained that she needed some help because she was bleeding and asked me if I'd assist her in the bathroom. We have procedures for that type of thing and I probably should have had a nurse take a look at her but the man was so agitated that I just went on into the bathroom to help her. Soon as we got in there she grabbed my pen and a paper towel and started writing as fast as she could. She told me to get this to you and that you would pay me. I told her I couldn't but she grabbed my hand and begged. When the man started banging on the bathroom door I just took the note and put it in my pocket." The young woman takes a breath and looks from me to Brianna and back.

I stand there with the note from my cousin in my hand, hesitant to open it. Dana is dead after all, what difference can it make now? I know I don't want to read this message from my cousin in front of a stranger. "Thank you for bringing me this note, Jasmine. You are right. It is important and it was kind of you to get it to me. Dana said I would pay you, so"

The girl stops me. "No ma'am. I wouldn't dare accept any money for bringing you that note. I'm sorry I mentioned the money. I just hope everything is okay. She seemed like a nice lady. Some of the patients can be testy but she was a sweetheart."

"Jasmine would you mind leaving us your full name and phone numbers," Brianna asks.

"No, I can do that. I'm not in any trouble am I?" The young woman looks terrified.

"No dear, I just appreciate you going to the trouble to get this to us. I'd like to send you something, not money but just a thank you."

"Like I said that's not necessary but I will text you my information if that's okay."

We thank the young woman again and she departs, giving every indication that she regrets her decision to deliver the note.

Once Jasmine has gone, I remain standing and stare at the piece of crumpled brown folded paper towel with my name and phone numbers written haphazardly on the outside. Brianna looks at me and asks, "Well, are you going to read that note or not?"

I smile and look over at my sister. "You think Jasmine really didn't read this. I don't think I could have been so ethical."

I sit down across from Brianna and unfold the crumpled paper and begin to read to myself. "Hannah Travis is making me go with him. He saw Blick in my room last night and says he'll hurt you

Dora Blick and everyone else I love if I don't go now. I'll call you as soon as I can. Don't worry and tell Blick not to worry. I'll get away from him. I love you and Dora so much. Pray for me."

I hand the note to Brianna who breaks down and cries for us both after she reads it.

The note answers many of our questions but not all. I tell my family and the Melancons about the note and its contents. We are so grateful to have received that last message from Dana that Brianna sends a letter to the hospital administrator with praise for Jasmine's care of Dana while she was a patient. Brianna makes no mention of the note in her letter. We also send Jasmine a one thousand dollar money order along with a personal note of thanks.

--

Blick takes time off from his job and visits my home every day until well after the New Year. If I didn't know better, I'd think he had moved in but he wants to know his child and I don't deny him that right. The more I see of Blick the less I see of Zeke. I've learned to heed Zeke's advice, most of the time, and although he doesn't stay around during Blick's visits he frequently makes an appearance.

It is well after the holidays before Blick and I sit down to discuss Dora who is breaking out of her shell daily. "I don't think I'm ready to take on the responsibility of raising a child," Blick tells me with a doubtful smile. It has become clear to me that he is quickly falling in love with his daughter but is not ready for the role of full-time parent.

"Dora will always have a home with me Blick. I know you need more time to settle into your role."

"I've started putting feelers out for permanent positions that won't require as much time on the road. My mother is nearing seventy and I don't want to take Dora so far away from you and your family. I know I want to raise Dora but I need more time to get situated."

"I'm fine with that. I'd just like to make things as easy as possible for Dora. It's important that she settle in with you before she gets too old."

"I'm looking for something steady here in Northern California."

I feel like jumping for joy but don't want to get ahead of myself. "That would be so nice. I'd love that. In the mean time she can stay here with me."

"Will you allow me to take her London?" Blick asks.

"I'll bring her if you take the necessary action to legalize your status as her father. I mean name changed and your name on her birth certificate as her biological parent. I won't challenge you. You're her father and she should be with you, just please let her always be a priority in your life."

"And I can visit her here as often as I like?" he asks for more.

"As much as you like but you can't move in with us," I laugh.

"I'd like to bring my mother to meet her and you also, if that's okay."

"Just let me know when," I tell him.

--

"Are you my Valentine?" I call and ask Zeke early Valentine's Day morning. I haven't seen or heard from the man in three days and I'd like to know if I have a date for tonight.

He laughs that beautiful deep laugh of his but simply says, "Hello, stranger."

"Will I see you today?" I ask.

"Do you want to see me?"

"Yes."

"I'll call you later and we can plan something." I can hear and feel the smile in Zeke's voice.

"I'll cook if you bring me something sweet," I negotiate.

"That's a deal."

Later that night after dinner, I ask Zeke, "Are you trying to drop me? I don't think I'll be so easy to get rid of now."

"I've been giving you space to get things straightened out without my interference. I hate it when you put me in check so I've been self-checking. How's that for growth." The man smiles at me and my heart goes all pitter patter.

"I like having you involved. You make me feel safe. I'd rather you do something I have to check you on than for you to stay away. When you stay away I think you might be tired of me. Sometimes I wonder if maybe you've just taken me on as a charity case." I tell him honestly as I watch his reaction.

This time he leans back in his seat and laughs. "Oh, Hannah, you amaze me. Do you think I've been here through all this crap with you because I feel sorry for you? I have a sister I used to sometimes feel sorry for. You're not my sister nor are you one of my students who may be trying his or her absolute best but still cannot make the grade."

Zeke leans forward, reaches across the table, and takes my hand. "I used to watch you so hard when I'd see you out walking on the trail that I became embarrassed. I'd see you from a distance and after a few times I could tell it was you from a long ways off. I always knew when you were aware of me. Once we'd get close enough for our eyes to meet, you'd drop yours until we got almost next to each other. That's when you'd look up at me, right in my eyes and smile. It got to the place where I'd find myself talking through that little ritual of yours. Later you started adding a little wave but that open direct smile of yours rendered me helpless. I knew I had met you before but couldn't remember where. When you walked off into Shantrell's that evening with that chicken, I was actually speechless for a few minutes. I just stood there looking at my phone like a dumb kid; remember that?"

I'm blushing and speechless now. I had no idea that Zeke had even noticed me other than to speak on the Coastal Trail. I can only smile and say, "Really?"

"Really," Zeke mimics me. "I thought the gods had smiled down on me that day."

Now I laugh. "Until all my family drama took over my world."

"I have to admit this relationship with you has been just about the hardest thing I've ever done."

"Too hard?" I ask.

Zeke shakes his head. "No, not too hard. I'm in love with you Hannah. I loved you before you ever walked into the house with that scrawny chicken and that sorry bottle of Moscato."

--

On a warm September afternoon, Zeke and I sit out of doors in the small Tuscan village of Populonia looking out at the beautiful blue of the Mediterranean. I hate to leave the beautiful place but tomorrow we leave for Tsilivi, Greece. We've been on vacation for three weeks. We spent the first five days in London where we left Dora with Blick and his mother, Laena. They've got big plans for our little girl. She's talking now and almost out of diapers.

It's been a busy summer. Zeke has taken a sabbatical until the spring semester. He spent a lot of time fixing up the duplexes he purchased with occasional help from Buddy and me. Miss Mel moved into one of the duplexes and she seems happy to be living on her own again. She likes to entertain and sometimes her old friends visit and stay for days.

During the early summer, I brokered a home purchase for Budrow and his girlfriend Denise, or Niecy as everyone calls her. Niecy is working hard with Budrow and I'm sure he will propose any day because she is an industrious woman who will not be denied her due. She is a registered nurse and part owner of a home health business. Budrow has been working two jobs for nearly a year now. In the spring, he will start classes at Monterey Peninsula College.

We all put in a lot of time over the summer helping Shantrell get her new business opened. I found the perfect building for the daycare and she had her grand opening in mid August.

Actually, this past summer belonged to Shantrell. Our hands were full with her agenda. The biggest news is that she and Mykol tied the knot in June. Their wedding was the event of the summer. Even Deidra and her newest love were in attendance. Shantrell's wedding was executed on a shoestring budget but every bit as lovely as Brianna's, which cost every person in my family a good portion of their life's savings and some blood. Both the ceremony and reception were so lovely that Brianna said Shantrell needed to consider event planning as a side gig.

Zeke finally moved back into his house. It's a lovely home with a beautiful view of the bay and more than enough room. Needless to say, Dora and I spend as much time at his home as we do ours. I'm finally making him a priority and it's not hard. He makes room for all the important things in my life, especially Granny and Dora.

Zeke told me once that he hadn't had a nice surprise in a long time. When I learned that he always wanted to spend time on the Mediterranean, I planned this vacation. This trip is our first opportunity to focus on each other. During this time, I can make Zeke my only priority. I love this man and I know he loves me!

~~~

About the Author

Cinda Brea is a native of the city of Carthage, Texas, located in the East Texas Piney Woods and grew up in the city of Seaside on the beautiful Central California coast where she attended Monterey Peninsula College. Cinda is retired from the United States Army after 22 years of service. She has degrees in culinary arts and restaurant management from St Philip's College. She is a wife, mother of four, grandmother of four, a family member and friend to many. She and her family make their home in San Antonio, Texas. *An Industrious Woman* is her fourth novel.

Novels by Cinda Brea
Romancing Retha
Sylvia's Story
Friends No Longer
An Industrious Woman

Contact Cinda
http://www.cindabrea.com
Follow Cinda on Facebook at: https://www.facebook.com/Cinda's-Books
contact via mailto:cindabrea@gmail.com